# PAUL QUARRINGTON

ANCHOR CANADA

Library and Archives of Canada Cataloguing in Publication has been applied for

ISBN 978-0-385-66601-5

This book is a work of fiction. Names, characters, places and incidents are products of the author's imagination or are used fictitiously. Any resemblance to actual events or locales or persons, living or dead, is entirely coincidental.

Printed and bound in Canada

Published in Canada by Anchor Canada
a division of Random House of Canada

Visit Random House of Canada Limited's website:
www.randomhouse.ca

TRANS 10 9 8 7 6 5 4 3 2

*Respectfully dedicated to the true King,*
*Francis Michael Clancy,*
*from whom I borrowed a nickname,*
*a birthplace,*
*and a bit of the blarney.*

*A sad tale's best for winter.*
*I have one of sprites and goblins.*

*—A Winter's Tale*

# ONE

I GET WOKEN UP by the telephone. I was having a dream, but I can't put my finger on exactly what it was about. It had something to do with Manny, with Clay Bors Clinton, the son of a bee who was my dearest friend, but the telephone rings and the dream is gone. All I know is, I wake up with my guts burning, my hands shaking, and the damn blower hopping all over my bedside table. I snatch the thing up and bark out a hello before I'm even sure where I am.

"King Leary?" asks a voice. I can't tell whether it belongs to a man or a woman.

"You got him."

"My name is Claire Redford." I still don't know whether it's a man or a woman. I've known a few mooks by that name. In fact, considering hockey is such a manly thing, there's a surprising number of Claires in it.

"What can I do for you, Claire?"

"Well, sir, I was reading a book recently, *Hockey Legends of Days Gone By*. By Clark Higham?"

"Never read it, no." Although I've looked at it. It's got some dandy photographs. It's got one of me airborne, executing the famous St. Louis Whirlygig, a maneuver of unspeakable beauty. It's got a picture of me in my New York Americans' uniform that was on a cigarette card back in the twenties. And it's got the photograph you've no doubt all seen, the famous one of Clay pouring champagne over my head.

"Well," says this Claire thing, "the book mentions a very interesting fact about you."

I should think so. "I am the King of the Ice! I am the high-muck-a-muck hockey player! I have an Indian nickname, *Loof-weeda* , which means "windsong," referring to the fact that I could skate faster than anyone else."

"*And*," this Claire says, cutting me off, "apparently you drink nothing stronger than ginger ale."

Now I get the scoop. This Claire person is from some antidrinking group, and they want that I should come say a few choice words antidrinking-wise. They want me to talk about Manny Oz, the Wizard, how he ended up, which I don't got the stomach for. He was all alone in a hotel room in New York, New York, and that's as much as I care to know. So I ask this Claire thing on the telephone, I says, "True enough, but do you know *why* I drink ginger ale?"

"Why is that, sir?"

"Because it makes me *pissed!*"

This is gospel. I get drunk on ginger ale, Canada Dry. I drank it when it had a cork. I drank it when it came in a clear bottle with a little marble in the neck. I drank it in dark green bottles, with tin lids I learnt to open with my teeth. I drank it in cans (which I couldn't open with my teeth) and I drank it in cans with pull tabs, and today I drink it in cans with holes in the top that I can't muster the strength to push in. And it gets me tanked, don't tell Nurse Ames. Always has. Makes me want to dance in the rafters. It got so I couldn't drink the stuff before a game, or else I'd be giggling and couldn't score a goal to save the old mother's life.

"Isn't that fascinating!" exclaims this Claire thing on the other end of the blower. "Is that fascinating, or am I out in left field somewhere?" Well, now, he or she isn't from no anti-boozing league, that's for sure, because they like to slam down the phone when I say *pissed*. "I mean," says the Claire thing, "this strikes me as a little strange."

It is a mite peculiar, I'll grant, getting blasted on Canada Dry. But there's people who get drunk on a lot stranger. My no-good son Clarence got drunk writing pornographic poetry. In a way, it's more strange that some people (like my other son, gormless Clifford) would pick something so mundane and bilious as beer. No, ginger ale is the boy for me. It's sweet and bubbly and makes your toenails curl. If you down a whole can, you can belch in a truly horrifying way, like a dragon about to eat a maiden.

"Here's the thing, King. I represent the bottlers of Canada's best-selling ginger ale beverage. We are currently planning next year's advertising campaign, and we're looking at television spots with identifiable sports celebrities. I took the liberty of mentioning your name at a strategy meeting."

"Did you ever see those adverts I made back in the fifties? For Leprechaun Laundries—seven locations to serve you. 'If it's good enough for the King, it can't be all bad.' I did radio adverts, too. 'Top of the day to you, Canada, and all my Newfie friends! Lads, when was the last time you told the missus that you loved her? Well, how's about doing it today, with flowers? Yes, sirree, Knight's Florists—' "

Bastard cuts me short, I don't care if maybe it is a woman. "Wonderful! You have experience."

Considering I was born in the year of Our Lord one-nine double zero, this seems a bit of an understatement. Anyway, I tell this Claire thing, "I can think of lots to say about the good old ginger ale. How's this? 'Hello, there! This is King Leary, *Loof-weeda.* You wonder where I get my pep and ginger? Why, from Canada Dry ginger ale, where the hell else?' "

"We'll have professional writers to supply that personal touch."

"Uh-yeah. Any money involved with this little scam?"

"Certainly. You'd be paid a flat rate of ten thousand dollars."

"Who do I have to kill?"

"I beg your pardon?"

"Nothing. That sounds about right. When do we do it?"

"Arrangements have to be made to get you to Toronto."

"Can't we do it here in South Grouse?"

"At the home?"

I guess it wouldn't make much of an advert. *Friends, they're dropping like flies around this joint, but listen, it's not the fault of this stuff, Canada Dry.*

"So I'll be in touch."

"You do that, Claire. I'm not going anywhere."

"And I must say it's been a real pleasure. I'm not just bang-ing a dream tambourine, I mean, it has been a real and true pleasure."

"Nice talking to you." I'm half inclined to ask whether Claire is a man or a woman, but that's not the kind of thing a person likes to be asked. Anyway, before I can, the Claire thing hangs up.

Blue Hermann is grinning my way like a cat with a mouse in its maw. Blue can't grin without spittle dribbling onto his chin. "How much?" he wants to know.

"Hermann," I tell him, "things has changed out there."

"How much?"

"Sounded to me like he said ten thou."

Blue nods, lights up a cigarette. This is quite the stunt, given his palsied claws. He smokes Export dead ends, but what the hey, there's not much point in switching over to low-tar filters at this stage of the game. Blue Hermann takes a puff, which provokes about ten minutes' worth of intense hacking. He spits stuff into his bedpan, wipes his mouth with the back of his hand, and announces, "If you're going to Toronto to make a commercial, I'm coming with you."

Blue has been my roomie for about seven months now. I've had nine or ten roomies since I first came to the South Grouse Nursing Home, and I've watched them pop one by one. That's what you get for being healthy and fit all your life—more of it, and it gets damn dull. Blue Hermann, now, he don't have that problem. In fact, I'm always amazed when I look over to his bed that he's survived since I last looked over to his bed.

When they first wheeled him in, he was doped up and passed out. I looked at his chart. EDMUND B. HERMANN. Meant nothing. His condition (I've gotten pretty handy at reading med-ical charts) was terminal, but so what, everyone around here is terminal, with the possible exception of yours truly.

This Ed Hermann had:

> *end stage liver disease, portal hypertension and ascites* (drank too much);

*Esophogeal varices, chronic obstructive pulmonary
disease*
(drank and smoked, too);
*positive* VDRL
(drank and smoked and hanky-panked with loose
women);
ASHD
(his ticker was about to go);
*Kersakoff's psychosis*
(he made up stuff and believed it);
*Wernicke's enesphalopathy*
(hot damn! you don't see that every day);
*affecting optic nerves.*

That's when it hit. "Bless my soul," says I, even though no
one else was in the room. (What are they going to do, lock me
up?) "Why, this is Blue Hermann."

Then I pretended that whoever I was pretending to talk to
had asked, "Who's Blue Hermann?"

"Newspaper man," says I. "One of the best. He chronicled
my career, Hermann did, and it's likely I never would have
been the King without him writing about my exploits. When I
got traded to the Amerks, Blue had a job in New York, writing
for the *Star*. When I went to Toronto with Clay, he gets hired
on at the *Daily Planet*. Almost like he was following me around.
And here he is again, except from the look of things, he's going
to get wherever we're going next long before I do."

I would never have recognized him. When I first seen him,
in New York City, he was young and mustachioed, and he
always had a big, bubbly-bosomed blonde hanging on to his
arm. Mind you, we was all very young back then. Now he
looks like a bum, only I don't say so to his face, and the reason
he isn't dead is that even the Grim Reaper has some pride.

It was the drink that done him in. The reason he's called
*Blue* is that early on the booze ruint his eyes, and he sees everything blue. As if he had blue-colored eyeglasses on.

Mind you, blue-colored eyes isn't that big a price to pay.
Consider what the booze done to Manny Oz. I myself have

only had one alcoholic beverage in my life, that being a glass of champagne when the Ottawa Patriots won the Stanley Cup back in 1919.

I scored the winner, you know. We were in overtime, in Montreal playing the Canadiens. What happened was, Cy Denneny took out Odie Cleghorn along the boards. Odie was one mean son of a bitch, but nowhere near as bad as his brother, Sprague. The puck pops out and I scoop her and go into the Bulldog. Then I see Newsy Lalonde coming at me. He was the King of the Ice before me, you know, and as nasty a piece of business as was ever turned out of Creation. Yes, sir, Newsy was intending to take me into the boards and probably into the Maritimes, that's how fast he was coming. But then I hear, "Psst, Percy!" and I know Manny is behind me. So we pull a stunt we pulled when we was playing together on the Bowmanville Reformatory's boys' team. Brother Isaiah used to call the play the Magic Stone, but I called it the Doorstep. I drop the rubber between my legs, and put a little spin on it so that it stops almost dead, leaving it at Manfred's doorstep, so to speak. I begin the double back, Manny comes up and collects the puck, and he takes the check for me. That's the point of the play, you see. Manny and Lalonde collide. My Lord, Newsy had his elbows up, and he took apart Manny's face with them. Manfred was fair handsome previous to that, you know, but ever afterwards his puss had an out-of-kilter aspect to it. Anyway, the rubber dribbles out from between their legs, and I've timed my circle perfect so that it tumbles onto my blade. Now there's just a lone defender, namely Bert Corbeau. Well, I go into the Whirlygig, and I pretzel the mook! I twist him around so good that his socks end up on different feet. The goaler is Nap Minton, the Little Napoleon. He moves out of the net, and I notice for the first time that his eyes are two different colors, blue and green. I clear my mind, the way the monks showed me. I shoot the puck into silence. Then I hear Manny shout, "Hey!" and from the stands I hear Clay Bors Clinton say "Yes!" and I know that the puck is in the net.

That's how it was back in one-nine one-nine. A marked improvement over how things is now.

# TWO

I WAS BORN AND RAISED in Ottawa, Ontario—Bytown, as we say. The Ottawa Canal was practically in our backyard, and the reason I say *practically* is that we didn't really have a back-yard. There was this little square thing that was full of bricks, because my father was always planning to build something. I never did learn what the Jesus he meant to build, but he certainly had the bricks for it.

I thought the canal was a beautiful thing. I spent so much time beside the water that it seemed to the young me that the canal had moods. Sometimes it would be whitecapped and rough, and I wouldn't think that the wind was up and blowing over a storm, I'd think the water was angry. Or sometimes it would be gentle, with little pieces of sunlight bouncing on it, and I knew that the canal was happy and that if I went swimming the water would play on my body.

But I loved her best when she froze.

A few nights of the right weather, and I'm talking thirty below, teeth-aching and nose-falling-off-type weather, and the canal would grow about a foot of ice. Hard as marble, and just as smooth. Strong and true. It gives me the goose bumps just thinking about it. Lookee there, see how goose-bumped I am right now.

I can't remember lacing on blades for the first time. Like-wise with hockey. I've got no idea when I first heard of, saw, or played the game of hockey. Some years back, Clay Clinton and I were invited to one of those hockey schools for a seminar. It couldn't have been that long back, come to think, because what we were discussing was something like The Development of Hockey in North America, which means we were trying to figure out a way of beating the Russians. So there was me there, and Clay (who was drunk much of the weekend, and occupied with the pursuit of somebody's floozy wife), and this young coach from Minnesota.

And the lad from Minn. starts talking about the *origins* of hockey. He went on and on about soccer and lacrosse, English foot soldiers playing *baggataway* with the Indians, some Scandinavian entertainment called *bandy*. I bit my tongue, but the truth of the matter is, I never knew that hockey originated. I figured it was just always there, like the moon.

Now, there was three of us Leary lads, Francis, Lloyd, and myself, Percival. We all early on got reputations in our neighborhood as good hockey players. Even though I was the youngest and the smallest, I was rated the best. Little Leary, they called me, a puff of Irish wind.

So one day—and this I remember like yesterday, better even, because what the hell happened yesterday other than Blue Hermann tweaking Mrs. Ames's enormous bub, eliciting a shriek that popped my eardrums—this strange young lad shows up at the canal.

The strangest thing about him was the way he was dressed, namely, a full-length fur coat with a matching little cap. We just wore sweaters, one for every five degrees she dropped below freezing, and on this particular day I had on maybe six. This boy in the fur coat and matching cap stood by the snowbanks and watched us for almost half an hour, not saying a word. I was pretending to ignore the lad, but really I was studying him. He was fat, but not the kind of fat that would get him called Fatty. Mostly what I noticed about him was his face, which was handsome as hell. The lad had gray eyes that seemed to have slivers of ice in them.

I decided to impress him, don't ask me why. The next time I got the puck I danced down the canal like I was alone. Then I made like Cyclone Taylor. I still loved Taylor even though he had, the year previous, abandoned the Ottawa Senators for the loathsome Renfrew Millionaires. As you may know, Cyclone claimed that he could score a goal skating backwards, and he did this against the Senators, and that's what I did myself, turning around and sailing past the pointmen, slapping the rubber with my heaviest backhand. The little boy standing between the two piles of snow that was the goal—who had been pretending to be Rat Westwick of the Silver Seven—just covered his head and let the puck fly by.

The boy in the fur coat seemed to nod a bit. He reached into his pocket and pulled out a handkerchief, one that had two fancy linked Cs sewn onto it, like this:

$$\mathcal{C}_C$$

and he blew his nose like your great-aunt. He studied the snot for a bit, folded up the handkerchief, replaced it in his pocket, and called out, "I say! Mind if I join you chaps?"

We said, "Huh?" because we thought he was speaking a different language. All it was was a classy English accent, but we'd never heard the likes. So he asked again, and Lloyd understood, and he says okay to the fat boy.

I naturally assumed that the lad would want to be on my side, but he skated right over to the other team. He skated pretty good, too, turning around and sailing backwards, showing off, positioning himself in the defense.

We recommenced the game of shinny. It wasn't too long before someone passed the puck over to Little Percy Leary. And I thought, all right, little fat boy in the fur coat and matching cap, maybe *this* will impress you. I took the puck and started downriver. I made it by everyone as though the world were standing still. The strange lad just kept backing up, watching me like a hawk watches a titmouse. Soon there was just him 'twixt me and the goal. He broadened out. I decided I'd get around him with one of my little tricks (I was born with tricks) flicking the puck between his legs and then hardstepping around him. I got the flick away and made my move. Then I fell down, filled with more pain than I'd ever known before.

I'd never paid my private parts any particular attention previous to that, other than noticing that in a warm bath they
tingled in a nice enough way. Now I realized there was something special about them, that being that if someone whacked
them with a hockey stick it could kill you. I was timbered as
though two-handed by Sprague Cleghorn, that black-hearted
lout. The strange little boy in the fur coat stood over me, saying
things in his funny accent like, "Most dreadfully sorry, old bean!
Are you all right?"

After a long time I got my breath back, and after a longer
time the pain eased enough for me to climb to my feet. Then I
cocked my fist behind my head. He hit me first, of course,
with a beautiful right hand that seemed to come from three
miles away. He caught me square on the beak, and there was a
gruesome crunching sound. I have never been considered a
handsome man and this is mostly because my nose is bended
and pugged. Popular mythology has it that my nose has been
broken something like twenty-four times, but the truth of the
matter is that it's only been busted the once, when I was a
sprout, and it was busted so thoroughly and convincingly that
no subsequent damage could be done. I keep that a secret
because the person who popped it was my dearest friend and
lifelong companion, Clay Bors Clinton.

When Clay died, in 1967, four thousand people came by
the Toronto Gardens to see his bloated body lying in state. I
asked if I could go in alone, and the police held back the multitudes while I did that.

And I looked down upon Clay Clinton, and I said, "You
bastard."

Now sir, after an introduction like that, it probably seems
strange that Clay and I became friends at all, let alone such
bosom buddies that there is a whole series of books about us,
Leary & Clinton and Their Various Fabulous Adventures.
These books are for kids, you know, but I like them. I got a
carton of them under the bed. Here's one, published in one-
nine five-one, my personal favorite, *Leary & Clinton Visit the
Dark Continent* (which, by the by, is your Africa).

> The King Cobra tightened around Clay Clinton's
> muscular body. "Ah well," Clay sighed musically,
> "I'm afraid I've about had it!"
> "Don't be so sure, Clay, me old son!" sang out
> Little Leary, his Irish blood at a boil. He swung down
> from the topmost branches at the end of a thick vine.

They keep writing Leary & Clinton books. The gormless
Clifford brings them to me, when he makes his visits. They are
getting stranger and stranger. I got one here, let me find it.
*Leary & Clinton Meet Michael Jackson.* Who the hell is Mike
Jackson? Whoever writes these books doesn't seem to know
that Clay is stone dead and I'm just a shriveled old mook who's
so scrawny I can't keep up *underwear*. Here's the latest in the
series here, which Cliffy brought to me last weekend. (Have
you ever met my gormless son Clifford, the fat, splay-footed
boy of some sixty-odd years?) Here we are, *Leary & Clinton
Fight the Dogstar People.*

> The Sirian sandworm tightened around Clay
> Clinton's muscular body. "Ah, well," he sighed
> musically, "I'm afraid I'm done for!"
> "Don't be so sure!" sang out Little Leary, his Irish
> blood at a boil. Actually, his Irish blood came to a
> boil very quickly because of the low-gravity
> atmosphere on the planet Quarm.

Seems the Earth is at war with some creatures from the
Dogstar Sirius. These Dogstar people, they're pretty sneaky
cookies. For one thing, they don't have bodies, making it very
hard to wage your conventional warfare. The Germans, now,
they had bodies, which is what we blew apart (them doing the
same to us), but these Dogstar People just float around in the
air like so much cigar smoke.

Anyway, me and Clay became fast friends.
Clay's father was some sort of undersecretary to such-and-
such, a Minister of This, That & the Other, and the Clinton
family was pretty well off. Besides Clay and his father, there

was Mrs. Clinton, who looked like a glass of milk, and his sister, Olivia. Olivia was in her teens, and I thought she was beautiful. Clay used to call her Horseface, and come to think of it, there was a resemblance.

Once we watched through a crack in the door as Olivia took a bath. I can remember it all. Not just Horseface bending over the tub, singing a little tune under her breath, I can remember the way the steam danced, the way the mirror was full of ghosts. Clay nudged me in the side and whispered, "What do you think of those bubbies, Percival my pet?"

One day after school the two of us laced on our skates and flew down to the canal. She was frozen hard and beautiful. The sunset lay across the river bright and heavy, like in one of those paintings so favored by Clifford's wife, Janine (who has abandoned him), paintings done mostly with a garden trowel. Clay Clinton set out the rules. "We're going to race, old fellow. We are going to race until we can't race anymore, until one of us drops dead from exhaustion. All right?"

I nodded. Clay tended to overdramatize. I figured we'd race until he got hungry.

"Also, Percival, my prince," Clay said, "all's fair." He pushed me into a snowbank and lit out.

I took out after Clay—I wasn't angry, because being pushed into a snowbank wasn't too bad compared to some of the things he did to me—and I went into the hardstep. Nowadays they got something called "powerskating." I used to watch the Maple Leaves learn this. The coaches had slide projectors set up to show diagrams of leg muscles and such palaver, and it made me laugh because it was just hardstepping, which I been doing since I was born. Here's what you do. You puff up your spirit till it won't fit into your body anymore. You get your feet to dance across the icebelly of the world. You get empty except for life and the winter wind.

Then you're going like hell.

I breezed by Clinton. He made a move to hip-check me, but Clay's hip was a big chunky thing and it didn't take much to jump out of the way. Clay couldn't stop once that hip of his got him moving sideways. He fell down on the river. "I'll get you for that, you scoundrel!" he hollered.

It didn't take long before the city went away.

Clay beaned me in the back of the head with a snowball, one with a quarter inch of ice formed around it. I wondered how he'd managed to make a snowball in the middle of a race— you have to rub them for upwards of five minutes to achieve that glaze—and when I got hit by another in quick order I realized that he must have made the snowballs sometime previous. Clay likely made them the night before and stored them in the icebox, a process by which snowballs can become deadly.

I went weavy so Clinton couldn't get a bead on me. A few more snowballs whistled by my ears, and one caught me on the fanny. That one hurt more than the two that got me on the head, which I suppose tells us something. Finally a few seconds went by without any snowballs, and I reasoned that he'd run out of ammo. I spun around and saw that I had a good thirty feet on him. "Drop dead from exhaustion, Clay!" I yelled. "I got you beat!"

The bastard had one behind his back. It came at me so fast that I'd swallowed the tooth before I realized what had happened.

When you lose a body part, even a tooth, it tends to slow you down. "Jesus H. Christ in heaven!" I screamed. I'd never screamed that before, I'd been saving it. When the old man bellowed out, "Jesus H. Christ in heaven!" my mother usually boxed him about the ears. Clinton skated by and give me a glance of some disdain. "And you call yourself a man."

Well, of course I never had called myself a man. I was the first to admit that I was just a pup. Still, I resumed the hardstep.

Then the night came, as quick as a greengrocer closing up shop. It came so fast there was hardly time for the moon and stars to get there, and all we had was black.

"Clay!" I shouted. I was ahead of him again, but not by much. Clinton was red faced, full of grit. "We got to go back, Clay!"

"Leary, I'm ashamed of you! You're afraid of the dark!"

That got me going. I never could stand it when Clay said he was ashamed of me.

I started thinking about this dropping dead from exhaustion business. I wondered if it was sudden or if there was some warning. I began to reflect on what difference Clay's fat would make. On the one hand, he had more of himself to cart around. On the other, he was likely warmer, and his lard could serve as extra fuel. And while I was thinking about all that, the world broke apart.

I could get technical on you, and explain about sudden temperature drops and pressure cracks and suchlike, but the truth of the matter is, I don't understand it all myself. Here's how it looks. In an instant, the river breathes up a huge wall of ice, and the water from beneath explodes like a fountain gone berserk. I had enough speed to glide over the crack, which was about three feet across, and then I slammed into the ice on the other side and got thrown backwards. Clay had more time to react, so he tried to stop. I suppose he panicked, though, and dropped onto his hands and knees, and there's no way you can stop in that position, so he didn't. He slid into the water, where I already was.

And here's what Clinton said, "Percival, old bean, I'm afraid we're done like kippers!"

You see, Clay was already living in those damn adventure books. He just said that because he knew it was a good thing to say. That's the way old Clay operated all of his life. Talk nice, fight like hell.

Mind you, I didn't relish the thought of becoming an ice lolly myself. But other than thrashing around and trying to grab a hold of the slick ice, there's not a lot can be done in that situation. Oh, you can bellow, I suppose, but that makes you light-headed. That is, howsomever, what I done, bellowed, and after a while, I began to lose consciousness, and then I felt a hand on my arm, the strongest hand I have ever felt before or since, and I thought it was God Almighty picking me up for to set me down in Glory, and I let myself slip into the darkness.

# THREE

HERE IS THE GORMLESS CLIFFORD, my child, stepping through the doorway. I can tell he's been wandering the corridors for the past few minutes, trying to find my room. It's been years he's been doing it, but Clifford always has trouble finding my room.

His fat hand is smoking. Clifford is convinced it's against the rules to smoke in my room. In point of fact, it ain't, or at least, Blue Hermann has been pretty militant about his right to puff, and the nurses, doctors, and orderlies all turn a blind eye, but Clifford hides the butt in his pudgy palm and looks so furtive you're convinced he just killed somebody.

"Hey, Poppa," he says. "Hey, Mr. Hermann."

"Hello, yourself," I respond.

"How goes it?" asks Blue Hermann.

"I don't feel very well," Clifford mutters. "Did I ever tie on one last night." With quite a length of strong rope, judging from the looks of him. There's an ugly scab on his forehead; he has done battle with another wall.

Blue Hermann, veteran of more hangovers than any man more or less alive, advises Clifford to recommence boozing immediately. Cliff shakes his head and says, "I got to go easy on that stuff."

You wonder how a boy can go from six to sixty and not change. Clifford's only accomplishment has been the acquisition of a truly monumental belly. I'm sure it must rank in the top ten worldwide.

"Hey, Poppa," says the gormless Clifford, "they almost won last night."

"They" being the South Grouse Louses. I am in this South Grouse Nursing Home mostly because Clifford lives in South Grouse, Ontario. The name of the South Grouse Industrial League Hockey Team is the Bullets. But it has been some time—more than five years, in fact—since they won a game. This is a world's record. You could look it up in your *Guinness Book* if you've half a mind to, "Longest losing streak in professional sports." They set that mark a little over a year ago, and ever since then they've been topping themselves. The South Grouse Bullets tied a game last season, but they at one time had a four-point lead, so the townspeople count that for a half loss instead of a half win. Anyway, nobody calls them the Bullets anymore. They are the South Grouse *Louses*. Even the local rag calls them that: "Louses Lose to Listowel."

But you know, the gormless Clifford is a big South Grouse Louse fan. His wife, Janine, too, may be even a bigger fan than Cliffy. She recently packed up and ran off with the equipment manager.

Clifford's cigarette is now burning the tips of his curled-up fingers and he's getting antsy. There's an ashtray over by Blue Hermann's bed, see, but Clifford can't use it, because he thinks it's a secret he's smoking in the first place. So Clifford shifts from foot to foot and sets his face in a sickly smile. Then he has an inspiration—same one he has every visit—and says, "Let's get some air in this place!" Clifford crosses over to the window, bangs it open, and flips out his little butt. Cliff takes a big breath of the fresh air as seven or eight resident ancients succumb to pneumonia.

"Close the window, Clifford," Blue Hermann snarls.

"Sorry, Mr. Hermann!" Cliffy swings it shut, comes over to sit in the bedside chair. The belly swells near to me. I am in awe. And I find myself all of a sudden surprised, I think, *where in the world did he come from?* I'm scrawny, always have been, my wife, Chloe, never weighed more than eighty pounds her whole life, and here's our offspring—two hundred and sixty pounds, six foot two. Clarence, now, was about my size. He had his mother's face, like a bird that just got a whiff of something bad.

And then no one says anything for quite a time.

Iain comes in with pills me and Blue have to take, fruit juice, and a couple of dailies, one from New York, one from Toronto. I don't bother with the newspapers, but Blue Hermann sets on them like a dog on a bone, ripping out the sports sections. He holds the paper in hands that shake so bad that he and it might as well be in different rooms. "They blew it," he announces. "They" being the Toronto Maple Leaves. "Six-zip to a suckhole team like New England." Hermann tsks his tongue, which echoes in his empty gobber like the night janitor mopping floors.

As if I care. While it's true that I'm the honorary president of the Toronto Maple Leaves Hockey Club, it was an honor bestowed on me so that they could relieve me of my previous job, being the *real* president. I couldn't tell you the names of more than about four players. I'm hardly sure who the coach is, being as they change him maybe twice a year. Actually, I tell a lie, the coach is a mook named Miles Renders, and I know that because he once came to the home in South Grouse to visit me. He wears spectacles and went to university. The man's even written books. He gave me one—it was called something like *Motivational Psychology in Professional Sports: An Overview*. Don't bother waiting for the motion picture.

Iain gives Clifford a tiny whack on the back of the head. "Hey, Cliffy," he demands, "have you been *smoking?*"

"Sorry," moans my son.

"Cigarette me, dahling," says Iain. Iain talks in different voices all the time. Don't ask me why.

Clifford chuckles, which the boy will do if presented with even a mouse-hole opportunity, and fetches out his pack. Iain lights up, inhales deeply, coughs a bit. Cliffy has one himself. He decides to enjoy it, he crosses his legs, he sets the smoke between his lips (which makes his right eye quiver), and blows a smoke ring toward the bathroom door. It's lopsided.

"You shouldn't smoke!" I tell them all. "It robs your wind. I wouldn't be *Loof-weeda*, windsong, if I'd smoked ciggies!"

Blue Hermann gives me a raspberry, his apparatus making for a real bone chiller. "Did I ever tell you, Clifford," he says, "exactly what *Loof-weeda* means?"

"Hmmm?" Clifford is something like an old dog, if you want him to pay attention, beat him over the head with a shoe.

" 'Windsong,' " says I. "Or, perhaps, 'wind music.' "

Blue Hermann isn't listening anymore. Something in the paper is making him mad, which has been happening quite a bit lately. "Hey, Iain," says Clifford. "The Louses almost won last night."

"Ahh, yes!" Iain's doing the old W. C. Fields. "The South Grouse Louses. A pitiful platoon of pusillanimous pissants."

"They almost won, though," persists Cliffy. "They only got beaten by two points."

Iain nods at my son. "Hey, I'll tell you what, boy," he says, "they didn't *lose*. They just plum *ran out of time*." Iain is making like one of those fat football coaches in the locker room. The lad's nice enough, but he's damn peculiar, that's my assessment. Once, just for an example, he marched into our room and aimed a little black box at Blue Hermann and myself. He waved it around and made a little beeping sound. Then he pretended to check readings or some such nonsense. "We're safe, Captain," said Iain. "No life-forms here." He's a strange-looking goomer, too. His hair is an eighth of an inch long. He's got plenty of it, but it's all an eighth of an inch long. Iain's head has more of a nap than a hairdo. Iain wears silly spectacles, and it seems like he's got thirty or forty pair, because he never wears the same silly spectacles two days in a row. He's a handsome enough lad, his nose is straight and his eyes are bright blue, but then he kind of goes out of his way to unenhance the effect, what with the nappy hairdo and the silly specs. On his right forearm Iain has a tattoo of a bird. The bird is in flight and savage looking. It is no type of bird that I have ever seen.

"Hey, Mr. Hermann," says Clifford, "how did Duane Killebrew do last night?"

Blue peruses the score columns and answers, "A goal and two assists."

"Lawdy, lawdy, *lawdy* !" says Iain. "Dat boy is shore a caution!"

"Which brings his yearly total to—" Blue Hermann has to do some arithmeticking in his head, and his wrinkles realign themselves with concentration—"forty-nine goals, seventy-four assists. And that's after sixty-one games."

"One year," I announce, "I had forty-nine goals." This is a bald-faced lie, but nobody's paying any attention to me anyway.

"Ladies and gentlemen," says Iain—he's gone into a television announcer's voice, all deep and golden throated—"we are here with two legends of the sports world, Ed 'Blue' Hermann and Percy 'King' Leary." Clifford is giggling. "We are here to discuss the rising young phenom, Duane Killebrew. Mr. Hermann." Iain is holding a pretend microphone, and Blue twists around, sitting up (a move that exhausts him) so that he can stick his mottled puss closer to something that isn't even there. "Mr. Hermann," says Iain. "You've seen them all. The Orrs, the Hulls, the Richards, the Clancys, the Shores, the Howes. In your opinion, is Duane Killebrew the greatest to ever play the game?"

"Sprague Cleghorn would have snapped the puppy in two!" I scream. "Eddie Shore would have made mincemeat out of him! I'll tell you that for free and give you change!"

Iain hushes me. "Mr. Hermann?"

Blue Hermann licks his lips and clears his throat. "It might be a little early to make a claim of greatest. He is without doubt the finest player in the game today."

"And the game today is nothing like the game that was! You put your midge Killebrew against a fellow like—"

"Like Manny Oz?" suggests Blue Hermann.

"Like Uncle Manny?" echoes Clifford.

"Like Manny Oz." My voice buckles, and something like a sob squeaks out. I just saw the strangest thing. As I said Manfred's name, there was a dark flash in the doorway, like someone poked his head in and out quick. It gave me a chill, and my throat choked up until it stung. I scuttle under the covers for warmth. "You put him beside Manny or any of the other old boys, and, sister, there's no comparing."

"Manny Oz," says Iain, filling in the make-believe audience, "the prodigiously talented young man whose love of the bottle brought him to an early end."

"Now interview Leary," instructs Blue Hermann. "Interview him right now."

"Yeah! Give me a blast, because Blue don't know what the hell he's saying. He's in a state of constant delirium on account of the dope you give him."

"Percival Leary. Little Leary. *Loof-weeda*. The high muck-a-muck of hockey."

"King of the Ice," adds the gormless Cliffy, my son.

"Tell me, King, in your opinion, is Duane Killebrew the greatest hockey player that ever lived?"

"In my opinion, ix-nay, nope, take a piss up a rope."

"Then who is?"

It takes about ten seconds before I can say it. "Me."

Naturally they start laughing, even my fat-assed boy.

"Damn it, it's true!" I holler. "And even if it isn't, I resent not being an option! Who potted the winner in one-nine? The King! Who led the Amerks to the Stanley Cup finals in thirty-one? The King! Who coached the Patriots to a divisional title? The King! If I'm not the greatest player, I am still the King! The King of the Ice! The King of All the Hockey Players!"

"Now, now," says Iain, his voice soft, "let's not start."

"I went toe-to-toe with Sprague Cleghorn. He couldn't stop me. Eddie Shore wanted to be the King, but I held him off. We would go into the boards and the earth would shake!"

I demonstrate, hurling myself against the wall. Iain jumps up, wrapping his arms around my waist. "Come on, Percy. Back to the real world, Percy. We don't want to have to give you a shot."

"Let him go," croaks Hermann. "He's happier in never-never land."

"Maybe I didn't score a lot of goals like Duane Killebrew, but I was too busy playing hockey to worry all the time about scoring goals."

"I'll go get Mrs. Ames," says Clifford.

Iain is grunting and sweating. I suppose I am putting up something of a ruckus. A familiar laugh fills the room. The son of a bitch always liked to see me get into predicaments. "Clay!" I bellow. "Tell them, Clay! I was the best you ever seen, wasn't I?"

"You're a prize, ducky, that's for sure."

Only that ain't Clay Bors Clinton, that's Mrs. Ames. She's got the hypo out and is making sure there's no air in it. This means I'll be sleeping for a while, that heavy black sleep that don't rest me at all.

"Tell them, Clay! Tell them I'm the King of the Ice!"

"Either you or Manny," returns a voice.

Mrs. Ames pulls down my pajama bottoms and lunges forward with a grunt. I feel a cold sting on my rump.

I go down as heavy as I did when Sprague Cleghorn two-handed me over the crown in one-nine two-six.

# FOUR

EVEN BEFORE IT CHANGED, Clay's voice had a richness to it, and your ears were drawn toward the rhythms, the rises and the falls, the way Clinton always seemed on the edge of tumbling into laughter. That's the sound I woke up to.

I opened my eyes, and the first thing I saw was Manny Oz—Manfred Armstrong Ozikean, really, because it would be some years before he became Manny "The Wizard" Oz, the Witch Doctor. It gave me quite a start, I'll say, seeing Manfred when I figured I was likely drowned and froze to death. Manfred's hair was long and red and appeared to be made out of wool. His eyes were black and a little crossed. Manny's nose was wide and flat, and fashioned so that his nostrils stared at you like another pair of eyes. Manfred saw that I was awake. His smile was vanished before I was certain that he had smiled at all.

There never was a book *Leary & Clinton Take a Tumble Through the Ice*, but if there was it would probably feature Clay Clinton saying, "That was as tight as my Aunt Rose's girdle!" because that's what Clay actually said.

The pair of us were naked and bundled in blankets, sitting on a short wooden bench. Clay had a cup of soup in his hand and Manfred handed one to me. "Soup," said Manfred.

"Luckily Manfred heard you shouting," Clay explained, as if we were in one of those penny adventure magazines.

We were in a shack not much bigger than the outhouse up at Clifford's cottage in the Muskokas. Much of the space was taken up by a black potbellied stove. Our clothes lay upon it, steaming and hissing. The hut had a floor of ice, and in front of us a square had been taken out of it. Water lapped over the edges, an odd glowing green. When he wasn't sneaking quick peaks at me and Clay-boy, Manfred hunkered over this hole in the world and stared down into it.

"I heard shouting," Manny whispered, talking more to the water than to us, "so I came and pulled you out."

"Thank you kindly," I said, the old mother having taught me to be polite. "I'm Little Leary."

He said his full weird monicker: "Manfred Armstrong Ozikean." His voice was so quiet you had to strain your ears to catch it.

Even that short conversation embarrassed poor Manfred. He took a huge gang hook, something that looked like an anchor with six sharp spikes sticking out of it, and dropped it into the glowing water. He fed out line in long, smooth movements. When he'd set the gang hook on the bottom of the river Manfred let it be for a bit, occasionally jiggling the line in his hands. Then he started it back up again, looping rope with quick, sharp turns, and in no time the gang hook was dangling above the water.

There were at least ten eels impaled on the thing, wriggling and squirming like a Blue Hermann nightmare. I could feel Clay stiffen up beside me. He was scared shitless.

Manfred grinned at us, his teeth arranged a little haphazard. Apparently this was a good haul. Clay and I managed a return smile, wondering what this lunatic might do next. What he did was open a little door at the side of the hut and one by one pick the eels from the barbs and fling them out into the night. Then he tossed the gang hook back into the water. "Eels," he informed us. "Do you want some?"

We declined with all the manners we could muster.

To avoid looking at the forthcoming eels (did you know that people actually *eat* those black wormy devils?), I took a gander around the hut. It was full of religious artifacts, twice as many as the old mother owned, and the mother was widely regarded as something of a crank. There was a painting of the

Virgin Mary hanging up. There was a particularly grisly statue of Christ upon the Cross that took up almost one whole wall. The wound on Our Savior's side was wide and gaping.

Manfred wore a crucifix around his neck. It cut the gloom like the North Star. It was big, too, almost big enough to nail up a midget. Had Manfred been of normal stature, the crucifix would have stooped him over, maybe even broken him in half. But Manfred was six foot two, two-hundred-odd pounds, most of it muscle. When I first set eyes upon him, Manfred Armstrong Ozikean was thirteen years of age.

After a time, Manny seemed to forget that we were there, or else he simply got used to us, because he started smiling (for no apparent reason) and laughing (ditto) and singing little songs under his breath. Mostly he sang hymns, and once or twice he broke into some strange stuff that I figure must have been Latin. He was raking in the eels like nobody's business, which, in my opinion, is what eel harvesting should be. Manfred nodded toward our ice skates. "I like to skate," he told us.

"Do you play hockey?" we asked, the realization hitting Clay and me that with this boy around we likely wouldn't lose another game for as long as we lived.

"Sometimes I play hockey," he admitted. "My Poppa Rivers showed me how to play. He used to play with the soldiers. But mostly I just like to skate. To go fast." Manfred shrugged.

"Is this where you live?" I asked, nodding at the tiny hut.

Manfred laughed. He had a boomy laugh, and if you weren't ready for it, it could make you jump a couple of inches. "No, I live over in the valley. This is just a fishing hut."

"Are you poor?" Clay wanted to know.

Manfred reflected on this and then shrugged. "I suppose."

"I'm rich," Clinton stated. "Little Leary is poor."

Manfred turned and looked at me. His dark eyes glowed with excitement. "Take some eels home for your family," he told me, as if this put the lid on the poverty issue once and for all. "Boil them up and eat them."

"We're not eel-poor," I told him. "Just Black Irish poor. The old man has a job, though, working for the Eddy Match Company, so we're not eel-poor."

"My father doesn't have a job," Manfred said, tossing the gang hook back through the hole in the world. "My father has no legs."

"Uh-yeah." I nodded. "My old man's got legs. Might not have any brains, but he's sure as shooting got legs."

"Hey!" shouted Manfred Ozikean. When something occurred to him, Manny let you know by shouting *"Hey"* in a very loud voice. "I have a whitefish, too. Do you want a whitefish?" Before we could say anything, Manfred had squeezed himself out the little hut door. He came back a moment later with a frozen-stiff fish in his hands. It looked to go three pounds. "This is good," Manfred said. "Take this home for your family."

Well, I'd be quite the hero if I fetched home a whitefish. I didn't know that the Ozikean clan totaled maybe fifteen people, and that they were mostly dependent on Manfred for their grub. I thanked him and took it. Manfred spent a few minutes pressing Clay into taking home some eels. "Give them to the servants," Manny suggested. Of course the Clintons had no servants, but Clay said nothing about that.

The potbellied stove soon had our clothes dry enough that we could don them and venture into the winter's night. Our teeth were chattering and it would be about a month before I got warm again, but at least I wasn't dead, for which I have Manfred Armstrong Ozikean to thank.

Clay told this story at Manfred's funeral. Manny died in a hotel room in New York, New York. Some say he had a broken heart. I disbelieve in the notion of dying from a broken heart. At any rate, the man died, and Clay spoke at his funeral (attended by thirty people tops, mostly drunken Amerks) and he told this story of how the three of us met. He somehow contrived to make it sound like it was Clay Clinton who saved Manny "The Wizard" Oz.

The Claire thing hails me on the blower. This is maybe two or three days later—I amn't sure. We don't put much stock in days here at the South Grouse. I was sleeping, I think I was having a dream, but it washes away as I pluck up the telephone.

"Yo?" The room is pale blue. They oughtn't to paint nursing-home rooms pale blue, because that's the color I expect heaven to be. They ought to paint the rooms lime green or purple, so when you wake you know you're still in the land of the living.

"Kinger-Binger?"

"Yes?" I take a glance sideways. Blue Hermann isn't in his bed. I hope he hasn't popped, I don't really want to be left alone. I look over to the other side, though, and see that our bathroom door is shut. If I strain my ears I can hear a weary grunting.

"Claire Redford *ici.*"

"The ginger ale person," I remember.

This makes the Claire thing laugh, and that in turn makes me rip the blower away from my ear and hold it out at arm's length. I give the Claire thing a few moments to calm down and then place the receiver back to my ear.

"—have a go-ahead!" Claire is saying.

"Go-ahead?"

"We want you in Toronto in two weeks." The Claire thing names some dates, Saturdays and Sundays, elevenses and twelfths.

I grunt out "Uh-yeah" and pretend that it all means something to me.

"Is there a problem?"

"Toronto's a long ways from here. I'd have to spend the night there, and I'm on medication."

"You can practically see Toronto out your window!" says the Claire thing. "We'll arrange for first-rate accommodation, and as for medication, well, my dear, who *isn't* on some damn thing or another? I mean, this is why God gave us little pills! And—here's the big surprise—Saturday night is going to be King Leary Night at the Toronto Gardens!"

"Oh."

"It is so exciting! It couldn't be more perfect!" I'm still trying to decide whether this Claire is a man or a woman, and when it gets going like this I get more and more confused. "Guess who Toronto is playing?"

"Who?"

"Ottawa! That means—drum roll—Duane Killebrew will be in town! The golden-haired cutie with the best buns around! I've managed to secure his services as well. I wish. I mean, he's going to do the commercial for us. Visualize. Two Ages of Hockey Legend. Duane Killebrew and King Leary, arm in arm. Flutter my heart. Is this not Pfeiffer Award–winning stuff, I mean, shouldn't I start dusting my mantelpiece immediately? What do you think?"

"Blue is coming with me."

"Who is this, your faithful hunting dog?"

"Blue Hermann. Newspaperman. He's coming to Toronto when I make the adverts."

"Not a problem."

"And—I think there might be someone else coming with me. One of the staff people here."

"Bring a staff person, King. Bring a fucking entourage, darling, because these ginger ale people pop coin like Penelope pops pimples."

"Okay, I'll bring him."

"Now get excited! King Leary Night at the Gardens!"

"They've had them before."

"You get to meet Duane Killebrew. This is excitement, admit it."

"All right, it's exciting."

"*Ciao.*"

I hang up on the Claire thing.

The toilet flushes, but it's minutes later when I hear the bolt get drawn back (what does Hermann figure I'm going to do, barge in on him?), and Blue comes hobbling out. Blue needs two canes to walk, both of them thick as oak saplings. He's got the Toronto *Daily Planet* newspaper rolled up and stuck in his armpit, a fate that even that rag don't deserve. "It pisses me off," he announces.

"What's that?"

Blue's got the john-to-bed lurches pretty well down pat. Anyone else would figure he was going for a tumble, but I know he'll make the mattress safe and sound. It's an alarming spectacle, though, particularly the way Blue Hermann allows himself to ricochet off the far wall. Once he's safe on top of his bed, Blue grumbles, "This new Canadian Sports Hall of Fame." He waves the *Daily Planet* at me. "Bullshit," he croaks.

"I'm in it, that's all I know. They got a whole display case for me."

"Clay's in it, too."

"What the hell for? He never did anything sports-wise, unless you count whacking me in the giblets one time when we were sprouts."

Blue tosses the newspaper over onto my bed. "There's a list of everyone who's in it."

The small print makes my eyes water. I manage to pick out a couple of names—Howie Morenz, Eddie Shore—but then I am wearied. I throw the paper into the wastepaper basket. "What's the problem, Hermann? Somebody there you figure shouldn't be?"

"Asshole," snarls Blue, and we both fall asleep pretty much simultaneous.

# FIVE

ONE DAY CLAY CLINTON INFORMED ME that the two of us had to defend the honor of his sister, Horseface. I never did learn the exact nature of the insult to Olivia, but I was more than willing to help. Clay told me that revenge had to be exacted. This is how he was talking, revenge had to be exacted, satisfaction given, recompense had for the besmirchment of the family name. I said fair enough. So, Clay told me, go get a bag full of dog dirt.

Well, a lifelong problem has been this inability of mine to think things through, but a bag full of dog dirt made as much sense as anything else back then. My next-door neighbor was an old widow woman named Mrs. Dougherty, and she had a dog. Her dog was a particularly gruesome thing, one of those wrinkled little brutes that God dropped on its face two or three times before setting onto the earth. This dog—I can even remember its name, Rex—spent all of its waking hours rooting in Mrs. Dougherty's vegetable garden. The beast was inordinately fond of radishes, so Mrs. Dougherty, having no one else to fuss over and being a motherly sort, grew the dog a whole backyard full of the little red things. Rex was out in the garden most of the time, chewing on radishes and passing them, and it was not a matter of much difficulty to go over into the yard and gather up a big sack full of shit.

Then, at night, after I was supposed to be asleep, I snuck out my bedroom window and carried this bag over to the house of Clay Clinton.

The first thing Clay did—and mind you, this is absolutely typical—is go on about how much I smelt. What the Jesus did he expect? First he tells me to get shit, then he's mad because the stuff stinks. He made me walk ten paces behind him. We walked straight downtown, across Rideau Street and into the market, just the place you want to be when you're carting a three-pounder of dog do. Then we went into a little residential area—poor people, I saw, but not as poor as my family, and certainly nowhere near eel-poor—and Clay Clinton stopped and told me, "His name is Humphries."

"Whose name is Humphries?" I wanted to know. It hadn't occurred to me that any specific person had insulted Horseface's honor. I sort of figured it was something that just happened.

"He lives," Clay went on, "right over there."

Clay pointed to a tiny wooden house with a rickety porch. There was a chicken tied up in the front yard.

Clinton produced a box of Eddy matches. It all became clear. This was how Clinton intended to avenge his sister, the old light-the-bag-of-dog-shit caper. Clay did his best to laugh ghoulishly. Even as a boy he was concerned mostly with style. Clinton pressed the matches into my hand and whispered, "Percival, the honor is yours."

"Horseface is your sister!" I argued.

"She's your betrothed, isn't she?" News to me. "You watched her take a bath."

I couldn't quarrel there. If watching a girl bathe meant you and she were betrothed, well, that's the way the world rolls. I took the matches and the bag of dog dirt up onto the little front porch.

The way the stunt works, of course, is: you light the bag aflame, knock on the door, and then scamper to a hiding place with a view. The victim opens the door and naturally starts stomping on the fire. He ends up with dog shit all over his foot. It ain't the people's choice for defending the honor of a young maiden, and maybe Clay hadn't put as much thought into the whole affair as he might have. It's all historical anyway. I set a match to the brown paper, knocked on the door, screamed, "This is for Horseface!" and then hightailed it to where Clay was hiding.

Naturally enough, Humphries wasn't home. He was likely out insulting someone else's honor. This might have been the best thing that could have happened. The paper bag might have burned and left behind a pile of smoldering manure and that would have been the end of it, were it not for Rex's strange diet. The ugly little beast ate nothing but radishes, and they rendered his shit volatile. All of a sudden there was a series of pops and fizzles coming from the front porch, and the air filled with a thick gray smoke. Great licks of flame started shooting from the bag. Then, with an enormous boom, the little porch exploded.

Clay Clinton said, with uncommon understatement, "Shit."

I ran for the porch, thinking that I might somehow be able to put the fire out. The house, however, was old and wooden, and the air was dry and hot, and it didn't take but a few seconds before the place was gone. I stood there and waved my hands, and about all I really accomplished was pointing out to all the neighbors that I was the one who had started the fire.

I didn't even bother looking for Clay. I knew he'd be long gone.


I was found guilty in the juvenile court of arson (I wasn't charged for killing the chicken) and sentenced to spend time at the Bowmanville (Annex) Reformatory for Boys. My crime was judged a serious one, and the judge shook his jowls somberly and said he thought it would be best if I stayed at the reform school until my sixteenth birthday. The judge kind of implied that when I turned sixteen he'd throw me into a real grown-up slammer.

Clay Clinton attended the court proceedings, dressed in a blue suit with short pants. He nodded judiciously throughout and seemed to think the judge's verdict was a wise one.

So they took me on the train down to Bowmanville, Ont. I was accompanied by a correctional officer, a fat man who smoked cigars and didn't say a solitary word to me. The general feeling was that I'd turned out bad, but this fellow seemed to think I was headed for the gallows. When he noticed people staring at us, and quite a few people did, the correctional officer would say to them, "Arsonist," and tip his head in my direction.

The first few times I tried to say, "I didn't know Rex's dung would explode!" but every time I said that, the correctional officer would give me a cuff on the side of the head.

At the Bowmanville train station, I was turned over to my new keepers. I thought things had gone from bad to worse.

They were *monks*.

There were four of them, all dressed in long black robes like they were waiting for a funeral to pass by. And as if them being monks wasn't bad enough—if the old man saw a monk he'd cross his fingers and wouldn't uncross them until he'd seen a horse sneeze—they were the oddest assemblage of monks the world has ever seen.

One was a great big cusser, ugly as all get-out. He looked like what dogs are dreaming about when their back legs start twitching. Another of the monks looked like a fireplug, short and squat, even to the extent of having a bright red face with a little yellow top, that being his blond hair. If this man of the cloth marched into any seaside groghouse, the drunken sailors would back out politely. The third monk was just barely there, that's how slight he was. He looked like something was eating him up from the inside. The skin on his face looked as thin as tissue paper.

The fourth was a regular enough goom, except for his eyes. They were crossed and bossed and weird in every way, a strange milky blue color. This was Brother Isaiah, about whom there were two schools of thought. The most popularly held position was that Brother Isaiah was as blind as a bat. The other school (Brother Isaiah himself being practically the only adherent) had it that Brother Isaiah could see perfectly well. To add fodder to this case, Isaiah was always saying sentences that began, "I see . . ." or "You look . . .". That's what he did now. He leant in real close to me and rested those egg blue eyes on my chest for a few seconds and then said, "I see you have arrived safe and sound, Mr. Leary."

I grunted, my old mother's admonitions of politeness be damned.

The ugly one made a big show of puckering his mouth. Speech took some preparation in his case. "Did you have a nice trip?" the monster demanded.

Next the tough little fireplug monk wanted to know if I was tired, and the skinny one asked, "Are you hungry?"

I didn't say anything. I was thinking of asking the correctional officer if he might be interested in adopting me.

The monks lined out (they couldn't walk to the icebox, I was to find out, without forming into a single file), and they led me to an old cart that was full of farming equipment, groceries, and gewgaws. There were two old horses hitched up front, and they seemed to get uneasy on our arrival, snorting and shifting their trembling legs around. I found out why. The blind monk, Brother Isaiah, climbed up onto the box. It took him upwards of two minutes to even find the reins, him groping with his hands, those two bossy-milk eyes of his no use at all.

Then the monk made a sharp chicky sound with his tongue and the side of his mouth. The old nags started moving forward and this Brother Isaiah started steering. If you want to call it steering. The wagon kept going back and forth across the road, and a few times we came within an ace of tumbling into the ditch. I was the only one who seemed to notice or care. One time the blind monk drove the horses straight for an old oak tree. I watched the two ancient beasts exchange glances, and I guess they decided that the time had finally come for rebellious action, because they pulled away just in time.

The three others sat with me in the cart and paid this wagoneer no mind. They kept trying to make conversation, but I wasn't having none of it. Instead, to keep myself occupied, I started digging around in all the junk, looking to see if there was anything interesting.

I found a hockey puck. It seemed a strange thing to find in a cart full of monks. I rooted around some more and came up with a pair of skates and a couple of sticks.

The ugly one, who'd told me that his name was Brother Simon, puckered up his face truly gruesome in order to ask, "Do you play hockey, Percival?"

I shrugged juvenile delinquent-style, but managed to sneak a little nod into it.

The fireplug, Brother Andrew, grinned and said, "Most excellent." He had a nice smile, except for the lack of teeth. He had the same amount of teeth as I do now, approximately one.

The skinny one—sunlight passed through the man—whose name was Brother Theodore, he asked, "What position do you play?"

"Mostly the centerman, but I can play the point or the cover-point. I can play the rover. I could play the wings. It none of it makes any difference to Little Leary. You could stick me in goal for all of that."

Brother Isaiah all of a sudden swung around and aimed his strange wally eyes somewhere in my general vicinity. "Mr. Leary," he said, "your new home."

Ahead of me, sitting at the end of a road and the top of a hill, was a castle. It looked like a picture ripped out of one of my brother Lloyd's storybooks, *The Knights of the Round Table*. The first time I saw it, the reformatory was golden in the autumn sun, all covered by clouds and ivy. It had turrets and round windows and even a moat, except for the moat was just an ambitious ditch. We had to cross a small bridge to get over, and then we had to pass under a gateway. I looked up and saw that someone had burned these words into the wood:

TO KEEP A BOY OUT OF HOT WATER, PUT HIM ON ICE

# SIX

THIS DREAM I'VE BEEN HAVING—I've been having the *same* dream over and over again, although I can never recall it on waking—has something to do with Manfred's funeral. Why in the world would I be dreaming about that? Clay and I went, dressed in suits as black as midnight. Jane came with us, and I was surprised that she didn't shed a single tear for the man she almost married. She seemed more angry at Manny than anything else, and I swear to God I heard her mutter "Christly bastard" even as the preacher said what a good man Manfred had been. There was weeping done, though, by some of the boys from the New York Americans (they attended the funeral pissed) and mostly by Hallie. Hallie wailed like an Indian spirit. The tears spilled from her and dropped onto her satin dress. Jubal St. Amour, the owner of the Americans, he made a small speech and said some poetry. Blue Hermann came, along with that bubbly-bosomed woman that was always on his arm back in those New York days. And after the funeral, after we'd laid Manfred in the cold earth, I remember Blue catching my eye. He gave me a look that made me shiver. I remember thinking, *son of a gun, that man hates me.* But when he worked for the Toronto *Daily Planet* and I ran the Leaves, we seemed to get along well enough, so I guess that was either my imagination or due to the fact that Hermann sees everything in a blue fog, as if he had blue-colored spectacles balanced on his grog-blossomed nose.

Blue is currently reading the sports pages, seeing them blue, his body crackling with the St. Vitus's dance, his face composed and scholarly. He's also doing a fairly masterful job of ignoring me.

"I am here to tell you, Hermann," I tell him, "that the Brothers of St. Alban the Martyr made me what I am today." Well, not actually what I am *today*, which is a shriveled old bastard who can't even summon the wherewithal to die, but those monks made me the hockey player I once was.

Blue Hermann lights a cigarette, a cunning strategy, as the first puff will start him hacking. He lets loose an assortment of horks and spews that drown me out. I persist, what the Christ, I got little better else to do.

"I was an extremely well rounded hockey player, thanks to Brother Isaiah and all the boys. Why, I once played *every single position* during a Stanley Cup play-off game. It was in one-nine two-three. Against the Hamilton Tigers. The Tigers were a tough aggregation, a bunch of plug-ugly larrikins, and they kept immobilizing us through checks and various murderous antics, and as our ranks thinned, Patty Boyle just kept shifting me about. 'Leary,' he'd say, 'you're on the left wing.' I'd move over there and do one hell of a job. 'Leary,' Patty Boyle would say, 'get back on defense.' 'Yes, sir.' And in the third period, our net minder, North Innes, took his stick and two-handed a goom across the back of the legs. The man crippled up and tumbled. North was called for a five-minute, and in those days the goaler atoned for his own sins. North stuck his goalie's stick in my hand. 'Look after the net for me, Leary,' he says. And I went into the goal, and the history books will tell you that I didn't let in a solitary puck. I am the only man to ever play every position during a Stanley Cup play-off game!"

Blue turns the page of his newspaper. "Manny got seven goals that game," he says.

"Yeah." That was, I'll admit, a keen stunt.

"Still the record," Blue mentions.

"Unless that punk Killebrew has smashed that one, too."

Blue Hermann suddenly looks up at me. His eyes are rheumy, squashed by all of his bad living, but he aims them at me and I find myself shivering. *Son of a gun, that man hates me.*

It was sometime in late October when the brothers started putting together the boards. They were usually a quiet bunch, but they got even quieter, all of them rushing around with hammers in their hands and nails sticking out of their mouths. The only thing us lads heard from them was pounding out in the playing field, pounding and the occasional grunt. I personally thought the monks were crazy, and I'll tell you why: they laid out the boards in a circle. A huge and, as far as I could tell, perfect circle. I even asked Brother Isaiah about it. He just grinned and fastened his strange eyes on my left shoulder. "Have ye not known?" he asked me. "Have ye not heard? It is he that sitteth upon the circle of the earth that bringeth the princes to nothing." That's the kind of answer I used to get from Brother Isaiah. So anyway, they laid out the boards in a circle, and around the beginning of December they raised them. The monks took the old horses off the cart. It took the horses and sometimes six or seven brothers to raise each section of board. The weather stayed pleasant for a week or two, the sun all biting and bright even though the trees were naked as firewood. We all waited; the monks prayed.

On Christmas Eve the temperature fell about forty degrees. The brothers rushed out with buckets and hoses. They stayed out there all night, and to keep themselves amused they sang. They sang strange songs with words I didn't understand. All night long the monks watered the world, and the winter air turned the water to ice. Blue-silver ice, hard as marble. On Christmas morning the round rink was ready. Brother Simon was out there skating, his face even uglier, reddened by lack of oxygen, his carbuncles polished by the stinging wind. For a huge, monstrous man he sure could dance out there on the ice! He had some figure-skating moves, dips and twirls, his arms raised slightly, the hockey stick acting as a balancing pole. And as I watched him, Brother Simon the Ugly became airborne. It seemed he was up there for a whole minute, and during that time he pirouetted lazily. This stunt robbed me of my breath

and made my knees quiver. I determined right then and there
to learn how to do that. It would be some months before I did,
and it would take a couple of years for me to refine it and come
up with the spectacular St. Louis Whirlygig.

Brother Andrew, the one who looked like both the fireplug
and the bulldog that might employ it, was streaking up and
down, dodging invisible opponents. Whatever he was doing,
it made my hardstep look like a cakewalk. I said to myself,
Leary, if you could do that, no one could ever stop you. It took
me some months to learn to skate like Brother Andrew the
Fireplug. I call it Bulldogging. Miles Renders, who is currently
coaching the Toronto Maple Leaves, calls it "achievement
through perseverance and mental imaging," and I say that one
of the reasons the Leaves are faring so poorly is that Renders
would call Bulldogging something like that. All it is, is, you
are at point one. You want to be at point two. The shortest
distance, as every schoolboy knows, is a straight line, but there
are no less than four big johnnies blocking the way. The secret
is, don't give a tinker's cuss, just go, man. Just go.

Brother Theodore the Slender, who seemed on the verge of
evaporation with all the rink-building activity, stood in the center of the round rink, his eyes half-closed, his pale lips moving
slightly in silent prayer.

And some of the other monks (there were twenty-odd
monks at the reformatory, regular fellows, especially in comparison to the four I knew best) were taking shots on Brother
Isaiah.

I have never in my life seen such a good goaler as Brother
Isaiah, and I have seen everyone from the Chicoutimi Cucumber to that tall slender fellow who looked like a schoolteacher
and played so well for the Montreal Canadiens in the seventies. Yet I am convinced to this day that Brother Isaiah was
blind as a bat, though he denied it. Isaiah might occasionally
admit to being "a tad shortsighted," but you'd have to catch
him walking into a brick wall. But the other monks couldn't
get a shot by him. Isaiah would just reach out and grab them
in his glove (and gloves back then didn't amount to much), or
else he'd get the toe on them, or the chest in front of them, or

bang them away with his stick. Brother Simon the Ugly tried to jimmy one by him, dancing right up to the goal crease, flipping the puck off his backhand as he made one of his ballerina twirlabouts. Brother Isaiah flicked it away with his wood. Then Andrew the Fireplug comes barreling along the wing, taking out a couple of bystander brothers just for style, and he unleashes a slapshot even though the damn thing isn't even invented back then! Brother Isaiah the Blind raises his left shoulder maybe a quarter inch and the rubber is dancing harmlessly behind the net.

But there was Brother Theodore standing in the center of the huge silver circle, and his eyes were popped open all the way and his mouth had ceased working. In front of him was a puck. Brother Theodore the Slender brought his stick back real slow, and then, with a motion that cut the air like a knife, Brother Theodore whacked the rubber. I swear to Jesus he hit that puck harder than Bobby Hull ever hit one, and it didn't even look like he was trying. Brother Isaiah didn't hear it or feel it, or however else he detected pucks, as I believe with all my heart that the man couldn't see the sun if it tumbled into his backyard.

There was a small smile on the face of Theodore the Slender.

I learnt how to do that, too. Some people (like scrawny Hermann over on the next bed) say that shooting was the weakest part of my game, but in my prime I could whistle the rubber like nobody's business. I scored on every goaltender there was in my day, and they'll tell you that I had one of the hardest shots going. Unfortunately you can only ask Hugo "Tip" Flescher, because he's the only one still breathing. What's more, you better hurry. But Theodore the Slender gave me the gam on shooting, which is this: shooting is more mental than physical. You just practice so much that you can feel the puck, like the blade of your lumber was the palm of your hand, and then you just inner-eye that puck into the back of the net. "See it there first," Brother Theodore was wont to say, "and then put it there." In other words, *wham, bingo.*

The monks left off playing long enough to tell us that there were plenty of skates in the recreational hall cupboards, so us puppies ran off to lace up. I had my own pair with me, of course. I'd brought them from Bytown, even though I'd had to leave out most of my clothes to get them into my suitcase. I was the first one on the ice with the Brothers of St. Alban the Martyr, and I commenced to hardstep. I flew around the circle. I got my speed up so that ice formed in my eyebrows. When I finally stopped, I saw that all of the other delinquents, and all of the black-robed monks, were staring at me.

Brother Simon the Ugly puckered hideously and made the following pronouncement. "It would seem," he said, "that Percival is something of a natural!"

The phrase just tickled me. One time I even asked my wife, Chloe, to put that on my grave marker: PERCIVAL H. LEARY, SOMETHING OF A NATURAL. But Chloe died many years back, done in by more diseases and ailments than I could count. I can't recall what it says on her gravestone.

Andrew the Fireplug divided us boys into two teams, and we had some shinny scrimmages. Periodically Isaiah would stop us and give us such coaching tips as, "Who through faith wrought righteousness, he quenched the violence of fire and waxed valiant in fight!" We quickly learnt how to nod politely (us little boys nodding at a blind man!) and then we'd get back to playing. I was the best pup on the ice, scoring four or five goals in as many rushes. Then I stole the puck from a boy named Billy and smashed him into the boards. Theodore the Slender rendered a two-finger toot that almost ripped the ears off my head.

"Leary," he intoned somberly. "Expulsion!"

"What?" I screamed.

All of the monks droned "Expulsion" in unison. It sounded like their strange singing.

"You mean I can't play anymore?"

Theodore the Ugly said, "You *weren't* playing."

I was mortified. I threw away my stick and left the ice.

You see what they were trying to tell me, don't you—that hockey is a team sport. I had forgotten that, because I was so damn much better than anybody else.

# SEVEN

BROTHER ISAIAH WAS THE HEAD HONCHO MONK. No one ever said as much, for theirs was an order that disbelieved in head-honchoness, but if there was deciding to be done, it usually got left to Brother Isaiah. He also did much of the actual teaching. There is a rumor that aside from the game of hockey I don't know a hell of a lot. But Brother Isaiah the Blind taught me all sorts of things. He taught me how a bird flies, for example, but it's too complicated to get into. He taught me history, mostly Roman stuff, great battles and whatnot. He made me read books, all sorts of them. Back then, I recall, there were books about a baseball player named Frank Merri-well. I read those all the time. He was a handsome do-gooder and always won the ball game with a grand-slam homer. They never did have any books starring a hockey player, at least not until they come up with the Clinton & Leary Farting Around series, which were pretty good. Here's how they used to go:

Suddenly, a scream pierced the winter air.
"Egad!" exclaimed Clay Clinton. "That sounded like Meredith Potter!"
"Faith and begorrah!" piped up Leary, his Irish blood at a boil. "It must be the blackguard Pierre LaFrance is arter her, t'be sure."
"Come on, Leary!"
Clay Clinton, his blond hair flying in the wind, ran off in the direction of the Potter home.

I only heard Clay say "egad" once. He had his arms wrapped around a toilet bowl, and I think it came up by accident along with a gallon of bad whiskey.

Another thing about Brother Isaiah the Blind. When a new boy would come to the reformatory, Isaiah would tell us the night before about the lad's arrival. He'd stand up, his strange eyes looking at nothing any of us could see, and he'd say how a new tyke was coming (he wouldn't say his name) and then he'd say what crime or crimes the fellow had committed. (A lot of the pups, by the by, were arsonists. I was sort of a hero for having ignited a house with dog dirt.) I think Brother Isaiah's reasoning was that we'd hear of the misdeed—robbery, say— and we'd get a mental picture in our minds of a Bill Dalton sort, and when the boy came in he was always just an apple-cheeked scallywag like the rest of us, so in that way we learnt not to tag people.

This one night, Brother Isaiah climbs to his feet and says that a boy is coming who was found guilty of car theft. Car theft might be pretty common stuff nowadays, but back then it was quite the caper. For one thing, only rich people had automobiles, so stealing one never seemed like a particularly good idea. Brother Isaiah said there was some evidence to suggest that the young fellow had need of the automobile, a family emergency of some sort, but we all thought, *They're shipping us a dope.* Brother Isaiah went on to say that when the fellow was apprehended he'd beaten the tar out of four or five peace officers. *Aha*, we thought, *they're shipping us a* Big *dope.*

So I for one wasn't that surprised when the four monks came back from the train station with Manfred Armstrong Ozikean in tow.

All us inmates gathered around to gawk at him. Manfred had grown a bit, which made him the biggest boy in history. He smiled at us, but his eyes were watering and his lips trembled. Most of the other boys were nervous around him, even outright frightened, so I decided to show off a bit. I stepped to the front of the crowd and gave a little wave, saying, "Ho there, Manfred!"

Manfred gave forth with one of his "Hey!"s. This scared the boys, not only because the "hey" was loud, but also because I don't think they'd figured on Manny being capable of speech. "It's my friend Percy!" Manfred told the trembling assembled.

"Percival," asked Simon the Ugly, "are you acquainted with Mr. Ozikean?"

"Sure thing," I answered. "We're both from the old Bytown. He plucked me out of the canal."

"Perhaps," suggested Brother Andrew the Fireplug, "you could take him under your wing."

"I'll do that." I waggled my fingers at Manny, and he came with me like a monstrous puppy dog. The lads gave us wide berth, and I reckoned I'd improved my status considerably.

"How's things in Ottawa?" I asked Manny.

Manfred thought about that for a while. He finally said, "Clay is fine."

Even at Clay Clinton's funeral, people were a bit guarded with their praise. The minister, for instance, said how Clay was a fine man, but how we likewise shouldn't forget that he was usually under a lot of stress. That's playing it pretty close to the vest for a eulogy. I was the man's best friend, his bosom companion, and even I have on occasion had a hard time saying something nice about him.

This wasn't the case with Manfred. To hear Manny tell it, and by jim he told it, Clay Clinton was perhaps the finest human being that God ever assembled.

It started that first night at the Bowmanville (Annex) Reformatory. We all went to bed in the bunk hall, but instead of talking about girls (which we didn't know anything about) or hockey (my favorite) or baseball (I was an excellent infielder, you know, and likely could have played in the major leagues) Manny Ozikean regaled us with tales of the great Clay Clinton. He said as how Clay was the best friend a guy could have. Manfred came from a huge family, one with aunts and uncles and kids in the double digits, and Manfred told us they might have starved to death if not for Clay Clinton bringing them food. (Likely stealing it from some other poor family, I thought.) It was sickening. We had to listen to how Clay played Rover-Come-Over with Manfred's baby brother, Oliphant. We had to listen to how Clay took Manny's sister Winnifred to the

parish hall dances. The other pups listened, their eyes bugged
and their jaws on the ground, like we were discussing King
Arthur or Lancelot, not some teenage porker from Ottawa.
But that's the way it was with Clay. People always talked
him up.

Manfred Ozikean set up a little private altar before he went
to sleep. He took his statue of Christ, the one where the wound
in His side was so gaping that innards were slipping out, and
nailed it to the wall. Manfred had a little model of the Virgin,
which he set on his bedside table. He took the huge silver crucifix from around his neck and laid it down gently beside. Then
Manfred took candles, five or six of them, and arranged them
in a circle on the floor. He lit the candles, but everything seemed
to get darker. Manfred took a photograph, a purple one with
dog-eared edges, and set that in the middle.

I took a gander at the photograph. It was blurry and filled
with strange clouds, because no one was much good at making pictures back then. It was a photograph of a girl. I understood why Clay had become so friendly with the Ozikean clan. I
knew this was Manny's sister Winnifred, and I also had a pretty
good hunch as to why her photograph was lying there in the
candlelight.

Well, I have to tell you that the team from the Bowmanville
(Annex) Reformatory was one hell of a hockey team, mostly
because of me, Little Leary. The year before we'd won the
county championship pretty handily, and that was against a
team with near adults and everything. We took hockey pretty
serious, we did, so the day after Manfred's arrival we practiced,
which is what we did every day.

We were in for another surprise. It won't be as much of a
surprise for some of you people, seeing as the name Manny
"The Wizard" Oz is almost as well known as mine.

We divided teams for shinny, which is how we warmed up
for the weird drills and maneuvers that Brother Isaiah would
put us through. For some reason Isaiah named his drills after
flowers, the Rose and the Tulip and such. I once tried to put
the Ottawa Patriots through the Rose when I was the coach
and I damn near had a mutiny on my hands.

So we divided for a warm-up game, and no one picked Manfred until the next-to-last call. He and I ended up on opposite sides.

Manfred looked mighty clumsy waiting for things to get started, his ankles all trembly, his upper body having to twist every so often so that he wouldn't pitch forward. It looked as if Manfred had trouble even standing in skates and, of course, that's entirely correct. Manfred had trouble standing in skates.

Brother Isaiah skated to the middle of the ice. His eyes looked like stones left over from digging a grave. Isaiah held out a puck over what was likely dead center of the round rink. He put two fingers into his mouth and tooted. We commenced.

I scooped the face-off. Down the boards I went in a Brother Andrew Bulldog. I mowed down two lads, stepped around another. Then I saw Manfred waiting for me. Well, my only concern is that he doesn't fall on me. I decided I'd take him out with my (still rudimentary) St. Louis Whirlygig. I went into the move, and all of a sudden I was arse over teakettle, and Manfred was waltzing down the ice like a ballerina. He outskated Brother Simon the Ugly! Manny spent more time in the air than he did on the ground. Every so often Manfred would set a toe to the ice, but it was more like how every so often a whale has to break surface to breathe. Manny cranked up to shoot and the goaler dropped his stick and covered his head, not that I could blame him. Manfred just floated the puck over the lad's shoulders, and his team was a point to the better.

Those four monks stood there looking like they'd died and gone to heaven. Even skinny Theodore was grinning. Manfred looked bashful. You might remember that look if you've got any great age to you. I recall when the Patriots tied up the Stanley Cup finals with Toronto in one-nine two-five. Manny scored the tying goal, one of the most beautiful I've ever seen, and while the crowd went wild, Manfred stood there looking like he'd just shit his drawers.

So we had another face-off. I won it, flipped the rubber backwards to a teammate, and then I hardstepped toward the other end. Manfred was nowhere to be seen, which I found a mite puzzling. I took a position near the side of the net, and all of a sudden I hear this cheer. I spun around, and down at the

other end the goaler was flipping the puck out of the net. Manfred wore the expression of a dog who'd just buried something
disgusting in the backyard.

Well, it wasn't all bad that day. I did score two or three
goals, but at dinnertime no one wanted to talk about me, they
all wanted to talk about Manfred. Except for Manfred, who
wanted to talk about Clay Clinton. I shoved some peas around
on my plate and then went to bed.

# EIGHT

"WHAT I DON'T SEE," says the gormless Clifford, cradling his monumental belly, "is what a castle was doing there near Bowmanville."

"A rich fellow named Jensen built the castle as a present to his wife," I answer. "It cost him nearly every penny he had, and when it was finished, the missus decided she didn't much care for it, and she took a scamper. Jensen had to sell the castle to the municipal government, and they annexed it for the reformatory."

"Oh." Cliffy is depressed by this, reminded of his own matrimonial hard luck. His wife, Janine, ran off with the Louses' equipment manager, you know. I thought the story might cheer him up, after all, if a goddamn *castle* won't do the trick, how the hell did Clifford think he could make a woman happy with a bungalow in South Grouse and a rinky-dink cottage up in the Muskokas?

The inability to hold on to women is nothing particular to the gormless Cliffy, although he takes it harder than most fellows. He is staring at the rounded toes of his boots as if they might tell him what to do. Clifford is a no-account, but I love him pretty much. After all, he's not as big a no-account as his brother, Clarence. Clarence never did nothing except write pornography and one episode for that teevee show *The Twilight Zone*. He wrote a book of poems that got his butt arrested, that's how filthy it was! It was in the newspapers every day how my son was being tried for obscenity. So don't be mean-mouthing the gormless boy Clifford. His mother disliked him, you know, for he is big and fat.

Mind you, if Chloe were here to speak for herself (instead of in the ground, massacred by disease), she'd rebut that I disliked Clarence, that I was unable to forgive Clarence for an incident that happened when the boy was only five. This is not the case. It was the other things I was unable to forgive him for, the way he affected the name of Rance and did everything in an abnormal fashion. Take skating. He had me for a teacher, and I tried to show him the hardstep, but Rance wouldn't have any of it. He moved around the rink with his hands held up for balance, pushing off from his back leg in short, sweet motions, in other words, skating like a girl! Sheer perversity on his part, and I swear to Jesus he enjoyed the way it grieved me. So don't get me going about my son Clarence.

What we got now is Iain coming into the room, armed with pills and fruit juices. "Cliffy," says Iain, "make wit da smokes."

My boy giggles and reaches for his cigarettes.

"So how's it going?" asks Iain, settling into a chair beside my son.

"I don't feel so good," admits Clifford. "I got corked again last night. I'm maybe going to quit drinking."

"Who gives a shit?" says I, but that's a bad thing to say. The boy's face is full of hurt and bafflement. "You just drink a couple of beer now and then, don't you, Cliffy?"

"Yeah." Clifford nods. "No big deal, eh, Poppa? I just quaff a few brewskies now and again."

"You're fine, son. Not like Manfred. He'd hit the bottle and you never seen the likes. Say good night, sister."

"Fuck yourself, Leary." This from Blue Hermann, who is reading his damn sports sections. Something's got his goat, but I pay no attention: his wrinkled brain is puffed up with pharmaceuticals and contraband whiskey.

"Iain," says I, "how'd you like to meet the puppy Killebrew?"

"Duane-o!" shouts Iain. "My main man!"

"I thought I was your main man!"

"King, you are my main hockey legend. But Duane-o is my main active player."

"Who's gonna meet Duane Killebrew?" asks Clifford.

"He's not so much," I tell them. "He's all flash, no grit."

Blue Hermann reports, "He got a hat trick last night."

"It likely wasn't a real hat trick!" I tell them. "A real hat trick is when you score three goals in a row, all in the same period. And what's more, if you scored a real hat trick, you got a goddamn *hat*!"

"A cornucopia of sporting lore!" says Iain in that high-pitched nasal voice all the radio guys had back in the thirties and forties.

"I had a number of real, true hat tricks," I recall. "Probably still got the real hats somewhere. It was a top hat they gave you, a fancy number. I imagine I have fifteen or twenty of them. I remember, I had a real, true hat trick in my first game with the Amerks. Three goals in a row, all in the third period. I only played the third period, because for the first two I was unconscious, rendered such by that son of a bitch Sprague Cleghorn! Anyways, I wake up and hit the ice with blood caked on my noggin. Some people say it was the best hockey playing they ever saw. Potted three goals, won the game for the pitiful New York Americans. And Jubal St. Amour, he—" I shut up as I remember Hallie's satin dress falling in the moonlight. "Anyways," I grab Iain's shirtsleeve, "you want to meet this Killebrew grub or what?"

"Who's gonna meet Duane Killebrew?" demands Clifford.

"Here's the scoop," I tell Iain. "The Canada Dry people want me to come to Toronto and make a small advert. I'm getting ten thou. I got to go for overnight, though, so I thought I'd need a staff person with medical knowledge, should I decide to croak."

Iain says, "You ain't about to croak."

"Yeah, but how about Blue?"

"Blue's going?"

"Damn betchas."

Blue Hermann says, "I want to see this new Canadian fucking Sports Hall of Fame."

I jerk a thumb at the wrinkled newspaperman. "Give this mook some horse tranks, Iain. He ties his butt in a pretzel every time he thinks about this new Canadian Sports Hall of Fame. I'm in it, that's all I know, one entire display case. I believe they got the actual one-nine one-nine lumber, the stick I used to score that overtime goal."

"So anyways," asks Clifford, "when is this?"

Iain butts the cigarette on the bottom of his shoe. From where he's sitting he can see the toilet through a small crack made by the bathroom door. He cocks the butt between his thumb and middle finger and spends a few seconds lining up and aiming. Then Iain flicks it away. The butt bounces into the toilet off the upraised throne seat.

"Rimmer," I mutter.

"Odd angle," he says.

"No excuses, boy."

"It was a tough shot."

"Tough shots the only ones worth making," I explain.

"Sounds like it could be a lot of fun," says the gormless boy.

"I don't think I should go," says Iain. "I, um . . ."

"Come on," I say. "You could have fun in Toronto. I'll pay for everything, maybe even slip you a few bucks bonus."

"Yeah, but, *Toronto* —"

"Maybe I could drive."

"We can stay in a fine hotel. We can eat good food."

"Hey, Mrs. Ames has a sister in Toronto," Iain mentions, "I'm sure she'd like to go."

Now Blue Hermann speaks up. "No." He's more than adamant.

"We could all fit in my car, no probs."

"What do you say, Iain?"

He stands up, smoothes down his trouser legs. "I shall dwell on it, my liege."

"You wouldn't have to spend all your time looking after me. Maybe you could meet some girls, go to a few bars or something."

"Bars," mutters Iain. "Just what I need."

Clifford climbs to his feet, too fast though. He misjudges and his monumental belly almost makes him topple over onto my bed. He steadies himself and says, "I gotta go, Poppa. The Louses are playing tonight. I got this feeling they're gonna win."

"All right, son. Thanks for dropping by."

# NINE

THE BOWMANVILLE (ANNEX) REFORMATORY hockey squad for boys sixteen years of age and under were the All-Ontario Champions in one-nine one-five, and to win that we had to go to a tourney in the city of Ottawa. The monks had to pull a lot of strings to get us there, because Bytown was none too keen on letting a bunch of juvies invade the burg. But news of me and Manfred had spread pretty good, the both of us born and bred in Bytown, so the city fathers decided to give us the green light.

I still get goose-bumped thinking about how good that hockey team was. Sometimes nowadays I'll wander down to the common room, and the ancients will be watching a hockey game on the color teevee. It might be, say, the Maple Leaves versus whatever the damn team from Los Angeles, California, is called. I'll watch for a bit, and then I'll start to hoot, and I'll say, "You boys is making one hundred thousand plus per annum, but you'd lose and lose bad to a team of pint-size hooligans, come-to-naughts, and arsonists that played back in one-nine one-five!" And I'm not just tooting my own trumpet, because I wasn't the only great one on that team. There was Manfred Ozikean, or Manny Oz as he came to be known, the Wizard, the Witch Doctor. (It's funny how they used to call him that. It started because before games Manny used to like to cross himself and mumble a few words to his Creator, but for some reason this started the fans calling him the Witch Doctor, as if he'd been strangling chickens and drinking their blood. Oh, I know that in the last years with the Americans Manny used to play along, spinning little circles, whooping

Indian-style and suchlike, but Manfred was pretty far gone
with the liquor by then.)

And, of course, we were well coached. None of the other
boys had the raw talent of me or Manfred, but they all learnt
the Bulldog and the Inner-Eye Fling. Some of them could even
execute a passable St. Louis Whirlygig, although none could
do what I did, namely, cast some doubt in observers' minds as
to whether or not I was ever coming down! And, during the
actual games, there was Brother Isaiah the Blind whispering in
our ears. He'd often tell us to pretend to be certain animals.
The games I liked least (although I can't say I've ever really
disliked a game of hockey) was when Isaiah would tell us to be
as a colony of ants, which meant a game of hard work and
drudgery, digging in the corners, checking every inch of the
way. When he told us to be as a swarm of bees I got fairly
excited, because this meant we would zip in their end to nag
and worry them, make the other team lose the puck through
general pestiness. But my favorite type of game was when
Brother Isaiah would whisper, "Be as a pack of *wolves*." That
was when we played our very best.

So we go to Ottawa, us Bowmanville Boys, and we play,
and none can even touch us, and we were the champs. They
held a big reception for us in my old neighborhood parish hall.
My mother was there, and Francis and Lloyd, and my little
sister Bernice, who later married a fellow with a withered hand.
(The old man, by the way, died during my first year at reform
school. He was walking along Hogarth Street when some biddy
opened her third-floor apartment window and knocked over a
flowerpot. The pot hit the old man on the bean and that was
that. I felt bad for the father. It was such a silly way to go.) We
go to the parish hall right after the final game (I'd scored the
winning tally, and a pretty one it was) and we no sooner set
foot inside when a horde of old ladies loaded down with cookies and refreshments surrounded us. I didn't want a cookie,
but I had quite a thirst to slake, so I grabbed a tall glass of
something clear, golden, and sparkly. I poured that down my
gullet and then went to say thanks to the blue-haired dowager
who'd given it to me.

*"Burrap!"* I let out a sound to wake the dead. It made the biddy stumble backwards, and a hand went to her heart. Everyone in the place turned and stared at me, except for Brother Isaiah, who didn't know where to look and finally peered cautiously towards heaven. I burped again, even louder. I tried to strangle this one deep in my throat. It made some odd twists and turns before it got past my lips. *"Eeeerrruppppaarrrhhh!!"* My head was light as a feather; there was a tingling in my ears. Something inside of me wanted to start fights, but only the good fights, fights with thugs, monsters, and dragons. I grinned at the people in the parish hall and then stumbled off to find adventure.

That was my first encounter with the good old Canada Dry ginger ale, and I hope they let me tell about it when I make the advert.

"Hello, old bean!"

I don't have to tell you who said that. Who else would call me "old bean"? I wasn't surprised to see that Clay Clinton was there, either, but what did give me the wet noodle to the puss was the way the boy looked. Sometime in the previous year Clay had shot up to his adult height of six foot even, and all of his baby fat had been used in the reconstruction, rendering Clinton lean and hard. His face was the handsomest I've ever seen on a man, handsomer even than Rance Plager, who you probably remember played on the Rangers back in the thirties and then went on and had a career in motion pictures. Or maybe you don't remember, no large difference. Point being, Clay was handsome. Most people remember him as he was just before he died, which was fat again, red faced and bloated, his nose all exploded and bumpy even though he only drank the finest cognac and champagne. That's a bit of shame, but I suppose it's only natural, and that's how most of us get remembered. Clay all fat and bloated. Manny scarred and black eyed. My wife, Chloe, consumed by disease. Jane pale as a sheet, both legs in metal harnesses. I hope people remember me as I was in the twenties, one hundred and forty-six pounds of shinny-playing Irishter, not pretty to look at, but a hell of a scrappy young donegan. I hope they don't remember me as I am now, which is maybe fifty pounds of skin and bone. I am so scrawny I don't even wrinkle the bedclothes.

"Hiya, Clay!"

"Does Manfred," asked Clay, "ever mention his sister Winny?"

"Manny doesn't say much that isn't about hockey or you. What's the scoop, anyways? Is she croaked?"

"Alas, yes," nodded Clay. He could say "alas" and get away with it, that's how good looking he was. "Cut down in the prime of her youth, Percival. Somebody should write a poem."

Clay was dressed in a suit, three pieces and all the accessories: collar stays, tiepins, a boutonniere, and a folded-up snotrag in the breast pocket. He had cufflinks that showed the two linked Cs that was his trademark.

I was wearing shorts and knee socks, which is what the monks had decided us lads should wear when we weren't in our hockey uniforms.

Clay said, "I must find the big Man-Freddy and congratulate him." Clay Clinton vanished.

What about congratulating me? That championship game I'd gotten three goals (one of them proving to be the winner, and truly radiant it was), but Clay hadn't said anything about that. One last ginger ale belch came up, and I spit it out with all my force. It silenced the room.

"Big storm coming," ventured Brother Isaiah the Blind.

The old biddies had hired this magician to put on an Entertainment. Wallace the Wonderful, he was called, and he was all right, if you happen to like magic. Myself, I can take it or leave it. Anyway, Wallace ran through some prestidigitations and thimbleriggery, and he even had one of the dowagers squawking like a chicken, which was the best part of the show. Then he turns all spooky, wrapping a black cape around his shoulders and hollering, "Now I shall cause a Spirit to become incarnate!" This made me chuckle, because Wallace the Wonderful had the aspect of an overfed hamster, and it was plain that all he meant to do was haul some tiny animal out of his top hat. "The Spirits are in this very room!" he chanted. "And I shall cause one to become flesh and blood!"

All of a sudden there was a crashing sound, and Manny Ozikean came flying through one of the parish hall's stained-glass windows.

Manfred landed in the glass, his hands and face all bleeding, and he moaned for a second or two. I can't remember exactly what he moaned—it was of a religious nature. Then Manny started puking, more watery green bile than I've ever seen before or since.

Brother Isaiah fastened his weird robin's-egg eyes on Manfred Ozikean. "It looks," said the monk, "as if he's a bit intoxicated."

Naturally this scandalized the old biddies something fierce, and whatever good reputation us delinquents had managed to fabricate went straight down the flusher.

Sometime later they found Clay Clinton asleep in one of the coat cupboards. He was curled up like a baby, smiling about Lord knows what. Clay's nose made little whistling noises while he slept, and sometimes they could sound quite musical.

We got them both to bed, at least, we got them stretched out and covered up on the floor of the hall where we boys were sleeping.

Later that night I snuck downstairs to the coat cupboard and rummaged around. I found what I was looking for, namely, a little pewter flask. The flask was empty except for fumes, but the fumes were enough to rot socks. The flask had this engraved on the side:

$$\mathcal{CC}$$

# TEN

THROUGH THE WINDOW OF THE BUNK HALL we could see the moon sitting in a tree like some stupid tomcat. One night Manfred got up from his cot and spent a long time looking at it. "Percival," he whispered, knowing somehow that I was awake, "I think I better go fight."

"Fight the Huns?"

Manfred nodded.

I'd been giving that some consideration myself. It seemed like a good idea. We were getting too old to be juvenile delinquents anyway.

When I left, the four monks, the monks that were closest to me, each gave me a small gift.

Theodore the Slender gave me a ring. I got it on now. It has a small stone in the middle. I don't know what kind of stone it is, but it's as bright as the sun. Andrew the Fireplug gave me a hat, a little coal miner's cap that became my trademark. Simon the Ugly gave me a new pair of boots, fancy jobs for perambulating about town and taking corners on one heel. Isaiah the Blind gave me a walking stick with a dragon's head carved on top. Brother Isaiah claimed to have made the thing himself, and while you don't like to disbelieve a man of the cloth, the dragon is so nicely rendered that it's hard to give the man's claim credence. I got the walking stick now. I use it on the rare occasions I go out. I don't need it because of any agèd and infirm hobble, mind you. I just need it.

They gave Manfred some gifts, too, damn strange ones. Brother Theodore the Emaciated gave him a little leather pouch full of money. That is, if you want to call twenty-six cents and some glass beads *money*. Andrew the Hydrant gave Manny a hat, a huge ugly goat-herder. It covered most of Manny's face and caused him to bump into things. Simon the Gruesome gave him a pocket watch. It was gold, and the back was engraved, but the face was busted all to Kingdom Come, and it was obvious that the timepiece was going to proclaim 3:26 forevermore. Brother Isaiah the Sightless gave Manfred a walking stick, a staff is more like it. It was bended and twisted, knotty and whorly, the length of it scarred by woodpecker and termite holes. Isaiah the Blind handed this ugly club to Manfred Ozikean and said proudly, "I carved it myself!"

So the two of us, Manfred and me, we walked from Bowmanville to Toronto. That took us three days, and they were pretty fine days. We'd sleep in farmers' fields, we'd help ourselves to apples and such.

Maybe I shouldn't say this, considering what I became to the city, but I didn't think much of Toronto the first time I saw her. Could be I was expecting too big a deal. At sixteen you think a city should be full of cowboys, bosomy ladies, Indians and scoundrels, carnivals and taverns, fistfights and love affairs, mooks with tattoos on their faces, women with garters above their knees—in short, the kind of place where Blue Hermann's been living most of his life, wherever the hell *that* is. But Toronto looked as if it had been designed and built by a committee of Sunday-school teachers.

Manfred, though, he was agape. He was all the time turning around and colliding with other pedestrians. Manny did a fair bit of damage to a couple of these unfortunates, not that he himself noticed.

We find the recruiting place on Spadina Ave., and the two of us go in there. Damned if there ain't a musical band set up in the corner playing these marches and things! The orchestra was made up of veterans of the Boer War, too old to fight but still gung-ho. Some of them were missing body parts, one of them had only half a face. A smart fellow might have thought twice about this army lark when he seen half a face stuck in a uniform, but I was just a ginger sprout.

Manfred and I march up to the sergeant at his desk and tell him that we want to fight. The sergeant looks up and sees Manny, and he starts grinning. Then he sees me and ceases. "How old are you?"

"Eighteen," I tell him.

The sergeant gives me the once-over and remarks that I'm a small git, whereupon I tell him I'm scrappy as hell and all Irishter muscle and blood.

Then he asks me if I have any experience with horses. "Yo," says I, don't ask me why, and that's how I come to join the Canadian Mounted Rifles.

They sent us to the Maritimes for training. It was kind of a perfunctory warfaring education. About all I remember is attacking straw men with our bayonets. After a couple of weeks of that, the superiors judged that we were ready. They took us down to the docks and put us on various ships. And while we sat there waiting, they handed out our Official Great War Stuff. They gave us each a Ross rifle. They gave us each a knife. Manfred laid each item aside as it was handed to him, without really looking at it. One of his hands was inside his shirt, touching the huge silver crucifix. Then they handed out the helmets. I got a regulation helmet, a green cloth affair. Manfred got one of the new kind, the kind they were experimenting with back there in WW I, a steel jobber. Manny put it on his knee, pinged it with his forefinger. It sounded like a bell.

"Hey, Percy," said Manfred. "My helmet is too small."

"You haven't even tried it on, Manny."

"I can tell. Yours looks like the right size for me."

"Yeah?"

"So trade me."

They were calling for the Canadian Mounted Rifles. I handed Manfred my lid. He gave me the steel one. "I better go," I told Manfred.

"Yeah."

"See you later, Manny."

We shook hands in a very manly way, and pretended not to notice that the other guy was crying.

They sent me to something called the Lille-Douai plain, along the border between France and Belgium. There a ridge shot out of the ground. It went up maybe two hundred feet, steep and more wooded than anything else in the neighborhood. I've seen more impressive ridges near Clifford's cottage in the Muskokas. The only thing different about this ridge is that when we got there, right around the beginning of one-nine one-seven, there was a lot of Germans huddled on it. Us Canadians got stuck with the job of taking it away from them. That's what your Battle of Vimy Ridge was all about.

Every year, right around Remembrance Day, the blower will start hopping and somebody wants to know if I'll come say a few words about my Great War experiences. I always affect to disremember them. It was a long time ago, I say.

But I do remember the attack on Vimy. We waited for a few months, just digging in and planning, and it was Easter Sunday, April 8—I'd turned seventeen the week before—when we attacked.

I was in the Eighth Brigade, which was made up of dismounted battalions from the Canadian Mounted Rifles. We formed the flank on the far right (kind of like a winger going up-ice along the boards) and it was our job to take out the Schwaben Tunnel.

That morning was gray and drizzly. We waited. The only sound was men breathing. One or two said prayers. I can't remember what I was thinking about. Likely not much. I've been more nervous before lots of hockey games.

Then we hit.

History books will tell you that it was the most perfectly timed barrage of the whole war, but that don't say the half. Brother, it was like God slapped the world with the flat of His hand. The ridge started screaming. It exploded with bits of German uniform and German flesh. We waited three minutes, as per our orders, and then we moved forward. I was in the front line, a creeper. We went out in lumps, a little clutch of four or five men, isolated and, we hoped, harder to spot. Our lump got pegged right away, but just by rifle fire. We hit the muck. I just kept moving forward, bulldogging through the mud on all fours. The lad beside me got hit. He didn't die right away. He lay there, breathing hard, and tried to pretend he was in a story in a CHUMS book. He thought about it for a long time, trying to think of something good to say. Finally all he could get out was, "To hell with this," and he died pissed off. I kept moving forward. Another boy got pegged. I didn't feel anything one way or another. I played a game in my head whereby God was handing out Major Penalties, and I thought that if I just stayed crawling on all fours through the muck and didn't do anything wrong I'd be fine.

We reached the tunnel so quickly that half the Fritzes were still in their underwear. It was then, while we were rounding up Germans, that I got shot. I got shot in the head, probably a ricochet off the wall, because the bullet just bounced off the steel helmet. It dropped me like a sack of bricks, and I had a doozy of a headache for two or three days, but it wasn't that big a deal. In a few years the famous son of a bitch Sprague Cleghorn would two-hand my bean and split it open like a nut, and this bullet was nothing in comparison. Still, the doctors figured I'd done enough fighting.

That was my war.

When I turned seventy-five years old, they had a big do for me at the Toronto Gardens, as if turning seventy-five had required some great skill on my part.

At the time I was living with my nephew Bernard, the son of my sister Bernice and her husband with the withered hand. Funnily enough, Bernard had a withered hand, and all three of his children have withered hands. One of these offspring has webbed feet to boot, and I understand that all three have married and I don't care to know what my great-grandnephews look like.

Anyway, because there was this do at the Gardens, Bernard goes out and rents me a tuxedo. I argued about wearing the monkey suit, but finally I was convinced to observe the

solemnity of the occasion. So I took out my WW I decorations—
two of them I've got—and I considered pinning them on my
chest.

I didn't do that. I put the medals away, and now I can't
even remember where they are. Probably somewhere with the
real hats they gave me, for scoring real hat tricks, which is
three goals in a row all in the same period.

# ELEVEN

I GOT BACK TO OTTAWA in the early summer of one-nine one-seven. I was thought of as something of a hero, and treated accordingly, although there was also a joke making the rounds that I was lucky to have been shot in the head or else I might have been hurt. Clay was away, attending military college in Kingston, so I didn't see anything of him. Clay Clinton, by the way, turned eighteen a month or two before the Great War ended. He was made a noncommissioned officer, and he spent a few weeks bossing people around at a training camp in the prairies, safest spot on the globe. How he parlayed that into an illustrious service career is a bafflement to me. Manfred Armstrong Ozikean, I should tell you, eventually got turfed out of the forces on some charge of drunk and disorderly (and that's going some when the army thinks you drink too much) but he still had a shoebox full of decorations tucked under his arm when he returned. Manny never said much about the decorations, or about the war. Then again, he was quiet on most subjects.

Sometime in August, Pat Boyle came to visit me at home. He was the coach of the Ottawa Patriots of the newly formed National Hockey League. I was reading, at least looking at, a book, staring at a color glossy of St. George with his foot on the dragon's head. The dragon's tongue was sticking out and blood was everywhere. The lad George held his sword in the air and was shouting to the world that he'd offed the effing lizard. The storybook had belonged to my brother Lloyd—he owned a number of them—and we just the day before received word that Lloyd wasn't coming home.

Pat was a handsome young man. Most people remember him when his nose had blossomed like a gray ghost squash and his teeth had turned black. Mind you, it was at age sixty-eight that Pat got arrested for child molestation, the sort of thing that tends to stick in people's minds more than coaching even such a legendary squad as the Ottawa Paddies. I don't know if Pat did what some claimed he did, but it hardly mattered, given how he looked, like Death waiting for a bus. He got shipped to Penetang and there he died. But I'm remembering him in his thirties, when he was a good-looking young mick.

So the old mother lets Boyle into the living room and he says, "What are you doing for the next seven months, Little Leary?"

I say, "Playing hockey for the Patriots, if they'll have me."

Patty says, "They'll have you right enough, Little Leary. And they'll pay you nine hundred and fifty dollars."

I jumped up from my chair and started pumping Pat Boyle's hand. I said, "I just wanted to put the lid on that offer before you changed your mind."

If I had my life to live over again (no thankee very much) I suppose I'd do pretty much the same, *except* for I would cancel the three weeks I spent at my rookie training camp.

I walked into the dressing room, strutting and puffed up like a prize gamecock. Most of the Patriots were older men (the younger ones either still serving in the Great War or dead), and I imagined they'd never seen the likes of me. I had my miner's cap tilted at a jaunty angle. My ring was tossing sunshine like a wet dog tosses water. The dragon-head walking stick was bouncing around as if there was a marching band in back of me. "The name is Leary," says I, tossing my gear into a locker. "Little Leary."

They didn't say nothing.

They grabbed me, stripped me naked, and shaved off my pubics.

The other rookie showed up two days late, bleary-eyed and unshaven. He stumbled into the dressing room, clinging to one of the walls. With effort he managed to pull his mouth together in a smile. "Hello, Patriots!" he sang out, and that made him laugh. The laugh made him stumble backwards. "Hello, Patriots," he repeated, almost a whisper. "Did you see what we did, Patriots? Can you believe what we did?" He struggled for purchase, getting a firmer grip on the wall. "My name is—" He hiccupped, a huge one that shook his throat. "My name is—" He looked up, bewildered almost, as if he'd forgotten.

"Manfred," I supplied.

Manny saw me and grinned. "Hey, Percy," he whispered, "you never told me you were a *Patriot*."

The goaler, North Innes, whipped out the straight razor. He grinned like a maniac, mostly because that's what the man was. The other Patriots stood up and advanced on Manfred Ozikean. I don't know what they could have been thinking. Timmy Finn tried to grab Manny's arm and he got thrown clear across the room. Three fellows came all at once. Manny started to bellow. I heard the crack of a bone-break, and Sully Fotheringham, a defenseman, started whimpering. The whole of the team set on Manfred Ozikean. By the time Pat Boyle broke up the fight, three men were injured for the season. Manfred was asleep, dead drunk.

Well, sir, that should have been the end of Manny's hockey-playing career, except for the fact that he demolished the lineup so thoroughly that Coach Boyle had no choice but to have a look at him.

The next day Manny showed up sober and quiet. He stepped onto the ice, skated the length of it, and fired a practice shot past North Innes. That's about all it took for Manfred to make the team.

For me, it was a different tale. They kept knocking me down. I kept getting up. My bony little arse was three different kinds of black. But I'd remember all that the monks had taught me—the Bulldog, the Whirlygig, the Inner-Eye Fling, and damned if I didn't do all right. They couldn't keep ahold of me, they couldn't stop my shots. And what I couldn't accomplish through the brothers' teachings I accomplished through pure Irish blockheadedness. Yes, ma'am, I done all right.

One time a reporter came from the Ottawa *Gazetteer* to ask about the new prospects. Pat Boyle says of Manfred, "The lad is a wizard." Of course, that play *The Wizard of Oz* was big news back then, and that's what started people calling Manfred just Oz, and that's how come today he's known mostly as Manny Oz, the Wizard.

Of Percival Leary, Boyle said, "A leprechaun."

Fully three-quarters of the boys were Irishmen. Not counting me and Pat Boyle, there was maybe eight all totaled, Finn, Denneny, O'Casey, and O'Sullivan, and some others whose names I could remember if there was any great reason to. We were as green as grass is what I'm saying, so much so that we were nicknamed the Paddies and our jerseys bore a big shamrock for the team emblem.

Many of that Ottawa Patriots team were pretty famous men. North Innes, for example, who was as good a goaler as there ever was, except for when I played with him he was fat, pushing thirty-five years of age. North liked to have a laugh, but he never laughed at anything that I thought was humorous. Shaving off people's pubics was one of his favorite activities. He also liked to cut your clothes into ribbons while you were showering, or dump itching powder into your uniform just before a game. North Innes died a young man, eaten up by cancer.

I made it through the training camp all in one piece, and then the regular season started. I rode the pines for seventeen games. It made me sick. I mean it. Sometimes I'd sit there wanting to throw up all over my skates. Lucky thing for me I never did eat too much, or that's likely what would have happened. Now, why Pat Boyle was sitting me out is still a mystery, because it's not like the Ottawa Patriots were tearing up the league. After seventeen games, our record was 4-11-2, which is piss poor, as you can see. And we're talking a forty-game season here! Manfred was the only bright spot, averaging a goal a game. But as quick as Manny could score them, our defense would open up and North Innes could only do so much.

Now, game eighteen was in Montreal, against the Maroons. I don't have to tell you who was on that team. Sprague Cleghorn, that's who. Sometimes I still have nightmares about Cleghorn. Don't get me wrong, I liked the man, but if there ever was a black-hearted shark-minded bastard, Sprague was it. I mean, his brother Odie would as soon cut off your balls as say hello, and we used to call him "the nice one."

In Montreal that night, Sprague is mowing down the lineup. He's just standing there chopping at us like we're so much firewood. Well, sometime in the second period, Sprague takes out Dan O'Sullivan with a two-hander to the kneecaps. Say good night, sister! Boyle starts eyeballing the bench. Then he says, "Leary."

This is peachy. I'm a center or a rover, but Boyle's putting me on the defense. Still, I'm not about to bellyache about it. I hop over the boards.

About a minute after play starts, Sprague gets the puck and starts down the ice. Now, the man could skate, but none too sprightly, and it didn't take me but a second or two before I'm right behind him. "Sprague!" says I, and naturally enough, he takes me for one of his teammates and drops the puck. I scoop it, tell him, "Thank you kindly, Spray-goo!" and I'm gone. Now was the time for everything I'd learnt from the Brothers of St. Alban the Martyr. I bulldogged, I hardstepped, I inner-eyed all the way. I blew that puck by the goaler! That was the best feeling I ever had in my life. Some of the Patriots skated over to congratulate me on my first NHLer. Then I heard a voice from behind me. "Hey, Percy!" I turn around, expecting a handshake, and the last thing I saw was Cleghorn's fist sailing into my face.

# TWELVE

LAST NIGHT, BLUE HERMANN TOOK SICK in a spectacular way. Blue smoked all his life, smoked too much and drank too much, and his insides are crumbly now as moldy cheese, and when he coughs he sprays them all over the walls. I don't mind that. I've seen worse. I saw Bullet Broun get his throat cut open by a skate blade. His gullet gaped like another mouth. I saw Rene LeCroix stop a puck with his forehead—his left eye flew clear out of its socket and dangled near his chin. Blue Hermann is just coughing up little chunks of his bad life, and I'm unaffected. But then he starts talking. Blue Hermann scares the bejesus out of me when he starts talking like that, nonsensical I mean, and soon he's screaming at the top of his lungs. I press the buzzer for the nurse and they come fill him full of dope.

I can't sleep after that. I take out the book *Clinton & Leary Fight the Dogstar People*. The Dogstar People float around the universe, they leak into things, trees and water and clouds. I shut my eyes. I'm back in this dream I've been having, the dream of Manfred's funeral. Manfred's spirit leaks out of his stone gray body. Hallie cries, the tears spill onto her satin dress, the dress becomes soaked, and I can see her nakedness. Clay Clinton begins to laugh, and that sound is in my ears when I wake in the morning.

Blue Hermann is looking at me.

"You had a rough one last night," I say to him.

Blue waves his nicotine-stained hand in the air. It's a spotted, twisted, palsied claw, and it barely looks human. Blue waves it in the air and I know not to mention anything more about his attack. Hermann reaches for his secret stash of whiskey and takes a long pull from the flask. His wattles tremble. Usually I'll have at him for that sort of thing, call him an alkie and whatnot, but today I just watch him out of the corner of my eye. The liquor seems to calm him somewhat. Blue lies down on his bed and folds his old hands neatly across his chest.

"Hey, Hermann," says I, "why do you want to come with me to Toronto anyways?"

Blue grins. He has a nice smile, considering. You should have seen that smile when he was a young man in New York, New York. "The thing is, Leary," Blue tells me, "Clay told me to look after you." Hermann makes a sound like an old Buick sinking in quicksand, which is what he uses for a laugh. "He told me to look after your spiritual needs." Blue turns away.

"It's King Leary Night at the Gardens. That punk Killebrew is going to be there. We're going to do the adverts together."

"I want to see this new fucking Sports Hall of Infamy," Blue suggests.

"Surely. Go take a gander at the one-nine one-nine lumber."

"We could visit the graves," he says in a near whisper.

"There's too many," I tell him. "We'd have to take a two-week excursion."

"And we could go to a *bar*!" Hermann's stony eyes acquire a sparkle.

"I don't think Iain's going to let you go to a bar."

"Did Iain say he was coming?"

"He's coming."

"Well, if he does," Blue tells me, "we lose him."

"You would, too!"

Hermann chuckles. "I would, too."

After a moment I say, "Iain says there's to be no croaking in Toronto."

We both nod, fair enough.

When I got off the plane in New York, New York, the first person I saw was Blue Hermann. He was standing on the tarmac, already scribbling in his little notebook. Blue had a cigarette dangling out of the corner of his mouth, so his eyes were all squinty as the smoke drifted into them. (Those dangling cigarettes likely account for the way Blue's aspect is these days, like that of a wax Chinaman that's been left out in the sun.) Blue Hermann had a green fedora cocked on his head. A card stuck out of the headband. Blue Hermann gave me a little wink.

"Little Leary!" called out the newspaperman.

"You got him! Also known as *Loof-weeda*. That's an Indian monicker meaning 'windsong.' "

I was twenty-six years old, at the height of my career. I bounced down the airplane steps with a Dublintown swagger, swinging my dragon-head cane. I'd have whistled a tune, except that I could never get the knack of whistling. I tipped my miner's cap to the stranger on the tarmac.

"Hermann from the *Star*," he informed me.

"Percy from the river."

"Let's clear something up."

"Let's do that."

"You and Clay Clinton are longtime friends, no?"

"Clay and I go back a ways."

"Don't you feel this sudden trade is something of a betrayal?"

"Clay's got the Patriots to worry about. He got ten thousand smackers for this little puff of Irish wind, and that's a fair bit. Anyone would have done it. Clay and I are still buddies."

"Do you think your play will be affected by the absence of your linemate Manny Oz?"

"I'll adjust."

"You won't miss him?"

"What do you mean, 'miss him'?"

"Is he still drinking heavily?"

"Manny's got the juice pretty much licked," I lied. The juice was licking Manfred like an all-day lollipop.

"How's your wife, Chloe?"

"She's good, mister. Why do you ask? That ain't exactly hockey related."

"Everything is hockey related. Do you agree?"

"I never thought about it."

"Yes or no, Little Leary."

"Wait up a minute, Hermann from the *Star*."

"You have a newborn baby?"

"Clifford."

"Do you miss him?"

"I just got here."

"Is Clay Clinton married?"

"Clay? No. He's a confirmed bachelor." He did get married later on, to Janey Millson, as you may know, but truth to be told, his marriage never affected his bachelor status.

All of a sudden this Hermann from the *Star* reaches inside his trench coat. He removes a pewter flask, unscrews the top— grinning all the while, staring at me, I didn't know he was seeing me all in a blue haze—and he takes a long pull. Then he shoves the thing in my face. "Care for a tug at the witch's tit?"

"No, thankee," I said, adding, for the benefit of the newspaper readers, "I do not drink. I have only had one alcoholic beverage in my life, that being a single glass of champagne when the Paddies claimed the Stanley Cup six years ago."

"And just when," Blue Hermann demanded, "do you think you might have another?"

"When the New York Americans claim the goblet at the end of this season."

Old Blue wrote that up in his column, and for a while it became quite a joke in New York City. All kinds of restaurants put bottles of champagne on ice, attaching little signs saying how it was reserved for Percival Leary on the cup-winning night. I received many letters, especially from ladies, telling me that I was welcome to have some champagne with them when the Amerks won. Mind you, that year the New York Americans were as pitiful an organization as one could care to see, the South Grouse Louses notwithstanding, so nothing ever came of that champagne lark.

The thing of it is, what gives me cause to wonder in these idle days, that single glass of champagne in one-nine one-nine was no big deal. I mean, it was fair bubbly, but weakly so, not like the throat-ripping gargles you could get from the good old Canada Dry. It tickled your throat like a puff of air. What the big deal on the champagne was, I never knew.

Clay Clinton loved the stuff. If Clay was eating a peanut butter sandwich, he'd want champagne with it. One time we went into some two-bit ramshackle groghouse—Manfred used to favor such establishments, even when, as in the case I'm recollecting, he was bone dry and off the juice—and Clay shouted, "Barkeep!"

The barkeep looked around, because he didn't know that's what he was.

"A bottle of the finest bubbly!" Clay never did lose his English accent, not in all his sixty-some years.

"Come again, mac?"

"Bubbly. The nectar of the gods. Pop off to the cellar and see what is nicely aged."

Lord knows what such places have aging in the cellar, but it ain't champagne. The bartender tilted his head like a quizzical dog.

"Champagne!" Clinton exploded at the top of his voice. "We want champagne!"

"Oh." The bartender had heard of it. "Someone get married?"

"The Man-Freddy is getting married to the lovely Jane. Isn't that so, Manfred?"

Manny blushed, which was right odd, given his complexion.

The bartender looked at Manfred, recognizing him. "I thought you didn't drink no more."

"Not me. But Clay likes champagne. If you don't have any champagne, it's all right. He'll have some beer."

"I will not have beer. Beer is swill for the hoi polloi. I want *champagne.*"

The bartender dried his hands on his apron, his eyes riveted on Manfred Ozikean. "I'll see if maybe there isn't a bottle somewhere."

"Thank you, buddy," said Manny, and the barkeep glowed.

"What's the big deal here, Clay-boy?" I asked him. "What are we celebrating? All's we need was whup the Wings. We been doing that all year."

"With the victory tonight, our lovely Ottawa Lily Pads mathematically clinched first place." I had no way of knowing whether that was true or not. It made scant difference to me.

Numbers and mathematics got no place in the game of hockey, that's the argument I got against that puppy Duane Killebrew. He's out to smash all the numbers in the record book, as if numbers could defend themselves.

"Plus," Clay went on, "I want to toast Manny and Jane."

"Why?"

"They're getting married."

"We've known that for a couple of months now."

"Shut up, Leary." The words came sharp and fast, like a bee sting. I wasn't even sure I'd heard right, but I shut up anyway.

Clay Clinton asked the publican for three glasses. He placed them in a row and filled them to the brim with golden bubbles.

"Clay," Manny whispered.

"One glass won't kill you," Clinton said. "There's less alcohol in that glass than there is in a spoonful of cough medicine."

"But I can't," Manfred said.

"Hell, Clay, if it means that much to you, I'll have a gobful." I went to grab a glass, but Clinton lashed out with his arm and sent all three flying. They smashed into the wall, covering the place with glass.

"Never mind," said Clay Bors Clinton. "It was a stupid idea."

# THIRTEEN

THE FIRST TIME I SAW Constance Millson, called Jane by all and sundry, she was in the company of Manfred Armstrong Ozikean. It was in the summer, the off season. I was taking a stroll around Bytown, which I did quite often, having nothing else to do. It was in those days that I perfected my swagger, the dragon-head cane flipping. The tykes would call out to me, "Hi, there, Little Leary!" this predating when I became the King of the Ice.

"Ho, there, young pups!" I'd call back, tipping my cap. "Eat yer veggies and you'll grow up like me."

The year was one-nine one-eight. The war was grinding down. The Paddies had finished in a measly fifth place, mostly, if you were to ask me, because North Innes spent too much time shaving pubics and suchlike, neglecting to keep himself in shape. Anyway, I'm strutting around the old town, cocky and all elbows, and I see this remarkable sight.

The first thing I see is Manny, because if he was anywhere in the vicinity, he was the first thing you saw. Now, usually Manny had the look of a sheepdog, but on this day Manfred had his hair all pomaded. It likely took a gallon of slickum to do it, but he had his hair greased down. Not only that, Manfred was wearing a suit, one of those three-piece jobbies. In his right hand Manny held a hat, a felt homburg, and I suppose he was carrying it in his hand because he didn't want to wear it on his head, thereby mussing the pomade. In his left hand Manny had yet another hand, a tiny white one. I stopped in my tracks.

I've known men who didn't find Janey attractive. Pat Boyle was like that. He'd see Manny and Jane together, shake his head, and mutter, "I don't know what he sees in her." I knew, and so did Clay Clinton.

She was a small girl, but you didn't realize that until you were standing right next to her and could get some kind of a reading off how far she came up on your chest. Even on me she only came up to about my nipples. Jane's hair was blond, and only a touch of color kept it from being snowy white. Her eyes seemed to change all the time, going from a blue to a green. When she was angry, Jane's eyes got gray as stones. Towards the end of her life her eyes turned gray and stayed that way.

"Hey!" sang out Manfred, catching sight of me. He dragged the girl forward. "This is Constance, Percy."

"*Janey*," she corrected.

"Little Leary, ma'am," says I, taking off my cap and crumpling it between my hands. Jane caused a lot of hats to be crumpled.

"Lucky number seven," she pointed out.

"Yes'm." It was in 1912 that someone decided that hockey players should have numbers stitched to the back of their jerseys. I was number seven all my years with the Paddies, but when I went to the Amerks, White Wings O'Brien was already wearing it (he was a superstitious son of a gun!) so I went to number nine, which I allowed was almost as lucky.

"It's jeezly hot out," Jane told me. "I'm sweating like a stuck pig."

Such talk would scandalize the old mother, that's for sure. The thought of Jane's little body sweating sort of discomfited me as well.

"What I'd really like to do," Jane announced, "is go swimming all in the buff-bare."

I didn't say anything to that. Manfred was nodding, but what the hell, the man was always nodding.

"Now, is it true, Little Leary, Lucky Number Seven," asked Janey Millson in earnest, "that they shaved your private parts?"

I must have pulled quite the face. Jane took one look and started laughing.

There never was a girl, especially not so small a one, who could laugh so loud as Jane Millson. Manfred A. Ozikean was looking mortified. "I didn't tell her, Percy!" he lied.

Jane was struggling to contain herself, but she couldn't do it. "Heee*yahhh!*" she started up again, and tears popped out of her eyes and stuff shot out of her nose. Jane folds in half and laughs on the intake now, mostly because she's gonna expire if she don't get any air. By this time we're attracting a crowd, people figuring the poor girl is suffering from some rare and fancy medical ailment. Jane is a right mess, and only thirty, forty seconds have gone by. A policeman wanders over, wanting to know what the trouble is. Manny leads the girl away.

I didn't see her again until a couple of months after that, at the season's Home Opener. I hit the ice and heard a shout. "Go, you Lucky Number Seven!"

I had one hell of a game.

Now, many times people have asked me outright and point-blank, they'll say, King, what the hell *was* Manny Oz anyway? Well, I never did get a handle on that. I seen his family, the whole crowded assemblage of them, and I'm still no closer to an answer. Mostly, I suppose, Manfred was an Indian. Some members of his clan were fine handsome people with coppery skin. But others were a lot darker, and his Uncle Silas looked for all the world like a Chinaman to me, and even if we riddled all that out, we'd still have to discover where in creation Manfred got that red woolly hair! Manfred was the only member of his family who had red hair, everyone else had hair as black as coal.

And, gracious, such names! Silas, Oliphant, Whitney, Grayman—that would be Great Uncle Grayman, a shriveled-up old prune who played the accordian, a talent he more or less passed on to Manfred. Manfred could squeeze out a few tunes and when drunk would do so for hours and hours. The music always reminded me of great disasters at sea, children and women wailing as they plunged into Arctic waters.

The females included Millicent, Ambrosia, and Conception. She was a pretty thing, that Conception, despite the fact that she had a big black mark clouding her face.

Manfred's father was named Hardy Ozikean. He would have been almost as big as Manny, except that he was missing both legs from just above the knees. He rode about in something that resembled a wheelbarrow. (Of course, as soon as Manfred started earning the long green, the first thing he bought was a fancy contraption for his old man.) Hardy Ozikean was extraordinarily happy for a man who lived in a wheelbarrow. His hobby was the weather, and when he cornered you, Hardy Ozikean liked to predict what was going to happen on the climate front for the next few months. He was always dead wrong, but Mr. Ozikean was a fearless and steadfast weather diviner. He'd sit in his wheelbarrow and predict sunny skies even as you stood there dripping all over him.

Mrs. Ozikean, Pantella her name was, was a small dainty woman who as far as I can recall never said one solitary word to me. Most of the females in that family were the silent type, although if they'd wanted to say anything they would have been hard pressed. Between Hardy and his oracling, Great Uncle Grayman and his accordian, Manny's brother Winslow (who blew the small talk issue right out of the water with his constant babbling about political issues), and the various squabblings of tykes, there wasn't much room for talk.

Manfred took after the ladies, that is, he didn't say much. But he was happy with his family, and I guess I understand how bad it must have been for him, later in his life, all alone in hotel rooms. He was in a hotel room when he died, a room at the Forrest Hotel in New York City. The official coroner blamed something called "alcoholic insult to the brain." I'm not sure what that is—it's never shown up at any chart here at the South Grouse—but I put no credence in the fanciful notion that Manny Oz died of a broken heart.

There is one more member of Manny's family who I should mention, Poppa Rivers. I didn't meet this man until later on—it was he who gave me the Indian nickname *Loof-weeda*—and the reason I bring him up now is that I just all of a sudden realized that he is in this dream I've been having, the one that takes place at Manfred's funeral. Poppa Rivers wasn't there in true life, mind you, the funeral was held in New York, New York, but in my dream he is there, keening like an old witch. He is naked and covered with dried mud. His skin has been scratched by thorns, stung by wasps and hornets. Poppa Rivers shakes a rattle made from the skull of a small animal. Every now and again he will launch into a dance, a wild and woolly one. The drunken New York Amerks cheer him on. Hallie doffs her satin gown. Her naked body is awash in moonlight. Things get out of hand. Clay Clinton, standing beside me, laughs, savoring my discomfort.

Poppa Rivers comes over and sticks a long finger in my puss. "*Loof-weeda*," he says, "you dumb fuck."

# FOURTEEN

TODAY'S THE DAY. We're going to Toronto. Iain's so het up that he's got Mrs. Ames doing his bidding, and that old marm don't do nothing nice for nobody.

"Dress them, Nurse Ames!" Iain shouts. "Dress them and dress them warmly! We'll have no chilblains on these chilluns!" While Mrs. Ames bundles us into our winter gear, Iain takes to strutting up and down the room, turning sharp and precise at each end, kind of like Napoleon. "The train," Iain says, "leaves at precisely sixteen hundred hours. That will place us in Toronto at eighteen-oh-seven. You boys will likely want to be fed then."

Blue Hermann takes the opportunity to dig his fingers into Nurse Ames's backside. He doesn't really want to do it, but it's required, given his reputation. "I want a steak!" Blue tells Iain.

"Indeed?" Iain stares at the ancient newspaperman. "And tell me this, Mr. Hermann. With *what* do you intend to chew this steak?"

"I'm just going to suck on it for a while."

"We go to a restaurant and eat gruel," Iain tells us. "Then we go to the Toronto Gardens, where it's King Leary Night!"

"Hooray!" says I. I can't help myself.

"And then . . ." Iain looks all around and whispers. "We hit the streets."

"*What?!* " roars Nurse Ames.

"Then we get some sleep," Iain says. "Because the next day, Kinger-Binger has to make some commercials."

"Friends," says I (I've been going over this in my mind), "this is your old friend, King Leary, the high-muck-a-muck of hockey. I been asked to say a few words on behalf of the Canada Dry ginger ale bottlers. I been drinking the good old Canada Dry all my life. People ask me why."

"Why?" asks Blue Hermann.

"Why?" asks Iain.

"Because it makes me *pissed!*"

"Hmph!" snorts Mrs. Ames.

"That's right, folks, it makes me piss, cleans out the system."

"Leary," says Nurse Ames, "surely there is more to recommend this beverage than the fact that it works as some sort of diuretic."

"Tastes good, too."

Mrs. Ames gives us all a look that could crack nuts. "I don't think this expedition should be permitted."

Iain ignores her. "Mobilize, men! Let's move out!"

Blue Hermann grabs his canes—he needs two thick industrial-strength jobs to keep himself upright—and he throws his hips back and forth, picking up steam, and finally he's motoring through the doorway pretty good. Myself, I launch into the old Dublintown swagger, my legs wide apart and my feet landing heel first. I curl my free hand into a fist and swing it about. I hold my dragon-head walking stick up and out, poking at the air in front of me as if provoking attack. There's very few gooms my age who could affect a passable Dublintown swagger, and I'm rightly proud.

Other inmates are lining the hallways, waving us good-bye. We're a goddamn parade!

"Make way for the hockey legend!" Iain tells them. "Royalty coming through here!"

I tip my coal miner's cap, I smile and wave. At least, I smile and wave until I see a pair of eyes, dumb idiot eyes stuck in a milk white face, eyes that don't understand or feel anything. My breath fails me. Maybe I'm going to faint. I start to fall but there's strong hands at my elbows.

"Steady on, my liege," whispers Iain. "You go down now and we're not going anywhere." Iain holds me up, but he's strong enough to hide it; it looks like he's escorting me the way any young man would escort an old fart.

"I'm all right," I tell him, but I don't shake myself free.

Blue Hermann's voice sounds like flat tires on a mud road. "King is going to meet Duane Killebrew!" This news is greeted by predictable *ooo*'s and *aah*'s. "It's King Leary Night at the Toronto Gardens."

"Give 'em hell, King!" someone tells me.

"Give 'em hell!"

Other people start nodding. They pick up the chant. "Give 'em hell, King! Give 'em hell!"

There's a taxicab waiting, steam pouring from its exhaust into the bitter wintry air. It must be twenty-five, thirty below out here. My nose freezes shut. My eyes sting like someone has stuck his thumbs in them. The trick is to let the sun sit on you. I tilt my head back and let the sun slap my face a little. My jowls start to tingle.

It's a bit of a stunt putting Blue Hermann into the backseat, on account of his legs don't buckle. The cabbie and Iain have to hold Blue on either side and load him in like a torpedo. I wait on the pavement, puffing steam upwards, trying to thaw my nose hairs. Finally they got Blue packed. I take a step and my foot catches a slick patch of ice. *Whooosh*, and I think, here it comes, say good night, sister, but somehow I end up in Iain's arms.

"King," says the lad, and his voice is loaded with amazement, "you did the St. Louis Whirlygig!"

"Damn right!" I scream. "You don't lose a move like that in a minute, you know! The monks showed me how to do it in one-nine one-five and I have just now executed it!" A couple of quick rusty wheezes come out of me.

"King," says Iain, "you *laughed!*"

"Put me in the car, felthead," I tell him. "We don't want to miss the train."

The countryside around South Grouse is farmland, barren and empty in the winter. We pass a little pond, and the pups are out on her. They've cleared the snow away, the ice is silver blue. Most of the lads have on Ottawa jerseys (the shamrock doesn't look like a shamrock these days) with the number double zero, which is what Killebrew wears. A few wear Toronto sweaters, a couple Montreal. I watch a lad score a goal, rolling the tennis ball slowly through another boy's legs. The lad flips his stick over and pretends it's a guitar. That's something Duane Killebrew does. When I scored a goal I didn't do anything, except maybe grit my teeth and say, "*Yeah!*" at whatever was out there.

On another part of the pond, all by herself, a young girl is figure skating. She does a turn in the air, a quick crisp thing. My wife, Chloe, could do that. Before she was set upon by disease my wife was quite the athlete. I wipe the fog off the window. I stare at the girl.

"Manfred could do some of that," says Blue Hermann.

"Like Brother Simon the Ugly," I say. "More like dancing than anything else. My boy Rance could skate all right, too, except he skated like a girl."

"Manny could do it drunk," Blue goes on. "Pissed out of his gourd. One time in New York, when he was with the Americans, me and Oz got pie-eyed. We could barely walk. But we snuck into an ice-skating rink somewhere, and Manny tied on some skates, and he hit the ice like a ballerina. One of the most beautiful sights I've ever seen, Manny skating like that. And he was shit-faced."

"Manfred drank too much," I mutter.

"And you didn't exactly help, did you, Leary?"

"What do you mean by that, Hermann?"

"I used to drink too much," announces Iain. "But not for a couple of years now. Not since I moved to South Grouse." Iain takes a cigarette out of the pack and fires it up. This is the first time I seen him with his own smokes.

South Grouse doesn't have much of a train station, just a little thing sitting on top of the hill, beside the tracks. It's quite a trek in from the cab to the waiting room, treacherous with ice. We get inside and Blue Hermann bolts for the nearest red plastic bench, his canes sounding loudly on the winter-wet tiles. "Whoo-boy!" sighs Blue, like he's been through the wringer. I imagine Blue has gone "Whoo-boy!" lots in his lifetime, but only in recent years has he gone "Whoo-boy!" on account of a cab ride.

Iain elbows me over to the bench, then says, "I'm going to go buy the tickets." We've already got it arranged that I'll pay him back when I get my ten thou for the adverts. Peculiar, isn't it? When Jubal St. Amour paid ten thousand dollars for me, it was ballyhooed all across the nation. Now they'll give that to an ancient mook for saying a few words about a soft drink.

"Uh-yeah." There's maybe fifteen other people in the waiting room. One is a mother with five kids, even though she looks to be about twenty-seven. The kids is racing around, staging a reenactment of some of history's great catastrophes. The mother sits, calmly smoking a cigarette. Every so often she'll say, "Knock it off, Jason!"

Iain comes back with three train tickets in his hand.

Then there's nothing to do in the waiting room but wait, unless you happen to be Blue Hermann, in which case you can fall into a sort of sleep, your limbs twitching electrically, sweat beading on your brow and upper lip.

Iain reaches into his coat pocket and brings out a little paperback. He removes a marker, folds the cover back so that he can hold the book in one hand, and begins to read.

I got nothing to do but remember.

Manfred Armstrong Ozikean hated trains. I think that's kind of odd. I can understand hating to *fly*—I was never too keen on it myself, several thousand tons of heavy machinery whistling through the air—but being afraid of trains is a little peculiar. If we were traveling to a game—meaning that Manny couldn't drink, although he did from time to time—then he'd sit in a seat, the curtains drawn, and thumb through a book. He was all the time trying to improve himself through various books. If we'd already played, and were on our way out of town, Manfred would bolt for the bar car as soon as the train made its first chunking sound. Manfred would buy drinks for everyone in the place. He'd play the accordian and lead his traveling companions in song. His favorite tune was "The

Church in the Wildwood." Manny could bellow this number for hours, the words becoming harder to make out as the booze dulled his brain. Sometimes I'd wake in the middle of the night and notice that Manny was nowhere to be seen. I'd go to the bar car and find him facedown in a puddle of wetness, booze, and, I should imagine, more than a couple of tears.

There's the whistle, carried on the ice-cold air.

Clay loved trains. Clinton would travel in nothing less than a stateroom, a full bar set up in the corner, a bimbo or two adorning the settees. He'd sit in there and scheme, which was Clay's hobby. He would scheme even if there was nothing cooking, or do other people's scheming on their behalf, or else just figure out the perfect bank robbery or murder, even if he had no intention of committing it.

The people are moving outside now, drawn by the train whistle.

Over there I see a couple not much younger than Blue and me. They hold hands and lean against each other, taking short painful steps and staring forward grimly. It's nice to have company.

The train comes to a halt with a lot of screeching and scraping, as if the brakes just but barely caught. A door opens and a conductor pops open the door, throwing a yellow step box onto the ground. The crowd jostles, the old couple gets shuffled to the back of the pack. We would, too, except that if anyone budges old Blue Hermann he raises one of his heavy-duty walking sticks and shakes it threateningly. And mind you, I got the old dragon-head at the ready, a stick that could do more than a little damage. Old people should feel safer than they do, considering how heavily armed most of us are.

It takes Iain, the conductor, and two more redcaps to get Blue Hermann into the train. I have to hold his canes. They weigh about twenty pounds apiece. When my turn comes, I labor upwards without assistance. Well, perhaps there's a hand on my elbow, but I don't need it. Another conductor inside the train is asking, "Smoking or nonsmoking?" He takes a closer look at Hermann, who has a nicotine-stained face, and directs us to a section of seating without saying another word.

There's a set of foursome seats at the end of the car, and we claim them. Iain brings up the rear with all the luggage, three traveling bags is all we have, and tosses them into the compartments above our heads. It would be nice to be able to toss traveling bags up into compartments. Iain's got the train tickets sticking out of his mouth. He sits down and looks at Blue and myself. "How's everybody feeling?"

"Tip-top," says I.

"One hundred percent," answers Blue.

"Jolly good show," says Iain, and I startle, because Iain sounds exactly like Clay Clinton. I can tell that Blue noticed it, too. "Next stop, Toe-ronno!" calls Iain.

I'm bored.

Train travel was the worst thing about my professional hockey career. Bytown to Montreal, to Toronto, to Hamilton, to New York, Boston, Chicago, and Detroit. I wish I could fall asleep like Blue Hermann just did, even if he does appear to be suffering the torments of hell.

Iain reaches into a pocket (the coat he has on looks to have about forty-odd pockets, and Iain has made use of each and every) and produces a deck of Bicycle playing cards. He riffles them so that they puff air into my face. "A game of chance, your highness?"

"I can play gin," I tell him, not letting on that I am by way of being a gin-playing genius.

"Gin it is." Iain starts to waterfall the cards, then he does a single-hand cut. He appears to have played before.

There's a little Formica table folded down between our seats. We raise and level it, and before long we're playing gin rummy.

Every so often I'll look up and watch through the windows. The forests are dead, drowned in snow. Starlings peck at the ground; otherwise, everything is as still as midnight.

# FIFTEEN

MANFRED A. OZIKEAN RAISED UP A HAND—the knuckles bruised from that afternoon's game against the Black Hawks—and poised it over his cards. The huge hand fluttered back and forth over the fan, sometimes darting in close for a possible pickup, always turning back. "My gracious," Manny sighed, "what a predicky-doo." Dainty talk from a man who that afternoon had situated Charlie Gardiner's nose somewhere near his hairline.

"Play," says I. I was one draw away from a lay-down, and I could fill it at either end of two straights or fill up my set of deuces. My little fingers had started to itch.

"A predicky-dicky-doo," says Manfred. Manny raised that hand again. It took a run at a card, even grabbed the top corner like it really meant business. Then, after a second's stillness, the hand retreated and began to beat on the tabletop.

"Manny," I said.

Manny looked up. "Yo?"

"Play."

I had a loathsome little seven of clubs that was eager to sacrifice itself on the refuse heap. I knew that the next card would fill up my gin. A feeling in my bones. Manfred likely had a couple of pairs or else was saving only one suit, something he did now and again, confused about the rules of the game.

Outside our window was Chicago on a Saturday night. It howled. But Manfred hadn't been drinking much since the beginning of the 1918–19 season (since he met Janey Millson, really), one of the main reasons that the Ottawa Paddies were currently tearing up the league. It was due to Manny and, I must say, Little Leary, a puff of Irish wind. I'd had a hat trick that afternoon against the Hawks, popping three straight goals all in the third frame. I was wearing the top hat in our hotel room, playing cards. If you could call what we were doing playing cards.

"*Hey!*" That blasted me and my seat almost two feet backwards. Manfred was grinning.

"Figured out a play, have we?"

"Gin." Manfred's hammy paw rearranged his cards quickly and laid them down on the table. I looked at them close— sometimes Manny left holes in the straights or confounded the suits—but this time he had it clean. I tossed down my cards and flipped him the quarter.

"Much obliged, Percival." Manny polished the coin on his shirtfront and pocketed it with glee. The Patriots were paying him plenty, but the only money that seemed to mean anything to him was the quarter we exchanged over card games.

Manfred scooped up the duckets and began to waterfall them. Cards dribbled over the top, and before long some were boxed. "You want another crack at me, Percival?"

"Naw." I flipped onto my bed, cradled the back of my head in my hands. The ceiling was cracked in more places than it wasn't. I shoved the top hat forward so that I wouldn't have the one light bulb burning into my eyeballs.

Manny flipped onto his bed, which could have been a serious mistake. The thing groaned and the room shook, but everything settled down. I counted two automobile accidents during the silence. Chicago sounded like a wounded animal.

"I miss Constance. Er, Janey." I was receiving a blow-by-blow account of Manfred's romance with Miss Millson, not that I'd requested it. We'd now arrived at a stage where Manny missed her every time he wasn't with her. Being a hockey player, that was plenty. "Do you miss Chloe?" Manny asked me.

Chloe was Janey's younger sister. She looked quite a bit like Jane, only she looked like she'd been salted and left out in the sun. Chloe's face was pinched and set like stone. When she walked, her cheeks jiggled. The best thing about her was her eyes, which were a very light blue. But, you know, eyes is eyes. If the big star is eyes, the show ain't going to Broadway. I'd been seeing Chloe since the summer previous. According to her, we had an understanding, although I had no idea what it was. Anyway, to answer Manny's query I produced a vague grunt that he could interpret however he wished.

Someone was screaming outside, drunken incoherencies, a foreign tongue.

At our Home Opener in Bytown that year, Janey Millson had single-handedly roused the crowd to near-riot pitch. She claimed a seat near the players' bench, one of the prime viewing positions, but she spent the whole game with her back to the ice, hollering upwards into the stands. She made us Paddies feel like a whole different team; even North Innes said, "We got to get *serious* out there!" The Patriots were in first place by a handful of points.

The door to our hotel room flew open, and there stood Clay Bors Clinton.

"*Asleep?!*" he demanded. Clay was dressed in his army uniform, even though the Great War was some time finished. He was going to milk that baby for all it was worth. Clay was sporting a handlebar mustache. He was all the time experimenting with facial growth, but the beards and mustaches just seemed to interfere with his beauty. "It's but nine o'clock on a Saturday night, and these two ponces are asleep!"

Manfred was off his bed in a second, scooping up Clay in a bear hug. I continued to lie there, although I did cock an eye at Clay and give him the old howdy-do.

Clinton sat on my bed. He regarded me archly.

"Is he exhausted, Freddy?"

"Could be maybe," Manfred noted. "It was a tough game."

"Did the Percival poppet play well, Freddy?"

"Three goals," Manfred announced proudly.

"Well done, Percy, my pretty!" Clay Clinton slapped my belly. Then he stood, straightened the crease in his trousers, adjusted his collar and cap, and said, "Leave us leave."

"I got shot in the head!" I piped up. "I got two decorations, Clay. I was at the Vimy Ridge."

"Percival, Percival, Percival," muttered Clinton quietly. "Do you really think I don't know these things?"

"I haven't seen you in some time."

"You're seeing me now."

I jumped off my bed. "I guess maybe I could go for some grub."

"I was thinking, Percival mine," said Clinton, "of refreshments that were more liquid." Clay grinned at Manny.

"Oh, listen," I said, "Manny doesn't—"

Manny cut me off, quick and clean. "Sure!" he shouted. "I could go for a glass of beer, maybe."

This was the early times with Manfred. I allowed as he probably *could* go for a glass of beer. We didn't know so much about the whole deal back then, didn't even have the word "alcoholic." That came up in the forties while my boy Clarence was busy becoming one. In the teens and 'twenties, someone who favored the whoozle-water was an "alcoholist," and what Manfred was wont to do, I hate to admit, was called "Indian drinking."

I flipped on my cap, picked up the dragon-head swagger stick. "I'll get a ginger ale and one of those pickled eggs."

"Still on the ginger ale, are we?" asked Clay, opening the door to the Windy City.

I nodded. "Can't quit the stuff."

The three of us went out into the night.

# SIXTEEN

THE TRAIN BURNS THROUGH THE HILLS. Every so often a town gets tossed in, but they're not towns like I remember towns. The towns I recollect had a town hall and a hotel, and houses used to huddle around for warmth. These towns are like dislocated suburbs, lost cows. The gormless Clifford lives in such a place, his tiny home looking identical to the one next door. I wonder how he can tell them apart, and then I think maybe the secret is that he can't.

A black man pushes a little silver cart down the aisle. The bouncing of the train makes the man lose his balance all the time, but he doesn't seem to care. The silver wagon is covered with miniature booze bottles, as if the train were full of miniature drunks. When someone asks for something, the black man stares ahead haughtily and grabs the appropriate little bottle without looking. The man can screw off the top with one hand and toss a cube of ice into a plastic cup with the other. Meanwhile the train bounces him around.

Blue Hermann wakes up and sees that the black man is headed our way. He gets excited, licking his lips.

I have just beaten Iain in a game of gin. Iain is reshuffling. He catches Blue's excitement, glances up, and sees the black man. "Ah," says Iain, "the candyman cometh."

"Can I have a drinky-poo?" Blue asks. His voice sounds like someone had thrown a scoopful of dirt up from hell.

"*Drinky-poo*," I repeat with some disdain. It's only the very serious booze hounds who use that word, "drinky-poo."

"Can I?"

Iain considers it, pulling on his bottom lip.

"Don't let him," I suggest. "He's an alkie."

Iain ignores me.

"Hermann might turn nasty," I say. This is just a lie. Blue turns nice when he gets a few drinks inside him, nastiness being his normal state.

Iain doesn't hear this either. He has arrived at some sort of decision. "Life is short," he says.

"Exactly," agrees Blue. "In my case, maybe a matter of minutes."

"You only live once, correct-a-mundo?" asks Iain.

"Once is an awful lot," I point out.

"Therefore," concludes Iain, "we should have some refreshment."

"Deal the duckets," I tell him. "You owe me fifty cents already."

The black man has about fifteen people to work through before he gets to us, but Blue and Iain stop dead and watch him. It's like time has frozen. I grab the deck out of Iain's hand and start to toss them myself. The hands lie on the plastic flipdown. Slowly Iain reaches out one hand and covers his cards. His sleeve is rolled up and I can see the savage-looking bird. God made no such bird, I'm fairly certain. It looks like a goose gone berserkers.

Finally the black man reaches us. He takes a long, slow look and starts to wheel his silver wagon away.

"Hey!" Iain calls out. "We want drinks."

The black man in the white coat shrugs.

"A double Scotch, straight up," demands Blue Hermann. He watches the black hand work the top of the silver trolley, fingering the tiny bottles and selecting the right ones. The other hand brings over the plastic glass and the drink is made. I've seen Blue dribble more booze down his chin.

"Kinger?" asks Iain.

"You know me, boy." My hand is a good one, full of possibilities, and I'm impatient to get down to it. "The good old stuff."

Iain tells the man, "He likes ginger ale."

A drink is set in front of me. I nod thanks, looking at my cards, plenty of royalty, jakes and ladies.

"And for you, sir?" asks the black man.

"Oh, yeah," says Iain. "I'm fine. Um . . . *yougotabeer?*" It comes out like one long word.

The black man names some brands unenthusiastically. Iain hasn't heard of one of them. "Well," says Iain, slapping his hands together like a Boy Scout troop leader, "I'll try that one, then."

The black man has the side door open and the beer out before Iain is through speaking. Then he pushes the silver cart back down the aisle.

Blue Hermann has his drink finished already, naturally. He's sucking on the ice cube, trying to get out every last drop. "I thought you didn't drink," he says to Iain.

"Oh," says Iain, pouring beer into the plastic cup, "not seriously. Not like I used to. You know. A beer now and then is no big deal. Right? A little brewskie every blue moon won't hurt me."

I take a look at my pop can. "Hey!" I shout. "What the hickory is this?"

The can is the same color as the good old Canada Dry, and the picture on it is the same, namely, a little map of the country, but something isn't right. Then I realize that my can doesn't say Canada Dry. It says, in exactly the same kind of writing, Acadia Dry. "What goes on?" I whisper. I feel like I'm in that television show, the one my no-good son Clarence wrote an episode for, *The Twilight Zone.* I pour some into my plastic glass—even the fizz is not quite right. I take a sip and almost have to spit it out. The stuff has an edge like a razor blade. "I'm going to die!" I scream, maybe a touch overdramatic.

Those two ignore me. We all have our problems. Blue's problem is that he doesn't have a glass of booze in his hand. Iain's problem seems to be that he does. He stares at his brew like he can't decide what to do with it.

"They're trying to poison the old King," I inform my traveling companions.

"*Moi aussi*," Iain says. He brings the cup to his lips quickly and his Adam's apple bobs a couple of times. "Aaah . . ." he sighs, wiping foam from his pale lips.

Manfred used to make a similar grand production out of taking a single sip of ale. The gormless boy Clifford and his cronies just toss the stuff back quick and natural, as if air had turned into golden suds.

"Veddy, veddy nize," Iain says, savoring another mouthful. He takes a glance at the skin on the back of his hand. "So far, so good. No signs of transmogrification."

"Mine's gone," snarls the Blue-boy. He looks about ready to eat his plastic glass.

"You want some of my ginger ale?" I offer nicely.

"Back to the cards," Iain says. He scoops up his hand. Iain sorts them, rearranges them, tugs at the corners for no good reason.

I start the play, tossing a three onto the flop. Iain ups it with a cackle, dispenses a seven. Sevens are as much use to me as earrings. I take from the draw pile, a miserable four of hearts. It gets heaped on the refuse. Iain's eyes light and he scoops the sucker. A king of spades gets thrown, and Iain is laying down his hand. "Gin, baby."

"No fair!" I shout. "*I'll* shuffle this time."

Iain grins. The white farmland screams by.

# SEVENTEEN

A BEER AND A GINGER ALE? was what Clay Clinton had to say. "How embarrassingly plebeian."

Manfred and I found it hard to argue the point, not knowing what the word meant. Clay had just ordered some house speciality. It was just like Clinton to know what the house speciality was, even though he'd never been in the house before. The particular house was in a huge hotel. There were chandeliers on the ceiling and oil paintings on the walls. There were men with waxed whiskers and women with bosoms making escape attempts from the bodices of frilly gowns. Clay Clinton sat in the midst of all that, waving and nodding. At first the patrons just stared at the boy quizzically, but before long they were returning his waves, and before much after that they were dropping by the table. Many people assumed that he had suffered some grievous injury during the war, a notion Clay wasn't anxious to dispel. "I'll heal," he told them all, "*physically*."

Meantime Manfred was trying like a son of a bitch to sip his beer. Manfred hiked the glass up slowly, placed his lips gingerly on the rim, and then *whoosh*, about half the ale shot into his mouth. His first beer lasted all of fourteen seconds. A waiter floated by and dropped another frosted glass in front of Manfred.

"Oh," said Manny, raising a hand, but Clay waved the waiter away.

My ears were buzzing on account of the ginger ale. I was spine-tingled and goose-bumped.

"I propose a toast!" Clay Bors Clinton raised his house speciality. "To the three of us."

We drank the toast, another beer down Ozikean's gullet.

Clay tapped his near-empty glass with his forefinger. Clinton had long, manicured nails. "Another," he snapped, always curt with the hired help.

"I'll try one of those," announced Manfred. "A house speciality."

"Drink while ye may," Clay chanted, "for I fear the dries shall rule the day."

Manny glanced up quickly. "You think there's gonna be prohibition, Clay?"

"I do, I do," answered Clinton. Then he slapped a dizzying smile on us. "And, my leaping lord, the money to be made!"

"You should hear the old mother on that topic." "Rabid" would be the word for the mother. She wouldn't have nothing to do with the Anti-Saloon League, which also billed itself as the "Protestant Church in Action," but aside from that she was doing everything she could to rid the world of the Demon Rum.

The waiter came back with house specialities and cocked an eyebrow at me.

"Naw," I muttered. "There's a game tomorrow."

"So?" That was Manfred. The word pounced.

I shrugged. "Just saying." We were playing back-to-back with the Black Hawks, Saturday and Sunday afternoons.

"I'll play good. Don't you worry about that, Percival."

"I was just saying," I repeated.

"Don't start on me, Little Leary," muttered Ozikean.

"Jumpin' Jesus, Manny, I was just saying!"

"How are the various loves of our various lives?" asked Clinton.

That softened Manfred some, and he started to smile. "Pretty good."

I managed a shrug.

Whereupon Clay launched into a long and windy tale involving his seduction at the hands of an older woman when he was stationed at the OT camp in the prairies. I suspect it was more fanciful than historical, but it got the three of us laughing and kept us engrossed for the better part of an hour. In that time, Manfred ingested four more beer and two house specialities.

"Hey!" Manny shouted, after the story was done. "Let's go somewhere else."

"What did you have in mind?" asked Clay, raising his glass to someone sitting across the room.

"You know," answered Manfred, "a tavern."

"Oh, Fred," asked Clay, "how do you expect to get any-where in the world?"

"I don't," admitted Manfred Ozikean. "I'm already some-where in the world."

I've just won a real battle. I won it when Iain tossed the queen of hearts, even though anyone with half a brain would have known I was saving the ladies. For the past few moments, Iain's been a bit distracted. I know what he's doing. He's looking for the black man with the little silver trolley. Iain spots him and waggles his fingers.

Blue Hermann is asleep, but his booze detector never rests. He opens one eye and mumbles, "Scotch. No ice," and then returns to slumber until it's served.

I shuffle the duckets. It's not my go, but Iain's not about to do it. Iain looks at me and shakes his head. "Let's give it a rest, my liege."

"You owe me money."

Iain goes for his pocket, but not to pay me, to pay the black man with his gleaming cart.

Blue wakes up long enough to slurp down his whiskey.

Iain lingers over his brew, savoring every mouthful. He lights up a smoke and begins to whistle.

I look out the window. We're moving through farmland. Things are darkening, the night is coming.

In the tavern, Manfred took over saying hello to everybody.

This was quite the place. There were men with waxed mustaches, but they'd been drinking so much that the booze had melted the wax and sprung all the hairs. And, with these women, one or two bosoms had made successful escape attempts from the bodices of frilly gowns. The walls and ceiling of the joint were covered with brickety-brack and purplish daguerreotypes of baseball players and naked ladies. There was, or so I seem to recall, a goat in the joint. It wandered around snacking on people's trousers and shoes.

The house speciality at this place was nickel-a-bottle hooch strained through an old sock. Manfred and Clay had about seven of those apiece, and twice as many beers for chasers. I nursed a single glass of ginger ale.

Two women appeared, Hermione and Ginger. They were older ladies, by which I mean they were in their late twenties, and they were heavily made-up. Both had waists so tiny that even I could have wrapped both my hands all the way around them, and both of them had bubbies so large that the rest of their bodies seemed tagged on as afterthoughts.

A little man wandered over and started yelling in my ear, addressing the Great Debate raging between the wets and the dries. He was a wet. His breath was bad, and he had a nasty habit of digging his forefinger into my ribs. Hermione and Ginger were giggling with Manfred and Clay.

The little man started to cry in my ear.

Manfred got raging drunk. Not mean drunk, though. Manny started laughing and pawing old Ginger right through her dress, not that she minded. Manfred and Ginger disappeared—Lord knows what diseases she might have!—and Hermione and Clay wandered off, and before I knew it I was out in the streets of Chicago. Damned if the sun wasn't coming up, making everything a wintry silver. I wasn't afraid to be out on the streets alone; back in those days things weren't half as rough. Oh, you might find the odd thug, but once you've gone toe-to-toe with Sprague Cleghorn, thugs don't seem like much. I understand Chicago is mean these days, a city full of bad blood. My no-good son Clarence lived there for a couple of years, writing his pornography and poetry, and he got mugged seventeen times! Once they even took a knife to his face, and he had a scar across his cheek. The scar looked like a garden slug clinging to his face.

Clarence was arrested and put on trial for obscenity. Most terrible day of my life, almost killed his mother. And it wasn't even good clean obscenity! That's what cities like Chicago will do to you. Full of whores and perverts. Mind you, Herm and Ginger were whores, so that much ain't new, and *who the hell is shaking me?*

I'm alone in the Windy City, just me and the gray morning, the empty streets and milk bottles. I need my sleep, that's for damn sure. A professional athlete needs his shut-eye. Listen to him, Blue says. *Blue Hermann?* Leave me alone, you bastard, I was out late last night. Sure, I'll score the hat trick again. I don't know about Ozikean, though. Looks like he spent the night in a suitcase. Just a bit of sleep, that's all I need. *Toronto?* What is this business about *Toronto?* We don't play those Toronto boys until Wednesday. Don't you read the schedule? You can pick me up and shake me all you want—it won't change the fact. *Look out the window?* How can I look out the window, my peepers is shut. I'll open them, all right, I'll open them. Whoa. Big black city out there. Breathing smoke into the air like a dragon. I don't know, I don't know where I am. Keep calm, King. Slip open one eye and take a quick gander. Train station. Biggest I ever seen. Maybe I died, maybe I finally went and did it, maybe this is the train to Glory—there would *have* to be a Jesus-big station for the Glory-train—but I recognize that wheezy braying, that there is Blue Hermann, newspaperman, and he for damn sure ain't bound for the Pearly Gates. There's arms around my chest, holding me up. Lookee there. A tattoo of a bird. The bird gives me the heebie-jeebies. Iain. All right. Let me take a couple of breaths. Just a dream, that's all.

"Just a dream," says I.

# EIGHTEEN

IT WAS IN MONTREAL, March 13 of one-nine one-nine, that I made my first move to become the King of the Ice. I did that by deposing the previous King, Lalonde. He was called Newsy, although his right name was one of those French affairs with too many vowels. Lalonde looked like God wrought him out of stone—except really Lalonde looked like God had thought better of the idea halfway through and gone out to a movie. In the middle of Newsy's face were two eyes, as black as a nun's habit, and when Lalonde was angry—all of the time—they acquired a distinct lunatic sheen. Many a player was beaten just by a look at those eyes. Mind you, Newsy Lalonde could play. He was what you might call a talented and sound hockey player, and when you combine that with largeness and the ability to scare the holy bejesus out of people, then you got something. In 1919 he was thirty-two years old, and that's when I went after him.

I was Little Leary, the heart and soul of the Ottawa Paddies. I wore the letter C over my heart, captain of the shinny-playing Irishters. I had the ginger back then, brother.

We were tied up in overtime.

Patty Boyle called for a time-out. The Paddies crowded around him at the bench.

Manfred looked at me and smiled that long crooked grin of his. "Let's do it, Percy," he said with a wink. "I'm getting hungry."

I nodded, stuff stirring in my guts.

"Here," said Manfred, and he stuck something in my gloved hand. It was his crucifix, the huge one. I noticed that Our Savior was not dying, He was stone dead. "Carry that," said Manny.

"You figure that's gonna help, do you?"

"You know what Brother Isaiah would say."

Manny had an uncanny knack for remembering the blind monk's drivel. I shrugged.

"Brother Isaiah would say, 'It couldn't hurt.' " Manfred winked again. "The Magic Stone, Percy."

"The Magic Stone?"

"Percival!" shouted Clay from the stands. He was sitting in the front row, having used some of his Bytown timber baron connections to get the ticket. "Score a goal, my prince! We're wasting valuable drinking time!"

"Go, you Lucky Number Seven!"

I dropped the crucifix inside my jersey. The metal felt cool and soothing on my belly.

We set up for the face-off. Newsy Lalonde was staring at me.

"Hey, newsboy," said I, "don't stand there. That's where I mean to skate with the puck."

"You are horsemeat, O'Toole." Lalonde always affected to disremember my name, or maybe he really did, and he just used any Irish monicker that popped into whatever he was using for a mind.

"Come on, guys," said Manfred, "let's not fight."

"Mind your own business, chief," said Lalonde.

Manny crossed himself.

I crossed myself, too, and I touched the crucifix.

The rest is historical.

I heard Clay Clinton shout "Yes!" with all of his heart and soul. Clay had just won a lot of money—this was the start of what is commonly referred to as his "vast financial empire"— but his shout had a lot more to it than that. And I heard Manny cry, "Hey!"—that big delighted bellow of his. I realized that

I'd scored, that we'd won the Stanley Cup. For that instant, we were three young men alone in the universe.

Of course the newshounds were barking in the dressing room. There must have been a hundred of them all shouting questions at me. One of them—and in my memory he looks a lot like the young Blue Hermann, although my memory may be playing a little trick on me—one of them demanded, "Little Leary! Who's the better player, you or Manny?"

"Hard to say." I shrugged.

"Come now," the newspaperman urged me.

"Time will tell" was all I said.

And time did tell.

It told in 1937. It was New Year's Day.

I'd woken early in the morning. Beside me Chloe slumbered deeply, because at midnight she'd tucked into the sweet sherry. We'd made a sort of love that approached wantonness, although I get the impression that nowadays it's what people do immediately after they exchange names. I studied Chloe's body as she slept. She'd lost a lot of weight, her dugs all but vanished, her rib cage plain as day. I got up, put on my gown, wandered into the living room. My knee still hurt like hell, even though a year had passed since the accident. The place was silent, the boys were out in the wintry sun, perhaps skating on the canal, Clifford spending most of his time dusting his keester, Clarence prancing about like a sissy. I switched on the radio. Hitler was up to more shit. Manny Oz had been found dead in his hotel room.

I took to the streets.

And everyone who passed me had the same greeting. "Happy New Year," they said. "Happy New Year, *King!*"

# NINETEEN

AS IT TURNS OUT, the Claire thing is a fellow. A most damn peculiar one, but a fellow all the same.

Claire Redford meets us in the train station, pushing through the crowd to get at us. He tells people, "Excuse me," very politely and then rams the ball of his hand into their backs and shoves. With the other hand, Claire Redford waves at us, and being as the Claire thing is well over six foot, the waving hand seems like a bird flitting above everybody's head.

The Claire thing has blond hair. Most of it is short, shorn up the back and sides, but there's a long shock that dangles down, covering his face. The first thing Claire Redford does when he gets to us is grab this shock and shoot it back up onto his head. "Hey there, hi there, ho there!" he sings. The Claire thing has a diamond stuck into a front tooth. "You're as welcome as can be!" Claire grabs Blue Hermann's wrinkled claw and begins to pump. "So here is the famous King Leary!"

"No, I'm not," Blue Hermann snarls, almost as if he's insulted.

The tone of Blue's voice startles Claire Redford. "You should do something about that throat," he advises old Blue, shooting the blond hank backwards. He turns to Iain and says, "Am I right or am I whistling 'Sweet Sue'? The throat demands medical attention." Then Claire grabs my hand. "All hail!" he says. "All hail the King!"

"This is Iain," I tell Claire. "He's here in case anything should go wrong. Blue and I are likely to pop off anytime now."

"Hiya." Claire Redford looks at his watch. It's an enormous thing and has tiny push buttons on the side. "Well, you people are all booked into the Oxford Hotel, that's all taken care of. What say we go eat?" Claire grabs our traveling bags and flits away. "I have a cab waiting." We follow. Claire would have us going at quite a clip, but Blue Hermann slows the whole herd down. The Claire thing circles around us like a buzzard. "How was the trip?"

"Leary had a nightmare," gloats Blue, concentrating on working the tips of his canes across the marble floor of the train station.

"It was that weird ginger ale they gave me," I explain. "Anyway, you're a fine one to talk, Hermann. You have seven nightmares an hour."

"Yeah, but I work for mine."

"If you have trouble with nightmares," Claire Redford says, "then you are probably sleeping with your head pointed in the wrong direction. All the forces in the world run up and down. North and south, you see, from the two poles. That's straightforward, no? We're talking grade three here. Now, if you lie down with the bonker aimed east or west, you interfere with these forces. Am I right or am I tap-dancing in zero gravity?"

"It makes a certain amount of sense," I agree. "I could always play better in an arena that ran north-south." Brother Isaiah, I remember, was a great one for going on about forces and suchlike.

And directions! For a man who didn't know which way he was going, Isaiah was surely fond of directions. Here's one of his coaching tips:

The little birds sang east, the little birds sang west,
and I smiled to think that God's greatness
flowed around our incompleteness.

I'm startled to have remembered the blind monk's doggerel so easily.

We have to go through a revolving door to leave the train station, but as much force as Blue's scrawny self can muster isn't quite enough to budge the contraption. Iain and Claire both try to spin it by hand, but Blue Hermann gets rattled about like a marble in a tin can, unable to keep up with his little wedge. The operation is slow and painstaking, Claire and Iain moving the door a few inches, Blue Hermann scurrying to center himself. I stand inside my own little piece-of-pie-shaped glass booth. In a while I get launched into the night.

Claire Redford leads us to a smoking taxicab and opens the rear door. He and Iain go into the loading procedure, stuffing Blue Hermann into the backseat. Then Iain puts his hands on my elbows and seats me. Iain gets in beside us, and the Claire thing jumps into the front.

"Chinese?" Claire asks.

"Sounds good," says Iain.

Blue nods, and I allow that Chinese is all right, as far as food goes.

"The Conqueror," Claire tells the cabbie, and we wheel out.

It's hard for me to imagine that this is the same town me and Manny came to to recruit ourselves all those many years ago. Everything is lights and loudness in the city. Many of the people are deranged. The psychiatric ward at the South Grouse Home got nothing on these sidewalks, that's for sure.

Blue had some good years here. In the sixties he was the big sportswriter for the Toronto *Daily Planet*. Blue Hermann got some of his best diseases in Toronto. After Clay died I didn't see hide nor hair of Blue until they wheeled him into my room at the nursing home. Some of the bars we pass are his old haunts, and Blue Hermann gazes at them sadly and lovingly. Every so often, he'll heave a sigh.

Next thing I know, we're in Chinatown. There's nothing but Chinese people everywhere you look, and Chinese writing on all the signs.

The cab pulls over to the curb. Claire and Iain unload Blue Hermann. I climb out unassisted.

Old men drift by on the sidewalk, little half smiles on their faces, like they just heard a good one. Chinatown hasn't changed much over the years. Same burnt-red ducks hanging by their feet in the windows. Same young moon-faced men scooping out noodles with paddles. Manfred loved Chinatown, you know, mostly, I expect, because it reminded him of home. It was just about as crowded and had the same general level of activity.

We move along the street. It's slow slogging. There's Chinamen here who look to have ten or twenty years on me and Blue, but they putter along like they're on wheels. I can't muster much of a Dublintown swagger. I drift close to Iain and hope he might put his hand on my elbow. Iain, though, catches the toe of his boot in a crack on the sidewalk and pitches forward. He spins around, tries to regain his balance, and this he accomplishes, except in the process he barks his knee on a fire hydrant. "Whoopsy daisy," he mutters quietly.

The Conqueror is down some steps. It's been around for close to forty years. Clay enjoyed the food, and they used to have a little gambling den in the back. Maybe they still do. Clay would go there and lose a lot of money, because in his fat years, Clay seemed to lose the ability to gamble. Before that, you know, it was like the man could make dice roll on his fancy, it was like cards would come shooting out of the deck if they were the ones he needed. I seen him pull to an inside straight more often than not. I seen Clay Clinton ride a number on the roulette wheel well past the point of foolishness and win. Then, after the Toronto Gardens was built and the Maple Leaves were his and he was all alone in the world—except for me—Clay Clinton seemed to lose this knack. He'd get dealt three aces and lose to four trays. Not that Clay cared particularly. The man never did care overmuch.

Blue stands on the top step and peers down cautiously. Claire Redford steps over to him and says, "Allow me, Old Yeller." The Claire thing scoops up Blue Hermann and cradles him babylike. "I hope you don't mind," says Claire.

"Naw," Blue snarls.

"Good boy." Claire fair skips down the stairs, sets Hermann on his feet, and pushes through the front door. "Table for four!" he bellows.

A little woman sitting behind a wooden desk scuttles off to find us one. The joint is packed.

Iain lights up a cigarette. For a fellow who doesn't smoke much, he's sure smoking a lot.

"A filthy habit," Claire pronounces. "Isn't it, your highness?"

"If you want to be an NHLer, eat yer veggies and don't never smoke a cigarette."

"I'm going to quit," Iain tells us earnestly. "I quit for a couple of years, you know, and then—" Iain shrugs.

We follow the little woman through the tables. The Chinese people stare at us even as they stuff rice down their gullets. We sit at a round table. A waiter comes with a pot that's full of hot green water. Another one comes and takes an order for drinks.

"Soda water, please," says Claire.

"Scotch, double, straight up," mutters Blue Hermann.

"Ginger ale," says I.

"Good boy!" ejaculates the Claire thing.

"Um . . ." Iain is chewing his bottom lip.

"I come back."

"No," says Iain. "I'll have the same as him." Iain levels his forefinger at the wrinkled newspaperman.

The waiter scurries. The Claire thing scoops up the menu and looks at it. Half of it is in Chinese, half in a strange sort of English. The Claire thing tries to start a conversation about what various food we should have, but it doesn't travel very far. Iain and Blue go dumb and wait on the little Chinaman with the drinks. I do my best to help, but food is food. I never did have a passion for it.

The drinks come. Mine is in a huge glass, but I can tell it's fountain ginger ale and watered down besides. Fountain ginger ale has got nowhere near the kick of the bottled or canned stuff, and you can't summon a healthy belch even after five or six big glasses.

Iain and Blue Hermann both have a couple of fingers' worth of stuff in dirty juice glasses. Blue tosses his down as it hits the table and barks out a reorder before the waiter has taken more than two steps. Iain has a small sip. His face wrinkles painfully and then relaxes. "Cheers," he mumbles.

"Same back at you, boy," I answer.

Claire says, "If it's all the same to you three, I'll just order at will."

There's some glum nodding. The Claire thing doesn't seem to realize that food ain't a big issue at our table.

Iain takes a larger sip. I seen this before.

# TWENTY

ONE SIP OF THE DEMON RUM—this is what the old mother used to say—is your first step toward the grave. My mother had a number of picture books that told tales of men and women whose love of liquor brought them first shame and infamy and finally death. My, how Death does love to get its hands on boozers. The last page of one of my mother's booklets showed a man dressed in rags, sitting in the fires of perdition, the Devil standing over him, chortling. I shudder to think of that picture.

The old mother wasn't alone in her thinking. During the Great War, prohibition seemed to work pretty good. I hardly even noticed, but there were people who could tell you that the crime rate dropped and worker productivity went up, so on and so forth, and it looked for a while like Ontario might stay dry for eternity. Then something happened, namely, they passed the Volstead Act in the U.S. of A. and America was all of a sudden dry as a bone. Certain people—the young Clay Bors Clinton among them—started a campaign to get the Ontario prohibition laws repealed, which they soon were. This enabled Clay to be about the business of his life, namely, getting filthy rich.

There was nothing illegal in what Clay did—at least, if there was, he never told me about it—and certainly the charge that Clay was a bootlegger is a false one. Jubal St. Amour, now, owner of the Amerks, that man was a bootlegger. Jubal started his career with an empty bathtub, some potatoes, and a lot of copper tubing. All Clay did was to take that money he won gambling on the one-nine one-nine cup series and open up a few taverns close to the American border in Ontario and Quebec. The Yankees would putter up and spend the day boozing. It could be that Clay sold a few bottles under the table, and I suppose it further could be that Clay sold the occasional truckload to some entrepreneurial types, but for the record, all Clay Clinton did was open seven or eight shanty groghouses, and that's when he started raking in the dough.

In the meantime, Manny and I were playing hockey for the Ottawa Patriots. In the season after we won the cup, we sank to fifth place.

Manfred was all the time on and off the water wagon. One time he even went to a clinic to dry out, but they had some strange notion about "maintenance drinking," and Manny was on a bender most of the three weeks he spent in there. Manfred went to the Oxford Group. They were church people, and their basic idea was this—you are a piece of dung, but God is willing to help. So they spent a long time convincing Manfred that he was a piece of dung, and it seemed like God Himself came around to this line of thinking, because He did precious little to help Manfred. It was after the Oxford Group that Manny really began to go on ragers. He got himself arrested two or three times—drunk and disorderly, creating a public spectacle—and once he disappeared for four whole days, missing two games. The assistant general manager of the Patriots fined him one thousand dollars for that scam! And if that seems like an overly stiff and severe fine, that assistant general manager was C. B. Clinton.

How that was exactly, that Clay became the assistant general manager, has never been too clear. The G.M., Frank O'Connor, was a good friend of the Clinton clan, but that hardly seems reason enough to install a young brash mook like Clay as your assistant. But things worked out. In that first year Clay Clinton arranged a trade. Clay traded North Innes, the Patriot star goaler, for four young players, none of whom showed particular promise. It looked like a rum deal until North Innes died in 'twenty-five. In 1926 Clay Clinton was made the general manager of the Ottawa Patriots Hockey Club.

His first move was to trade me.

Now, before all that happened, I should point out, I got married. I married Chloe Elizabeth Millson in the summer of nineteen twenty-three. How this event transpired is still something of a mystery to me.

I liked Chloe well enough, I mean, she was pretty in a pinched sort of way and quite the athlete, an excellent skater and skier. In the summer, there was nothing she liked better than to go to the small lakes in the Gatineau and swim all day. Come to think, it was at one of these lakes that the true nature of our "understanding" reared its ugly head. The deal was, Chloe would have no compunction against stripping off and swimming in my sight all in the buff-bare—not an unpleasant sight, I'll admit, Chloe being slight but muscled—and I in turn would join her in holy wedlock. Back in those days, that was the kind of deal you made.

We were wed in late August. I could likely remember the exact date if I put my mind to it. Some geese, worrywarts, were already heading for Florida.

The groom's side of the affair didn't amount to much. My mother, sister (with her boyfriend, a friendly young buck with withered fingers), and my brother Francis were there, naturally, and my friends Clay Bors Clinton and Manfred Armstrong Ozikean. Patty Boyle came to represent the Patriots. There were reporters from the two Bytown newspapers, because I was a celebrity. I wasn't the King of the Ice back then, but I was making my move, brother, you can believe me on that account.

The bride's side, I was alarmed to find out, was enormous. Not only that, it was largely women. Not only that, all the women were variations on Jane. Some were older, some were younger, some were bigger, some were slighter, but basically Janey was your basic Millson. These women buzzed around the front yard of the big Millson homestead while the men stood in the shade of an oak tree and drank lemonade. Mr. Millson, a fat man whose joy in life was the cultivation of a heroic handle-bar mustache, would occasionally walk over to me, wrap his arm around my neck, squeeze it hard, and make a peculiar growling noise. This was meant as affection, or so I took it. Mrs. Millson—Jane with gray hair, a powdery face, and thirty extra pounds—would come over and press on me various foodstuffs. Aunts would walk over and inform me, giggling, that I was a professional hockey player, but mostly these aunts confronted Manfred with the same information. Manny stood there looking nervous, intrigued by something held high in the branches of the oak tree. Clay Clinton held court for the matrons, and was as charming a bastard as the sun ever shone upon.

Chloe disappeared early on. She touched the back of my hand lightly and said, "Pookie, I'm going to lie down."

Pookie, that's me. Don't even ask.

"Uh-yeah," I grunted. It was about five-thirty in the afternoon. I've ever had a reputation as a man early to bed and early to rise, but this was pushing it. "I'll be along."

Chloe did look nice in her bridal gown. Don't think it never occurred to me that the girl deserved better than to marry yours truly.

When I did go to bed, some hours later, Chloe's face was creased by slumber, and a little line of spittle fell from her mouth. Her nightgown had ridden up, and her buttocks were naked to the world. The skin was very, very pale and seemed almost to shine in the gloom. I peeled off and got into the bed beside her. Her breath was heavy and regular. I mumbled a good night and closed my eyes. Chloe set upon me like a dog on a bone. Neither of us knew what we were doing, although Chloe seemed to have an intuitive grasp on things. Anyway, we worked it out pretty good. Afterwards, Chloe cried, but she insisted she was happy. We slept in each other's arms.

At the reception I had a talk with Jane. She came up to me, walking a little unsteadily. Janey was into the lemonade. The Millson menfolk were spiking the stuff, adding whatever liquor they'd brought with them. The lemonade kept changing color and consistency, and Janey had a glass of stuff that was bright orange and as thick as blood. "Brother-in-law!" she hailed me.

I hadn't thought of us in terms of this new relationship. "Sister-in-law," I said, more to hear the sound of it, and I toasted her with my glass of well water.

"I'm right corked," Janey confided, pressing her lips into my ear. "I'm pissed, Little Brother. Isn't it wonderful?"

"Watch your tongue."

"Answer me this, Lucky Number Seven. How's come when I get a snootful I start feeling all warm and happy, and when Manny ties one on he is as nasty a piece of business as you'd ever care to see. That's a poser, isn't it, Little Brother?"

I shrugged. Janey's bosom kept brushing against my arm. She took a tug on the lemonade. "Why don't you drink, Little Brother?"

"As the old mother would have it, I would not put a thief in my mouth to steal my brains."

"Brains," Janey scowled. "Who gives a spit about brains?"

"What do you mean?"

Janey decided to sit down. Actually it was more like the gods decided that Jane should sit down, because she plopped onto her backside like a sack of oats. Janey patted the earth beside her. "Sit down, Little Brother, Lucky Number Seven. Sit down and hear my problems."

I crouched beside the girl. "What problems, Janey?"

She hefted a finger and waved it at the general activity. "There they are yonder."

"What are we looking at, Little Sister?"

"Now, the one of them," said Janey—she crossed her arms on her knees and cradled her small head—"is standing there thinking about whether or not to have a drink of lemonade. That's all he's been thinking about, all day. My guess is he won't. Tonight, though, he'll go over to Hull and get so drunk he can speak French! Right now, though, everyone in the family thinks he's a proper eejit because all he does is nod and grunt." Jane did an imitation of Manfred's attempts at politeness, which sounded like a Barbary ape long deprived of creature comforts. "Some of the men here—like my Uncle Donald—want to start a fight with him. Isn't that queer? How's come so many men want to fight him, just because he's so big?"

I shrugged again. "Cleghorn sure has it in for him."

"You be careful of that Cleghorn, Little Brother. He means you harm."

"I can handle Spray-goo, Sister."

Jane held my hand briefly. I wondered at this for a while. "Now," she went on, "my other problem is standing there making my Aunt Sarah turn purple with laughter. The smooth son of a bitch."

I guess I looked a bit surprised. Janey thought I was gaffed at her language (which, frankly, could be quite unladylike). She burst out with a short laugh. "You know what he is, Little Brother."

"I didn't know Clay was complicating things."

"Clay Clinton complicates everything. That's what he's best at is complicating things."

Clay glanced up from Aunt Sarah and saw us watching. He raised his glass and turned on that smile of his.

Jane Millson sighed. "It's hard, Little Brother. Jeezly hard. I think I'll get so drunk that I sleep for four days." Jane struggled to stand erect. I could see almost the whole length of her legs. Janey picked up her lemonade glass and drained it. Then she looked at me. Her eyes were a hard, dark blue. "Little Leary," she asked. "What's wrong with you, anyway? How's come you didn't fall in love with me?"

"Couldn't say," I told her.

"Well, now you've got Chloe."

"Yep."

"But I've got bigger bubbies than her." Janey used to say things like that just to watch my face. I'm not sure what my face did, but it surely started the girl laughing.

# TWENTY-ONE

BLUE HERMANN, HAVING INHALED a couple of whiskies, lights up one of his dead ends and leans back. "I used to come here with Clay Clinton," Blue whispers. He's not whispering for secrecy, he's whispering because a coughing jag has deprived him of gas.

"Clay liked it here." The food's arrived, although no one but for the Claire thing is happy about that. I've sucked on a few pale noodles, crunched on a baby corn, that should do me fine.

"One time," Blue remembers, "Clay sat right where you're sitting now and cried like a baby."

"Uh-yeah? I imagine he'd just seen some motion picture. Those motion pictures could surely make him blubber."

"No." Blue Hermann shakes his head. "We'd been drinking all day." It might be my imagination, but I swear that when Hermann just shook his head, all of the liver spots and various mottles shifted position.

"Right. Clay would get drunk and then start crying over some silliness. He'd sing songs and say poetry. The man was mostly hambone, Hermann."

Blue Hermann spears a piece of meat and tosses it into his maw, satisfying his daily requirement of seven calories. He talks while he's chewing, as disgusting a sight as you'd ever want to see. "Not this time, O your royal highness, King of the Ice. This time Clinton was crying about specifics."

"Never happened, Blue-boy. This is liquor- and drug-induced fabrication. Hey, Iain! Hermann is commencing to hallucinate."

"*Specifics*," Blue Hermann hisses.

"Like what?"

"Something you and he did."

"Clay himself done a lot of things, and sometimes I was around. But we were never in cahoots."

Blue lifts his trembling hand and manages to snap his fingers. Before long there's more drinks on the table. I guess Hermann's finger-popping has a kind of alcoholic authority. "It happened in 1933."

"In one-nine three-three I was coaching the Ottawa Patriots. Clay was general manager. We won the divisional championship that year."

"True. And you lost to the Americans in the first round of the play-offs."

"If you say so, Hermann."

"I was there."

"So was I."

"The Paddies sure could have used Manny Oz."

"Uh-yeah." I spear an onion, ain't onions supposed to be good for the blood, but to hell with it, I toss her back on the serving dish. "The world don't always shake fair, Blue-boy. Look at me, for an example. The year previous, 'thirty-two, I'm playing as good as ever I was. I think I had twenty-some goals already that year. I was so full of ginger I could make a horse sneeze at thirty paces. And what happens? I break my kneecap all to bits, and that's the end of the song. I'm hung out like Wednesday's wash."

"And you didn't even break your leg playing hockey," says the withered scribe. "Ironic."

"Yeah. Things get ironic every now and then."

Blue sticks out his warted chin and scratches at it. He's affecting a poor memory, but I know the booze sops everything up like a sponge. "Now, if I recall, it was your son Rance—"

"His name was *Clarence*. And it don't matter. All that matters is, I busted the 'cap, Jubal St. Amour turned me loose, and

I likely would have starved to death if Clay hadn't said to me, King, old buddy, old pal, come back to Bytown and coach the Pats."

"He had a job he wanted you to do."

"What do you mean by that?"

"Yep," says Blue, "Clinton sat right where you're sitting and cried."

"Could be his bunions were acting up. The man's feet were in sorry shape. You know what else he had? Gout. A disease no one's had since King Arthur and his Round Table stopped drinking the hard stuff."

"And he called you a little Irish bastard."

"Is that a fact?"

"Yeah." Blue Hermann polishes off his drink. His hands have stopped shaking so much. Now they just modulate back and forth. Blue's eyes are rheumy and his wet lips press outwards. "He called you a little Irish bastard and said, 'Why didn't he stop me?' "

"Why didn't I stop him?"

"He said, 'All the little Irish git had to do was say no.' "

Iain asks, "What's the matter, Kinger?"

Clay asked, "What's the matter, Percy, my pet?"

I says, "Are you sure it's a good idea? You know, the Amerks are a wild crew. There's always booze around. Jubal even puts it right in the dressing room!"

"If you don't think we should do it, just say no."

"King?"

"King?"

"It's rather interesting, about Leary's nickname. The King." That's Blue Hermann speaking. Don't listen to him. They've been giving him some very nasty drugs at the home. "Now, some people have pointed out that there is an allusion to the Bard, but such subtleties are lost on Percival himself. It was, coincidentally, myself who popularized his nickname, but I cannot be given credit for having originated it." Yeah, don't listen to him. He's got the heebie-jeebies, he don't know what he's saying. "That dubious distinction goes to a young hockey player named Richie Reagan." Voiceless Richie Reagan was a winger with the Amerks, I remember him. Nice enough fellow. "This was in New York City. Percy Leary was the star of the New York American hockey franchise, owned by one Jubal St. Amour." Sure, Jubal St. Amour and his moll, Hallie. Hallie would come into the dressing room after games, and the whole entire team would hush up like we'd gone to church. Hallie used to dress in silver and gold. When she passed by a light, you could see the shadow of her nakedness. "They were holding scrimmages at the end of a practice. I was there, from the *Star*." That's right, always standing off to one side, trench coated and fedoraed, scribbling into a little notebook. You were a good-looking young charlie, Blue, you always had that bubbly-bosomed blonde on your arm when you hit the streets at nighttime. "Leary was on the blue team." Blue versus red. Red, white, and blue for the Americans. I was always blue. "And they take the puck down the ice. Leary applies the St. Louis Whirlygig to his cover and *poof*, he's in the clear." One of the great wonders of the world, the St. Louis Whirlygig! It's a spit in the eye of gravity and sundry physical laws! "And Leary starts pounding his stick on the ice, you see, so that his teammates will pass the puck." Boys, I'm by my lonesome over here! Give us the rubber, lads, I'll tally one sure as shit. "But they ignore him. They pass the puck back and forth a bit and then shoot it at the net. The goalie stops it." Of course he does. The shot's got no mustard on it, a weak drive from a piss-poor angle. "Leary throws down his stick in digust and marches off the ice." Damn right I do.

"And Richie Reagan says, 'Well, who the hell does he think he is—the King of the Ice?' "

# TWENTY-TWO .

CHLOE AND I LIVED WITH MY MOTHER AND MY SISTER, Bernice, in the Leary household until Chloe pointed out that I earned a fair salary and said as how the two of us should probably find a place of our own. It's not that there was any friction in the domicile, mind. On the contrary, the mother was very partial to Chloe—as was Bernice—and often the joint was nothing but those three giggling and conducting womanly business. But Chloe had a certain idea in her mind of what married life should be, and heading the list was that we two should live in our own place. Anyway, they'd just finished building some luxury apartments over on St. Nicholas Street, the Sherwood the building was called, and I took out a lease on one of them.

So one day Manfred came over with the largest of the Ozikean family farm carts, and we loaded all our belongings into it. Now this is slightly humorous, because all our belongings amounted to diddley-squat. After everything was loaded, it was apparent that Manfred could have borrowed the family wheelbarrow. Myself in particular owned nothing. I scoured the household in pursuit of items I might lay claim to, but about all I came up with was my skates and some hockey sticks, my hat and dragon-head cane, a few of Lloyd's storybooks. Chloe had more stuff—mysterious boxes on which she'd written room names—and my mother pressed on us a set of dishes and some silverware. But that was it. Rather than being depressed by this state of affairs, as I was close to being, Chloe was delighted. It suited her mental picture of young newlyweds that they should be impoverished, I suppose. She turned right romantic on me during the move, throwing her arms around my neck for no good reason and covering my cheeks with lipstick. Manfred was his usual self, pointing out that the more things one owned, the greater the risk of loss through theft, fire, and acts of God. At any rate, we threw this meager assemblage into the Ozikean cart and hauled it through the streets of Bytown. Kids ran alongside, chattering to me and Manny. We told them to eat their veggies. When the tykes called Chloe "Mrs. Leary" she beamed, telling them to eat their veggies and always brush their teeth. The children wondered how brushing their teeth would make them better hockey players, and I thought they made a point. But Chloe told them to brush their teeth and clean their fingernails, for Jesus' sake, and in like manner the mule hauled us across town and down St. Nicholas.

The doorman, Johannsen, eyed our cartful and raised a single brow. "Delivery for the Leary household?"

"What do you mean?" I asked him. "We are the Leary household!"

"Oh?" Johannsen looked confused. "But—"

"Come on, Percival," said Manfred, jumping off the driver's bench. "Let's take this stuff up."

"Right." Manny and I grabbed some stuff (Manfred toting most of the cart's contents) and we went up in the elevator. Chloe thought the elevator was rather stylish, but it made quite a few noises, odd groans and such, and I never did feel at ease in the contraption all the years we lived in the Sherwood. We went up to the fourth floor, which is all the floors available, and went to the door marked 4A. The letters were done in burnished brass. Manny and I set the stuff down, and I opened up the door.

Well, sir, it was as big a surprise as I've had in my lifetime, and you're talking to a man who once found some baby mice in his underwear drawer. The place was done up like in a magazine. There was a sofa, a love seat, a little table, and that was just what I could see from the hallway! "What gives?" I wondered aloud. Manfred started to laugh, he pushed me into the apartment so that I could see a big oaken table set up in a dining area. The far wall was almost completely taken over by a spectacularly large mirror. The kitchen was through a little doorway, but I could see pots hanging on the wall, a block of knives sitting on the counter. "This must be the wrong place," I whispered to Chloe, who was holding on to my arm, her eyes bugged open and her jaw slack as an ape's.

"Wrong place," chuckled Manfred, steering us down a hall-way toward a bedroom.

Lying on top of a huge four-poster, rumpled and a little drunken, was Clay Bors Clinton.

"You don't mind if I break it in, do you?" he asked. A glass of bubbly sat on a bedside table. "There's nothing worse than a virgin bed, except—never mind." Clay swung his legs around and sat up. "Welcome home, Mr. and Mrs. Leary."

The toilet flushed down the hallway and a moment later Jane rushed into the room. She gave out with a short "Oh!" Janey's flowery dress was cockled up and creased.

Chloe burst into tears right then, and she and her sister embraced each other. The happier Chloe got, the more she cried. Chloe was perverse in that regard.

"And now," Manfred announced, "I'm going to cook."

"Allow me to assist," said Clay. He got off the bed and smoothed his trousers. He winked at me. "A bit nonplussed are we, Percy, my prince?"

"I'd say so."

"Into the kitchen with us," said Clinton. "Leave these women to blubber in peace."

"You should have seen Percival's face," said Manfred. "And you know what? He thought we were in the wrong apartment."

"He was right, of course." Clay would sometimes say strange things like that. It was best to ignore him.

I said, "It's the fanciest digs I ever saw."

"I have a certain flair for home decoration," Clay admitted. "That impossibly gaudy mirror over there, that is Ozikean's doing."

"You need a mirror!" said Manfred, in that overexcited way he had. "When a room doesn't have a mirror, bad things can't get out, and good things can't get in."

"What sort of things did you have in mind?" I asked Manny.

"It is aboriginal mumbo-jumbo," stated Clinton.

"What do you mean, aboriginal mumbo-jumbo?" Manfred had colored slightly.

"Isn't this something you learnt from your bizarre Grandfather Rivers?"

"You know who told me about mirrors? Brother Isaiah."

"Oh, no. Not the blind monk creature again!"

"If Brother Isaiah says a room needs a mirror," I said, "she stays right there on the wall. That boy knows his stuff."

But the mirror didn't stay on the wall. It was, I'll own, an extremely large affair, that mirror. Often people will stick up a mirror and other people will say, "It's like there's a whole other room over there." In this case, it was like there was a whole other universe. So Chloe had me take it down, and I stored it in the Sherwood's basement. And I often wondered what sort of bad things were trapped inside our apartment, and what good things were banging on the walls, trying to get in.

# TWENTY-THREE

THE TORONTO GARDENS WERE BUILT IN 1947. WW II was good to old Clinton, he spent a lot of time building an airbase near Regina that never received a solitary airplane, he manufactured a certain flywheel necessary to some bit of machinery inside some piece of weaponry. At any rate, by the time Adolf was put down, Clinton had greenbacks popping out of his ears. So Clay announced the building of the Toronto Gardens, which he said would be the finest hockey arena in the world.

The construction of that edifice set some sort of record for safety—the lack of it, that is. There were scores of injuries and no less than seventeen workers died. There is a story that one death was no accident, that a worker pushed another off the high scaffolding during an argument about a woman. This started the rumor that the Toronto Gardens is haunted. I believe a ghost is wandering around the place, but I don't believe it's an offed construction worker. No, sir, I think it's just some old-time hockey boy who's got no place to go. If there is life after death (what a thought), I know where I'm headed.

It used to be that there was a secret entrance to the Gardens, which was used only by me and Clay, and women either too well known or too unsightly to be seen with Clay Clinton. This entrance led first of all to a tiny apartment that the architect had secreted away at Clay's behest, and then there was a long hallway, dark and always smelling like mud, that led to a private booth at the north end of the ice, where Clay and I and the occasional visiting potentate could watch the action. But after Clay's death, this secret entrance was bricked over, Clay not wanting people to discover the dirty socks and underwear that lay scattered about his little hallway.

So we pull up to the front main entrance. The sidewalk is packed with people, shoulder to shoulder. As bad as the Maple Leaves are (and they would have a tough time mustering a win against the world-record losers, the South Grouse Louses), the Toronto townfolk always turn out to see them. I've heard it said that Torontonians wouldn't show up in such numbers if the Leaves were any good. People go to see them for the same reason that some people watch automobile races, the possibility of great catastrophe.

It's like stepping into a wind-whipped ocean, we get swallowed up by the throng. I watch Blue Hermann's bald and speckled head bob away. He's calling out for help, but it's a small sound against the rumble of the crowd. The Claire thing reaches over people and manages to lock his long fingers around Blue's collar. Iain squeezes next to me and wraps his hand around my elbow. I don't shake him off. For one thing, it's better than being trampled and/or crushed to death. For another, Iain is none too steady on his own pegs, and I would hate for something bad to happen to the lad.

I see something that stops me dead in my tracks. There's a beggar standing in the middle of all this commotion. He's being whipped around like a dead leaf in a hurricane. In one hand a battered tin cup rattles to the tune of maybe eight cents. In the other hand this beggar holds a stenciled sign that reads: BLIND AS A BAT.

What shocks me is this mook's face. He is Brother Isaiah.

The beggar breaks into a broad grin and shakes his tin cup with enthusiasm. "Blind!" he sings out. "Blind as a bat! Couldn't see the sun if it landed in my backyard! Amblyopic to the max!" Mind you, the beggar is about the same age as Brother Isaiah was when I knew him, somewhere in his midthirties.

I point him out with my dragon-head walking stick. "Iain," says I, "give this bum a copper or two."

"How come?"

"The King always gives out a copper or two."

Iain reaches into one of his many pockets and comes up with about sixty-five cents. He tosses it into the tin cup.

"Hey, thanks heaps!" says the beggar. "*But*—this won't get you through the Pearly Gates!"

"Who asked you?" I demand.

The beggar gets bounced away. He calls out, "Blind! Blind as a mole! Couldn't see the moon if it fell on me!"

We make it through the front doors. Claire and Blue are standing off to one side, squeezed into a corner. Blue Hermann is breathing heavily and sweat is beaded on his upper lip. The Wringer of Life has wrung him again.

The walls of the Toronto Gardens foyer are covered with pictures. The biggest is a painted portrait of Clay and Jane Clinton. They're posed with Clay sitting down, one leg draped easily over the other, Jane standing behind him and resting a hand on his shoulder. This painting is a heap of lies. Clay's potbelly is gone and the artist has lightened up the rum-ruddiness of Clinton's face. Around the age of fifty-two, blood vessels started exploding on Clay's face, and sometimes his aspect was like a road map. The other lies have to do with Janey. Not that the artist hedged on the weight or changed her complexion or anything. No, the big lie is that she was there at all, with Clay.

Over there is a photograph of Manfred Armstrong Ozikean. I look back at Clay Bors Clinton. He's still grinning.

*No*, I tell him.

No, I don't think we better had, Clay-boy. He's doing fine right here. Everybody's happy. It's a bad idea. What the hell was you thinking? I believe I'll put the kibosh on that deal pronto.

Hand on the elbow.

Blue, I got a quote for the *Daily Planet*. Take this down. Clay Clinton came up with an idea for a trade, but the King ix-nayed it. I said no, forget about it, and it never happened. Print that up in the *Daily Planet*, will you, Hermann?

I know Hermann will run that story, because I'm director of hockey operations here at the Toronto Gardens. That's my job. My office is right down this way. I notice that Blue Hermann is following along. Lord, he looks awful. He must have caught a hangover that won't let go. He likely wants a scoop. All right, Hermann, I'll give you all the gen on the Toronto Maple Leaves. You want a quote about tonight's game against the Canadiens? Surely. You know me, Blue, I got the gift of the gab and I've kissed the Blarney Stone. Step into my office. Well, sir, the Montreal defense is a little like Old Mother Leary. Ancient and holy. That's a quote for you, Hermann, print that up in the *Daily Planet*. Wait a second. Lonny Chandrian is in my office. What can I do for you, Lonny? Why haven't you got your head usher's outfit on? You can't do tonight's game in that fancy checkered sports jacket. By the by, what the hell happened to your *hair*? You just got two little gray strips that circle around your sticky-out ears. Not many boys go bald at sixteen, Lonny. I think maybe you better see your family doctor.

Now, Hermann, what was I saying? Oh, yeah, about to-night's game. Run along now, Lonny. Change into your head usher's outfit. If you see Mr. Clinton, tell him I'll be along directly. I'm just having a chat with Hermann, star reporter from the *Daily Planet*. Who's that over there? That there is the Claire thing, Lonny. *That* is Iain. You surely ask a lot of ques-tions for a head usher. Director of hockey operations? Wait a second here.

Hand on my elbow.

I'll go sit on my chesterfield. Yes, all right, that's a good idea. Iain, I hope I don't have to fire Lonny. It would break his mother's heart. What do you suppose got into the boy? He dresses like an oddball, he thinks he's got my job! Rest for a while? Are you crazy, Iain? Big game tonight, Leaves versus Canadiens. Traditional rivalry. Ottawa? No, we played Ottawa last week. Got stung for seven goals, mostly because Jim Mc-Mann stank up the joint. What's that, Lonny? McMann died? McMann might have played like a dead man, and if he ever plays another game like that, by Jesus he'll wish he were dead, but as far as I know he's fit as a fiddle, although I'm putting the rookie Linehan between the pipes tonight. Iain, can I go back to my room now? I'm a wee bit slackered. Maybe Mrs. Ames could give me a little something. Blue Hermann, I got a quote for the *Daily Planet*. Take this down. "Leary Says No. En-Oh. No." I put the kibosh on that deal, Blue-boy. Good idea, Iain, I believe I will stretch out. It's been a long day. Always a lot of excitement when the Canadiens come into the Gardens. Traditional rivalry. The best kind. Traditional rivalry.

# TWENTY-FOUR

MANNY, CLAY, AND JANE took to hanging around our apartment on St. Nicholas. We played a lot of card games (mostly Bugger-Your-Neighbor, which Clinton was especially good at), and then we'd sit around and not do much at all.

This one evening, Manny and Jane were sitting on the sofa hand in hand. Chloe had caught a chill and was taking a hot bath. She caught an awful lot of chills, it seemed, and took a corresponding number of baths, languishing there in the steam with her teeth chattering. I myself was putting some electrical tape around the blade of my hockey stick, which was fad back then. (The lads still do it, which means it caught on pretty good.) Clay Clinton was pacing up and down in our little apartment, deep in thought. Then he stopped dead. "I'll tell you what, large Man-Freddy," he said. "Let's you and I have an arm wrestle."

"That's an excellent idea, Clay," I muttered. "Why don't you have an arm wrestle with Manny, and then you can have a head-butting contest with a trolley?"

"Care to place a little wager on the outcome?" Clinton demanded.

"Manny ain't about to arm wrestle with you," I told him.

"Let's let him make up his own mind, shall we? Manfred!"

"Hm-mmm?"

Janey said, "I hate it when you get like this, Clayton."

"I'm bored," the man responded.

"Read a book," Manfred suggested. That's what he was doing. He was reading a book Jane had recommended, *Man's*

*Descent From the Gods*, by Anthony Mario Ludovici. Actually I hadn't seen him turn a page for quite some time.

"I don't much like books," announced Clay.

"You got all sorts of books," I pointed out.

"Doesn't mean I like them, does it?"

"Why don't you sit down quietly," Janey suggested, "and try to figure out just why you act the way you do."

"Oh, you have some objection to the way I act? You didn't used to, Janey. You didn't have any objection as recently as, let me see, yesterday afternoon." Clinton turned back to Manfred. "What do you say, Ozikean? How about it?"

"How about what, Clay?"

"An arm wrestle, you bloody berk. My Lord, you have an attention span of about three seconds."

"Why don't you read a book?" Manfred suggested.

"Think of it as training," Clay said. "It will strengthen the arm. Ergo, you can shoot the puck harder."

"Right-o," mumbled myself. "That's just what the Wizard needs, a harder shot. Why, that Hamilton defenseman who went down to block one last week, he says Manny needs a harder shot, because the puck didn't quite knock out all of his teeth. There's still a couple of molars poking around back there."

"Yes," Clay argued, "but muscles atrophy with lack of use."

"Clay," I told him, "I don't see how an arm wrestle with you is going to give Manny much of a workout."

"Yes, yes, Percival, my pest, you've voiced your opinion. What you haven't done is backed it up with lucre."

"All right, then, Clinton. Ten bucks says Manfred rips your arm out of its socket."

"Little Brother!" scolded Janey.

"Heck, it's as easy a ten spot as I'm ever likely to make. Manfred will crank him down in no time."

Janey said, "Manfred, tell them you don't care to do it."

"I don't care to do it," said Ozikean, not looking up from the pages of his book—he wasn't engrossed, mind you; it was more like he was afraid that the words might melt away if he took his eyes off them.

"Why not?" we asked Manfred.

"Why not?" Manfred asked Jane.

"It's stupid, that's why not."

"It's stupid, guys," Manfred told us.

"Since when, Man-Freddy," cried Clinton, a touch exasperated, "has *that* ever stopped you?"

"Yeah!" Manfred turned over his book. "I say, okay."

Manfred and Clay wandered over to the big dining table. They set chairs so that they faced across one of the corners. The pair of them gripped hands and clutched the table's edge with the other. Clay and Manny spent a long time working on the clasp, releasing and curling their fingers. Clay was especially persnickety, pushing Manfred's elbow an eighth of an inch this way, moving his own elbow an eighth of an inch back. It took a couple of minutes before the two of them were prepared.

"Percival, my prince," whispered Clay.

"On your marks . . . set . . . *go.*"

Manny threw Clay's arm over like it was a blade of grass. But just before Clay's hand was to hit the tabletop there was a sound—half sob, half scream—and Clay's hand stopped. Clinton's face had reddened and his gray eyes turned a lunatic black. How in creation Clay held his hand like that, an inch away from beaten, Ozikean bearing down with his full and considerable strength, is a mystery I'll never figure. Say what you will about the man, Clay Bors Clinton had grit. That's how he died, too. Disease started knocking him over with flying tackles and leglocks, but Clay Clinton just kept rolling along. Finally disease talked Clay's heart into helping, and in 1967 the heart more or less exploded. I may not believe in *broken* hearts, but I believe they can go up like trod-on land mines, because I seen it happen to Clay.

Ozikean's jowls were vibrating, so you know he wasn't fooling about. Clinton's face was beaded by sweat at this point, and he was squeezing his eyes shut, trying to rid them of the sting. Clay managed to gasp out a small call—"Leary." I went into the kitchen and soaked one of the little tea towels under the faucet. I took it back and wiped Clay's face, the back of his neck. Janey took the tea towel from me and did the same for Manfred.

There was no sound in the room except for breathing.

Then Janey whispered, "Draw."

Manfred nodded. "Draw."

Clay ushered out a smile. "No draw."

This was errant foolishness on Clinton's part. It was obvious that something was going to give. If Clay was lucky, his energy would give out, and then he would end up no worse than exhausted. Or Clay's spirit would buckle, which would render him petulant and sulky for at least three days. As it was, Clinton's wrist gave way. It did so with a nasty cracking sound.

Manfred placed Clay's limp hand on the table gently.

"Good show, old boy!" said Clay, his voice strangled somewhere in his socks.

"Jesus, Jesus," sang Manfred miserably.

"Well—" Clay Clinton stood up, or tried to. His legs wobbled on him and he had to sit back down. "Fortunately," he said, "Grim Jim lives fairly close by."

This was the medical doctor who worked for the Ottawa Patriots. His right name was James Grimm, you see, so we all called him Grim Jim.

"He would be the boy to see," I admitted.

This time Clay managed to stand. He threw his good arm around Janey Millson's shoulder for support.

I went to the bathroom to get a big towel to use for a sling. Chloe was there in the steam and the bubbles. She was ghostly pale, no color in her lips or her nipples. Chloe's teeth chattered, but she tried her best to be chipper. "Hi, Pookie!"

"I'm taking Clay over to see Grim Jim," I explained.

Chloe screamed and splashed the bathwater. She was an excitable lass. "What happened?"

"Well," I took a deep breath, "Manfred just broke Clay's wrist."

Grim Jim lit a cigar and settled back on his chair. "Why is it that nothing in my medical training prepared me for this?" he asked. "You've been arm wrestling with Manny Oz, correct?"

Clinton nodded.

"And now you come to me with a *sore wrist.*" Grim Jim chuckled a bit and rotated the stogie. "I'll have to write this one up for the journals."

Clinton wore no expression on his face, meaning he was angry as shit. "Yes, well, Dr. Grimm, I have to tell you that it hurts quite a bit. Your flippancy is a slap in the face of the Hippocratic Oath."

"Would you like some aspirin tablets, Clay?" cooed Grim Jim. "Would you like me to kiss it better?" Grim Jim was a gaunt, balding cuss who resembled the Great Leveler more than it was good for a doctor to do.

"I would not like aspirin, Grimm," said Clay.

"Laudanum?"

"I would like you to put a cast on this." Clinton waved his wrist in the air.

"A cast." Grim Jim sucked on his stogie. "And why would you like me to do that, Clay?"

"I believe I sign your paycheck," snarled Clay. "Please address me as *Mr. Clinton.*"

"*Mr. Clinton,*" said Grim Jim, "a cast is warranted in the case of broken bones. It is a measure taken to ensure immobilization of the affected limb, you see. You have no broken bones, Mr. Clinton. You have a sore wrist. It will be better in the morning."

"A cast," repeated Clinton. He whacked his forearm up toward the elbow. "All the way to here."

"The muscles will atrophy."

"And you can be the first to sign it," said Clay. "Just as I sign your paycheck."

"Is he serious about this?" Dr. Grimm looked over to me.

"Couldn't do any harm," I ventured.

Grim Jim set about preparing the plaster.

# TWENTY-FIVE

I HEAR A VOICE, a loud booming voice that seems to fill the air like thunder. "Ladies and gentlemen," the voice says, "*King Leary!!*" Then there's applause, thousands and thousands of people clapping for me.

Aha and hallelujah. I've done it. I've given up the ghost.

The King has died and gone to Glory.

Who'd have thought they'd give me a big intro like that? It's going to be nice to see them all again. Manfred, how the hell are you, brother? You're looking fine. You got some spark back in those coal black peepers of yours. Chloe, my wife. Are we feeling any better, Chloe? And lookee there, Jane, Jane, beautiful Janey. Clarence, you no-good so-and-so. Who taught you to drive? Drunk as a skunk you were, and don't bother denying it, I've read the police reports. Oh, there he is. Clay. You bastard. Man, it's good to see you.

The people are still clapping. I'm some sort of big deal, even up here. I had no idea. Someone whispers in my ear, "Wave." How silly of me. The King starts to wave to the multitudes. Wait, wait! Oh, how perfect is my paradise! Heaven is a huge skating rink! There's hockey players on it now, all the beautiful, golden-haired men. They are banging their sticks on the ice for me, hail, hail, all hail to the King!

A red carpet is laid at my feet. The King waves with both hands now, and every so often I'll take a humble little bow. The crowd rises to its feet. The huge voice—do you think it's Himself giving me the big play-up?—says, "*King Leary!!*" one more time, and now there is whistling and cheering. It seems to go on forever. I'm a trifle embarrassed.

"At this time," says the huge voice (I've decided that it's likely just one of the higher-up archangels), "we would like to ask the captains of both teams to step forward for the ritual opening face-off. King Leary will drop the puck."

Oh, boy, gonna be a hockey game. All the old boys, all my friends. Newsy Lalonde will play. Dirty Joe Hall. Howie Morenz. In goal, maybe Vézina and Charlie Gardiner. All the former Kings. And—

Wait just one second here.

I'm still waving with my hand. It's a wrinkled old claw, liver spotted and blurry with palsy. What gives? Why ain't I the Dublin Hurricane, one hundred and forty-six pounds of fighting breezy Irishter?

And these two fellows skating toward me, I don't recognize them. They're just young puppies, and they got hair like girls'. Hold on, I do recognize one of them, from his pictures in the dailies. That there is Duane Killebrew. I think I jumped the gun here.

I take a look to my right. There's Iain grinning at me. "You're doing good, sire." His breath is sharp and stale and snaps my head back as though a bottle of smelling salts was passed beneath my hooter.

I sigh wearily.

The two team captains get to me. The Toronto captain I don't know from a hole. He takes off his hockey glove and offers his hand. I shake it. He winks. He's chewing gum and winking, for Jesus' sake. He's got no sense of tradition.

Duane Killebrew is a lot more humble. He takes my hand and pumps it up and down, saying, "This is a real thrill for me, Mr. Leary. King. I've read all the books about you. When I was a kid I read all those Leary & Clinton adventure books."

"What's your favorite?"

Duane Killebrew shrugs, and his hair wiggles like a fat girl in a sideshow. "I dunno. Maybe *Leary & Clinton Climb Mount Everest.*"

Clay Clinton's long fingers trembled and his grip on the sheer face loosened. "Well, Leary, my friend," he said, "it looks like I might not get to watch you win that game after all."

"Don't be so sure, me old son," said Little Leary, his Irish blood at a boil. Leary took the rope from his hip and tossed it down the mountainside.

"Have you read *Leary & Clinton Fight the Dogstar People?*" I ask Killebrew. "Damn peculiar. These mooks from the Dogstar Sirius, they don't got no bodies. They float around the galaxy like beerfarts."

"You're looking very well, sir, if I may so say. Very fit and all. I understand we're going to be taping a commercial together tomorrow. I'm looking forward to that. Maybe we'll get a chance to talk further." Killebrew squeezes my hand, and with an imperceptible motion of his ankles he sails about five feet backwards and gives a tiny bow.

I look at Iain. "Nice lad," I comment.

Lonny Chandrian appears and hands me a puck. The feel of a hockey puck has changed over the years, but I'd be hard-pressed to tell you exactly how. In front of me Killebrew and the Maple Leaves' mook assume the traditional half crouch and poise their sticks above the ice. I hold out the puck and let it tumble. Killebrew bats it in the air, bouncing it upwards, and then he catches the rubber on the blade of his stick. It's a fairly keen stunt. Then Killebrew flips it again, catching it in his glove. "I'll keep this one," he tells me. Killebrew turns around and skates back to his mates. His stride is long and leisurely. He looks like a fellow out for a Sunday pleasure skate on the canal. Duane has got the big double zero on the back of his jersey.

The Voice gives forth with another "*King Leary!!*" and the applause comes again. This time it's halfhearted. The people are waiting for the game to begin. More to the point, they're waiting for Killebrew to hit the ice in earnest. Truth to tell, I'm looking forward to that myself.

# TWENTY-SIX

AROUND THAT TIME, ALL THOSE MANY YEARS AGO, a doctor diagnosed Chloe as possessing a heart flutter. This terrified the girl, she gave the impression that her poor heart was like a canary in a coal mine, a breath away from death. Chloe turned ever paler. Then she got pregnant. Having the baby inside made Chloe feel mighty poorly, the morning sickness lasting all day and all night. I was always having to tend for her, because Chloe was running fevers, throwing up, worried past sense that the baby was going to be stillborn. If she'd known she had Clifford in there she could have relaxed, I suppose, because Cliffy was his big gormless self even as a newborn, but all Chloe knew was that she was twenty-one years old and mostly felt like a bucket of homemade manure.

Now me, mind you, I was flying, I was playing like a son of a bitch. For one thing, I was pushing one-fifty weight-wise, something I never did again. And it seemed like everything that the monks taught me had become second nature. I didn't have to think about bulldogging, I just bulldogged. When I skated for the net my inner eye would pop open automatic. My mind was blank when I played back then, as empty as a frozen lake. Sometimes I'd savor the cold sting on my skin, listen to the *loof-weeda*, song of the wind.

Don't believe anything Blue Hermann might tell you contrariwise. *Loof-weeda* means "windsong."

Here's how I got my nickname. Manfred informed me, after a game, that his great-grandfather, Poppa Rivers, was there to see me.

As he told me this he was sitting naked on a bench trying to rub rum-sickness and bad sweat out of his eyes. Manfred was hitting the bottle hard, and I don't believe he was having any fun doing it. Drinking appeared to be as much drudgery as working for the Eddy Match Co. or going down the mines.

"What's he want to see me for?"

"How should I know? All I know is, he wants to talk to you."

"Probably wants my autograph. The old P. H. Leary." I was showered, I was drinking a bottle of Canada Dry, I felt like a fine piece of work. I started climbing into my civvies.

"Hey," said Manfred, "how's Chloe?"

Her tiny fluttering heart and ballooning tummy notwith-standing, Chloe was beset by any number of medical devil-ments. I was confused and confounded by them, so I gave Man-fred a shrug, saying, "She's all right."

"You see Janey lately?" Manfred asked, assuming an air of nonchalance, a bit like a buzzard trying to look cute.

"She was over last night. We played cards. I beat her four games straight playing the old gin rummy."

"Clay there?"

"Oh, yeah, he was over." Holding Janey's hand, rubbing the soft white skin, but I didn't tell Manfred.

"That's nice." Manfred pulled on his trousers. They were shit-stained from a drunken tumble.

Poppa Rivers was standing down the hallway.

He was as ancient a bugger as I'd ever seen. He looked like God Almighty had forgot to punch his time clock.

"Christ," I muttered.

"He's old," said Manfred. He was wont to say that sort of thing.

"Old? If his life flashed in front of his eyes there'd have to be an intermission."

Poppa Rivers smiled, that is, he pulled the corners of his mouth apart and demonstrated the fact that not only did he lack teeth, he didn't even have much gum to speak of.

"Are you going to introduce us?"

"No," Manny told me. "The thing of it is, he's not speak-ing to me."

"How's come?"

Manfred shrugged. "Just go talk to him, Percival. He won't bite."

"No, I can see that. Where are you off to?"

"I have to see a man about some land." Manfred liked to give his drinking expeditions an air of business and enterprise, and was constantly claiming that he had to see a man about some land.

Poppa Rivers lifted this bird's-claw jobbie that he was using for a hand and waved at me. I nodded, but stuff was stirring around inside me that was best left unstirred.

"Go," said Manfred, pushing me forward.

Despite his decrepitude, Poppa Rivers was a big man, largeness seeming to run in the Ozikean family. He held himself upright with a cane that was more like a totem pole, birds and animals carved the whole length of it. His hair, and he had plenty of it, was gossamer, and represented the stage in the graying process that comes after white as can be.

Manny ducked out the other way, leaving me alone in the hallway with the graying specter. I swaggered over, hitching my drawers and giving my dragon-head walking stick a little Chaplin twirl. I was pretty good at that. "Evening."

"We have to get out of here," Poppa Rivers said urgently. "*Loof-weeda.*"

"How's come we have to clear out, and what's this *loof-weeda?*"

All of a sudden a smell grabbed hold of my nose. It was like someone had made a stew with potatoes, death, and cow dung.

Poppa Rivers was fanning the air and grinning sheepishly. "Let's go," he croaked. "Sorry about that."

We managed to escape the hallway, and although I'm sure you think I exaggerate, that was the closest I been to death, certainly up to that point in my history. Blue Hermann can let loose some beauties, it's true, but even he's got nothing on Poppa Rivers. It was a nice night, almost balmy despite the time of year, and I thought it would be best if me and Poppa Rivers just walked the streets. I wanted to keep him outside in case he decided to float another.

"When I was a boy," Poppa Rivers told me, "we used to play hockey. Except we didn't call it 'hockey' back then. And we played with a ball. And the sticks were different. We played on the river, with the soldiers. We had one goal at one end of the river, and the other goal would be maybe two, three miles down the way." Poppa Rivers waved his bird's-claw jobbie, indicating great distance. "I remember one time, I had a breakaway. And I remember thinking, 'Oh, no, a fucking breakaway.'" Poppa Rivers laughed. "I skated and skated and skated, all alone on the river. Then I see the man between the stones. The goal, I guess you would call it. I shot the ball at him. He caught it." Poppa Rivers shrugged and sighed.

We walked in silence for a few minutes. Poppa Rivers seemed to be baffled by something in the sky. He kept taking peeks up toward the stars as if their alignment was wacky.

Poppa Rivers said, "Tell Manfred to stop drinking."

"Come again?"

"Say to him, Manfred, stop drinking liquor. Do not drink it anymore."

"A lot of people have said that to him."

"No." Poppa Rivers shook his head. "No one that he loves and is part of his life has said that to him."

"We're all the time saying—"

Poppa Rivers wasn't a great one for waiting on the end of sentences. "You say things like, Manfred, you drink too much. Or, Manfred, you should cut down. But no one has said this to him: because you love me I'm asking you for this promise, that you will stop drinking this liquor that hurts you so badly."

"Why not Jane?"

"Someone else should shoulder this one. If Jane and Manfred marry, there will be many promises made between them, and promises need some looking after."

"How about Clay?"

Poppa Rivers looked at me, cocked a single eyebrow. "I don't think so. Clay has many schemes and plans to separate Manfred and Jane. No, Clay Clinton won't do it. And now you won't either."

"Who says I won't?"

"If you were going to do it, you would have said yes. But you haven't. So you won't." Poppa Rivers was really quite perplexed by something in the heavens. He walked with his neck craned backwards, staring at the inky sky. "Oh, I suppose you might say, 'Hey Manny, go easy on the boozing,' but you won't make him promise, and it won't work. You won't do it, you *loof-weeda*."

"What is this *loof-weeda* business?"

"It is what I have decided to call you."

"An Indian name, huh?"

"Right."

"What does it mean?"

"Oh, a literal translation would be something like 'wind music' or 'windsong.' "

"Because of the way I skate?"

"For sure." Whatever was wrong with the sky, it was making Poppa Rivers tired and sad. "The way you fucking skate."

"*Loof-weeda*."

Then there was a hint of that smell again.

# TWENTY-SEVEN

LORD, LORD, THE PUPPY HAS IT ALL! He's got the Brother Simon Ice Dance, he's got the Theodorian Inner-Eye Fling, he's got the Brother Andrew Bulldog and Hardstep, he's got Brother Isaiah the Blind's Mystery. That is, every time Killebrew does something, you say to yourself, "How in the world did he do that?"

The fans is going wild in the stands. After one period the score is one-zip for the Ottawa Pats, so low mostly because of the Maple Leave goalie, a Czechoslovakian player with a name that has no vowels. He stops Killebrew at point-black range a couple of times. The lone tally belongs to Duane-o, of course. It was a beautiful backhander, hard as shit. My own backhand, I have to admit, was a trifle weak.

The Maple Leave big gunner is a Russian defector name of Serge Mikaloff. He's fancy and sneaky as hell, and he manages to pot a goal early in the second period, tying up the game. Then Killebrew feeds one of his own teammates. This makes me giggle, because Duane sets up *behind* the net and passes out to his man. I've heard that on account of Killebrew this has become a fairly common practice, but we certainly didn't do it, matter of fact, it never even *occurred* to us. Anyway, its two-one for Ottawa, three-one for Ottawa, and then Toronto scores late in the period to come within a tally.

Between frames Lonny takes me into the private hallway where we can chat without being disturbed. Except he and I don't have much to say to each other. Even with his executive baldness, Lonny still looks to me like head usher material. He smokes huge stogies and wears an expression of consternation. Lonny asks me a lot of questions about my health. I just shrug, not wanting to get technical.

In the first minute of the third period the Maple Leaves get lucky. The Leave number 27, that uppity captain who has the name of Dickie Dauphin, a poncey monicker if ever there was one, he throws the rubber near the Ottawa goal and it bounces into the net off one of the Bytown backenders. Now she's tied up like a sneaker, and the stands are buzzing, maybe the Leaves will even win this one. But Duane hits the ice with a glowing in his eyes. Then I know he's the right man, because he's got the cold fire. The Rocket had it, Sprague had it, Manny had it, Newsy Lalonde had it, and now I see that the Killebrew puppy has it. Duane-o gets the puck in his own end and it looks like he's starting upriver, because his hair's blowing and he's grinning and hardstepping like a six-year-old.

Now, what does Duane do here?

*The goddamn St. Louis Whirlygig!!!*

The crowd cheers, and I wonder how many of them know it's my patented move, and I wonder also if maybe Duane didn't do it because I was in the stands. It's a thing of unutterable exquisiteness, that St. Louis Whirlygig, and I certainly am glad I got an opportunity to see the damn thing.

The other Leave defender has to come a-sprawling, and Duane simply jumps over him. Now it's just Duane-o and the Czech goaler, whose name sounds like Blue Hermann coughing. The goaler stays with Killebrew, and then Duane pulls off one of his feats of sorcery, one I seen Manny execute, the stoppage of time. Shutting down, freezing out the whole factory. It's like Duane has stopped dead as coffin nails with just the tip of one skate holding the ice. The whole world comes to a standstill, and then the Czech net minder keels. Duane Killebrew flips the puck into a net that is gaping like a dragon's maw. Killebrew flips his stick and cradles it like a guitar. He strums it a few times and looks momentarily pixilated. Then he unflips the stick, grins sheepishly at the cheers, cruises back to his own end.

I nudge the ancient scribe. "Well?"

Blue Hermann produces a puff of stale air and shrugs his shoulders. He almost rattles, that's how frail and brittle he is. Blue doesn't know what to say. Duane Killebrew has produced in Blue Hermann of the *Planet* a loss for words!

The lad is a Wizard.

Lonny Chandrian tells me that the people from the Canadian Broadcasting Corporation want to do a wee small interview with me. This means the hockey game ended about twelve minutes earlier than it should have. I tell Lonny it's all right with me. I used to give interviews all the time when I was director of hockey operations.

I get led down a hallway. Bright light is spilling out of a doorway up ahead. This is where they got the teevee studio set up. I get put in a chair, someone clips a little microphone to my lapel. A voice asks me to count to ten. I do so. The voice says thankee. I say don't mention it.

There's a young charlie in the chair beside me. He's smoking a cigarette and looking at a clipboard. I'm transfixed by this fellow's hair, every single strand in place.

The young man puts down his clipboard and turns to me. "Hello, Mr. Leary."

"Hey." I nod.

"It's Ben. Ben Jimson."

"Benny Jimson who was one of the worst defensemen who ever played the game?"

"Yeah!"

"You got a job on the television now?"

"That's right. Color and postgame." This fellow grins at me.

I snap my fingers. "Hey, now. Ben Jimson didn't have no full set of chompers."

The young man spits out teeth into the palm of his hand.

"That's a bit better. Now ruffle that Toni Home Perm of yours."

Benny pulls his fingers across the grain of his perfect hair. It hackles like the back of an old and stupid hound.

"Ben!" I slap him across the knee. "How you been, Benny-boy?"

"*And* camera." A finger appears out of nowhere and points at the pair of us. Ben Jimson stuffs his teeth back into his mouth and shakes his head. The hair realigns itself. "We are here," he tells the home viewers, "with one of the all-time great hockey legends, Percival 'King' Leary. How are you tonight, King?"

"Right as rain."

"Did you enjoy tonight's game?"

"I enjoyed it tremendously, Benny. I never seen the likes of that boy Killebrew, except—" I remember a round rink in the middle of winter and the dead of night, five shadows moving on it, but the teevee audience wouldn't be interested.

Jimson just asked me a question. I got no idea what it was. I interrupt. "Did you see Duane-o do the St. Louis Whirlygig, Benny-boy? That was one of my moves. I thought it was dead and forgotten, but Killebrew executed it flawlessly in the third period."

"When was this, King?"

"When he potted the go-ahead. There was a defender there and Duane got around him by means of the wondrous St. Louis Whirlygig."

"When he . . ." Jimson wrinkles his brow. He still has a boyish aspect, except he has more wrinkles than when he played for me. "Oh! You mean when he did the *Nureyev.*"

"How's that again?"

"When he jumped up and twirled around the defenseman?"

"The unspeakably beautific St. Louis Whirlygig."

"The Nureyev."

"What is a Nureyev?"

"You know. The ballet dancer."

"Benny-boy, you're making no sense. Seems like you're no better a teevee man than you were a shinny player."

"Have you never heard of Rudolf Nureyev?"

"Who's he play for?"

"He's a ballet dancer!"

"A ballet dancer."

"So, when Killebrew jumps up in the air and spins around—"

"The St. Louis Whirlygig."

"—we call it the Nureyev."

"I see."

"King, I was wondering how you feel about the recent controversy concerning Manny 'The Wizard' Oz?"

"The man's been dead since 'thirty-seven, Ben. You telling me he's still managing to get into trouble?"

"Well, there's been an official protest over the fact that he has not been put into the new Canadian Sports Hall of Fame."

"Manfred isn't in the Sports Hall of Fame?"

"No, sir."

"I didn't know." I shrug my shoulders, shake my head. "That explains why Blue keeps losing his goat."

"Sir?"

"I just assumed Manny was in there."

"You feel he deserves to be?"

"Manfred was—" I feel quite odd. "You see, Benny, I am King of the Ice. But Manfred could have been King, except . . . I never thought that they wouldn't even vote him into the Sports Hall of Fame. I never thought he'd come out of it with nothing."

"It's presumed to be because of his lifestyle."

"How's that? Because of the booze?"

"Yes."

I nod, lace my hands together and play a little Here's the church, here's the steeple.

"But I take it you are in favor of the induction of Clay Clinton?"

"I suppose. He gave me one hell of a whack to the bollockers when we were boys."

"His main contribution to Canadian sports was this building, and the glory teams of the fifties and sixties."

"The glory teams were my doing, for Jesus' sake. I was director of hockey operations. Clay was too busy with those young fillies he used to squire about."

"So you *don't* feel he belongs there."

"Don't be stuffing words down my gullet, Jimson. Clinton did a lot for hockey. But Manfred. . . He danced like flute music. He was big as a mountain, but he moved like the wind. And tough? Lordy Lord. Him and Lalonde collided and made a sound like thunder. The arena quivered and the ice cracked. Pandemonium. The world was naught but chaos and ruination. The air turned heavy with power and fury. The—"

"That's all we have time for. Good night, King."

The lights go down.

# TWENTY-EIGHT

THE RINK THAT THE BROTHERS of St. Alban the Martyr built was round. Hockey rinks are curved in the corners, as you likely know, but basically they should be squared. Our rink was a circle.

One night, I couldn't sleep. I didn't usually have that problem (I do nowadays, in my dotage—I have actually snoozed for periods of seven seconds and been wide awake for the rest of the night) but that evening, there in the reformatory, I was restless. There was a full moon, and it filled the window across from my cot, and for some strange reason I could make out all the mountains and craters. The moon was a strange color, too, a silver like a nickel had been flipped into the sky.

Then I heard the sounds, the soft windy sweeping of hockey sticks across ice. At first I thought I was dreaming, but then I recalled that I never did dream to speak of. I moved across to the window, soft on my feet so as not to wake the other delinquents. The moon was so bright that I do believe I squinted up my eyes. I have never seen it like that since.

I could see the rink, and I could see the shadows moving on it. The monks were playing a little midnight shinny. It quickened my heart. I threw on some clothes and flew outside.

There were five of them. I watched from a distance at first. I couldn't understand what sort of game they were playing. The action would move erratically within the circle, and sometimes the five would split so that three men would rush two, or four would rush one, and then sometimes the five of them would move in cahoots, the idea seeming to be to achieve a certain prettiness of passing. Then a man would break from the pack, and another man would chase him around the circle, and as quick as that happened they'd rejoin the three in the center. There were no goal nets on the ice. Just five men, a puck, and a lot of moonlight. They played in silence. I moved closer.

Simon the Ugly was the easiest to pick out, because he was the biggest. He was dancing, jumping into the air, and sometimes I could see his monstrous frame silhouetted against the trout silver moon. Theodore the Slender cut a shadow so fine that it was hard to pick out, but I could tell him from the quick, precise movements of his twiggy arms as he took a shot. And Andrew the Fireplug, it was he who was likeliest to make a break for the boards, to drift like gunsmoke around them. I watched him scoot off with the puck, and then I watched a man slip up easily behind Andrew and relieve him of the rubber. That was Isaiah the Blind. I could scarcely credit it. Playing goaler is one thing—I mean, at least Isaiah was standing still between the pipes, and you could always convince yourself that he was simply the luckiest son of a bee *ever*—but here he was skating around like a madman, stealing pucks, passing and receiving, and the moonlight was sitting on his dead eyes like it does on the still surface of a lake. I crouched down behind the boards. Brother Isaiah had an aerial maneuver that made the Whirlygig look like tumbling down a flight of stairs, he had dekes and fakes that would have baffled God! Whatever the hell game they were playing—and I never did come close to figuring it—Brother Isaiah was the best. In fact, Brother Isaiah was the best I've ever seen, bar none. That includes me, Duane Killebrew, and the fifth man out on that moon-washed rink, Manny Oz.

# TWENTY-NINE

WE ARE SITTING IN THE POTBELLY LOUNGE of the Toronto Gardens. There's me and Blue here, the Claire thing and Iain, and we also have Lonny Chandrian. I'm recounting a bit of the personal history, telling them about the wild New York Amerks, but no one is paying much attention. Claire is sort of listening, but he find this sports stuff as interesting as wallpaper. Lonny Chandrian is looking consternated. Iain and Blue, those boys is boozing.

Then Duane Killebrew appears beside the table. He looks to have on three jackets, and they all seem to be four or five sizes too large, and are mostly comprised of buttons and zippers. He wears his hair the same as my wife, Chloe, did.

Lonny Chandrian is on his feet in a second. "Duane!" he explodes. "Please! Join us!"

"Thanks." Duane jumps into the seat beside me.

His arrival has set the lounge buzzing. Over in the corner is a clutch of young girls, huddled together and staring Duane's way. They are about fifteen years of age and they have not yet tamed their laughter. Duane Killebrew doesn't seem to know they're there. He orders a beer.

"You done good, boy," I tell him.

Duane nods.

"This man is Blue Hermann. He was one of the finest sportswriters that ever worked. He chronicled the rise of the King. He's seen them all, Duane, and he can tell you, you don't got to take a backseat to nobody."

"Pleased to meet you, sir."

"Hi, Duane." Blue Hermann, I'm sorry to say, has somewhat the same aspect as the schoolgirls. He lets loose with something alarmingly close to a giggle and shakes Killebrew's hand.

"Have you met the Claire thing? Claire Redford, from the ginger ale people?"

"Oh, yes. We've talked on the phone. How's it going?"

I swear to Jesus the Claire thing bats his eyelashes!

"That down there is Iain, from the home."

Iain laboriously raises an arm and gives a little wave. "Harya!"

Lonny Chandrian says, "Boy, oh, boy, were you ever good. Mr. Leary has been saying how much he enjoyed it when you did the Nureyev."

"I enjoyed it," I put in, "but that there is a St. Louis Whirlygig."

Duane considers something. "Not exactly."

"Say what?"

"A St. Louis Whirlygig, you cross your legs and get the push from the right foot. In a Nureyev, you keep your foot back. You don't get as much height, but it's quicker." Duane-o has been demonstrating all this out in the aisle, on a toned-down scale, of course.

"Technical niceties of no import!" I shout. "The point of a St. Louis Whirlygig is that it happens up in the air! How you get there don't matter squat!"

Duane sits down and takes a sip of his newly arrived brew. "I have seven airborne maneuvers," he tells me.

"I only had one," I tell him. "Leaving the ground."

One of the young girls comes over for an autograph. She's got a color eight-by-ten of Duane. In the picture, he's got no shirt on, and he's got his thumbs in his belt loops, tugging down his jeans. Any more tugging and he'd be parading the pecnoster. Duane-o signs the photograph for the girl, and he's very nice about it. He asks what her name is, that sort of thing. Manny used to do that, too, except he could be so plodding and painstaking with his penmanship that people were telling him, "Never mind what my name is, just write yours." Part of the reason

Manfred started calling his last name just Oz is that it cut down on autographing time by about forty percent.

Me and Duane get back to talking about hockey. I tell him about the greats and the near greats. I tell him of the time I pretzeled Howie Morenz, of the donnybrooks I had with Cleghorn and Eddie Shore. I point out some of my better scars. I got a three-incher on my calf, so I hike up my trouser leg and show it to him. Duane rolls up his pants, too. He's got the one knee there, looks like nothing I ever seen. Inside it's mostly plastic and metal. I wish they'd had that in my day, because that's what ended my career, you know, a busted knee, and I wish to God they could have plugged it up with some metal and plastic and made it good as new.

My spirit was busted right along with my knee. The peculiar thing is—ironic, as Blue Hermann would have it—I didn't break my knee on the ice. After all I'd been through playing-wise, the age of thirty-two found me hale and hearty, if a little uglier than I might have been otherwise. It was Christmas Day. I was sitting in the kitchen of the Sherwood apartment on St. Nicholas Street. I got up to go to the john, and quick as a wink I was pitched forward and my kneecap crushed up on the floor. I lay there filled with more pain than I'd ever known. I didn't scream or yell, because Chloe was out with the children (tobogganing they were, they'd both gotten toboggans for presents), and there was no one around to hear me. And as I lay there, a little red fire truck rolled slowly in front of my eyes. I grabbed it and went to hurl it across the room. Something caught my eye. I didn't even know he could write—he was only a five-year-old, and one I'd never heard speak more than seven words—but the tyke had taken a laundry pen and quite nicely printed his full name across the side of the fire truck. CLARENCE ARMSTRONG LEARY. I lost consciousness with the toy clutched in my hand.

Iain stands up. It is strenuous and newborn coltish, as if Iain had observed people standing up but had never attempted it his ownself. "I got to make a telephone call," Iain tells us. "Transmogrification is starting. I have to phone my personal physician and have him arrest further development."

"Oh, dear," says the Claire thing. "This sounds serious."

"It's ugly," admits Iain. All of a sudden Iain finds his legs, skipping and hopping, even spinning little pirouettes so that he doesn't collide with tables. Except one of the pirouettes is a little late in coming, and Iain rams his hip up against a table corner. He knocks a drink into the lap of an overweight businessman. The businessman makes a lunge for Iain, but the boy's already careening away.

It was my wife Chloe's opinion that I never forgave Clarence, but he was a willful, headstrong, contrary lad. At the age of nine he was caught distributing filthy stories at his school! Can you imagine that, him becoming a pornographer so early in life? Clarence had run off the stories on a Gestetner and was selling them at a nickel a pop. I'm not saying the boy wasn't enterprising. If I didn't know better, I'd swear he was some blood relation to his godfather Clinton. He had no interest in sports, Clarence, except he liked to skate, but he skated like a girl! It is a most distasteful sight, a lad skating like a girlie, arms held up like seal flippers, the short sickly sweet strokes of the legs.

Clarence quit school at sixteen, insisting that he wanted to become a writer. Well, sir, I know the sort of life a writer leads. Wasn't I a familiar of Blue Hermann's, one of the finest newspapermen ever? Didn't I see Blue drink, smoke, and work his way through the *Dictionary of Medical Diseases* all the way to the letter *W*? But Clarence—Rance as he called himself—was determined. During his late teens and early twenties he wrote a huge book, must have been four thousand pages, and of course no one would publish that. Then he became a beatnik and wrote peculiar poetry, and he had one long poem published and he was arrested and charged with obscenity! Can you imagine his mother's grief? All right, I tell a lie, his mother seemed to think there was some merit in this poem thing, "The Stink of Grace." But I am here to tell you that every four-letter word you ever heard was in there, and there was so much sex going on that it made me dizzy. I was a laughingstock down at the Gardens, you know. The trial was in the papers every day, and they always said, "Rance Leary, son of hockey great Percival Leary."

It was big news, because famous writers—pornographers too, if you want my opinion—came to testify on Clarence's behalf. One of these mooks had even been awarded the Nobel Prize, some Swedish fellow who made six suicide attempts daily. He said "The Stink of Grace" was a beautiful work of art. Now have a tug on the other one so I don't walk around in circles.

Clarence was acquitted, but I never spoke to him again. He racked up his sports coupe on a telephone pole in Vermont. I don't know what business he had in Vermont, other than reckless drunk driving.

So I had plenty not to forgive Rance for, the least of which was leaving a toy fire truck lying around our St. Nicholas Street apartment. And, if you ask me, Chloe could never forgive Clifford for being a big gormless oaf, which is what he is. Chloe had high hopes for our offspring, based on what, I'll never know, she went on and on about how they would be both athletic and artistic. Well, there you go, Chloe. Clifford played some high-school football, mostly because he was so big and fat. Clarence wrote smut, except for one time he wrote an episode for *The Twilight Zone*. That was pretty strange, but it was semirespectable. What happened in the show was, an old man and a young boy bickered for the whole half hour, and then at the end you find out that the two of them are stuck in some peculiar kind of time-warp affair, and they're really both the same person.

Well, I'm not saying the lad didn't have an imagination.

# THIRTY

THE FIRST TIME IT HAPPENED it made me spit orange juice all over Chloe and Clifford.

We were sitting at the table eating breakfast. Chloe was nursing Cliffy. He was a big, gormless child, and he pulled on my wife's teat until she was pretty near robbed of all substance. Chloe did her best to look and sound happy, but her skin was white and her hands trembled. She had a frightened little bird of a heart. Chloe was experiencing twinges in her lower back, and in a few months she would have full-blown arthritis. She'd given up calling me Pookie. She had started calling me Perce or Percy, and in time she'd be calling me Percival like she was a Sunday-school teacher. So anyway, Chloe had Clifford sucking away at her—him making horrid mulching noises—and I was reading the Ottawa *Gazetteer*. I took a sip of orange juice and flipped into the sports pages. The name Clay Clinton leaped off the page, and that's when I spat orange juice at my spouse and offspring.

The rest of the sentence read: "Appointed general manager of Pats."

"What is it?" asked Chloe.

"Clay's the new G.M., " I answered.

"Good," she responded. "You can get more money."

I ignored that. Chloe was always after me to make more money. I was never a millionaire, but I made fairly good jack for all the ages I lived in. Say now, wasn't the Great Depression right around the corner, and didn't I keep Chloe and the boys in food and clothes? There was plenty of mooks back then who didn't have two nickels to rub together.

"Clay says," I told Chloe, "that he's working on a block-buster of a trade."

"Good," said Chloe. "Maybe he'll get some quality back-enders."

I just let her rant and rave. "Trouble is," I said—more to myself than to her, seeing as she largely didn't know what the Jesus she was on about—"he's got nothing to trade."

That statement brought along a frosty stillness. In point of fact, Clinton had a couple of good cards in his otherwise plain hand.

Chloe pulled the gormless baby off her tit and pressed him up against her. She gave his back a few little taps and he covered her shoulder with milky blue puke.

The telephone started ringing. I let it go seven or eight times, and back then a single ring was a lot longer than it is nowadays!

"Aren't you going to answer it?" asked Chloe.

"Nobody's got any business calling at this time in the morning."

"Answer it, Percy."

It wasn't even Clay, which stung. It was Frankie O'Connor, Clay's former boss, now one of his underlings. I nodded and said quite a few "uh-yeahs." Clifford started to wail. The way Frank told it, there was so much money involved that Clinton had no real choice.

"By the by," I asked, even though my throat was knotted and speech was painful, "you didn't say where I was going."

"Oh, right." O'Connor came up with a lighthearted laugh, as phony as they come. "You're going to be an American!"

"*What?!* An Amerk? You can't do that to me! They are the sorriest collection of trash ever assembled!"

"That's why they need you."

"Where the hell is Clay? Is Clinton in the same office as you are now? I got a hunch he is."

"What? No. No, Clay is somewhere else."

"I'll tell you why you lost your job, Frank. You're one lousy liar."

"Swear to God. He's gone—"

And then there was Clay's sweet voice filling my ear. "Con-gratulations, Percival, my prince!"

"What the Christ are you doing, Clay? You sold me down the river."

"At twenty-five thousand per annum, laddy-buck. Hardly slave wages."

"Yeah, but . . . Jesus, Clay. I'm the *captain*. Ask Pat Boyle, he'll tell you. I'm the heart and soul of the Patriot lineup."

"Go to New York, my pet, and be the heart and soul of the American lineup."

"They're bums! Most of them are too drunk to play. I fit in with the Paddies, Clay-boy. But—"

"Little Leary, I have something to tell you. Papers have been signed. Money has changed hands. This discussion is not going to lead us anywhere. How's the babe, Clifford?"

"He's throwing up right now, Clay. I feel like joining him."

"You're going to thank me for this, Percival."

"Uh-yeah." I cradled the earpiece and went back to the din-ing room table. "New York," I told Chloe wearily. "Twenty-five thousand per."

She was impressed by the figure.

"Money's not everything," I muttered.

"I'll miss you," said Chloe. She couldn't have held on to Frank O'Connor's old job either.

I went into the bedroom and started to pack.

By the time the airplane landed in the Big Apple, I'd resigned myself to the trade. At the airport I met Blue Hermann for the first time, granted him a short interview. Then Blue hailed a taxicab, and he had it drive me to the Forrest Hotel, where I would be living. Many of the Amerks lived in this place, mostly because Jubal St. Amour owned it, and rooms were therefore dirt cheap.

One thing you got to understand is that back then hockey players were young Canucks from small towns, if they hap-pened to be from towns at all. Many of the lads came from farmhouses so isolated that the cows had to ask directions home. Howie Morenz, for instance, was from Swastika, Ontario. Pleasant-sounding place, eh? Bullet Joey Broun was from East Braintree, Manitoba. Jacques La Rivière was from St. Louis-de-Ha!-Ha!, which gets my vote for the all-time strangest place name, even if it is in Quebec. Anyway, the point is that the Amerks were young boys from small Canadian towns and outposts, plunked down amidst the bright lights of New York City. This is why they went how they went. Which is hog-wild.

They all lived on the seventh floor.

When the elevator doors opened, the first thing I saw was Voiceless Richie Reagan chasing a naked bimbo down the hallway. This bimbo had a certain heft to her, and the sight of her running naked down the hallway transfixed me for a moment or two. I stepped out of the elevator (there was a sound—maybe a champagne cork popping, more likely a gunshot) and moved down the hallway checking room numbers. I wanted number seven-oh-three. The first one I come to is seven-three-something. White Wings O'Brien was standing there in his gotchies, pissed as a newt. White Wings grabbed me, pulled me into his room, insisted that I have a drink with him. I escaped and resumed my search for 703. Farther down was an open doorway. I looked in and saw seven men crowded around a small table. Bollicky Bill Stubbs was dealing cards. The room was so thick with cigar smoke even Blue Hermann would have gagged. I recognized several of the boys from hockey games and gave them all a little nod. There was a ton of moola on the table. I moved away. At 712 a tall man wearing little round glasses came out. He held a leash attached to one of those tiny white yap poodles. The poodle took a nip at my ankles as I walked by. I peered through the doorway. There was a buxomy lady reclining on a sofa, and while she wasn't naked, she was undressed enough that I wondered if there wasn't some sort of female nudity code enforced by the hotel. The bespectacled man caught me looking and chuckled. By the by, that was Damon Runyon, the writer. He never did like hockey, you know, which I think was due to the razzing he received for having to walk the silly little poodle. Runyon tried to tiptoe past the room containing Bollicky Billy and the stud-poker players, but the poodle cut loose a yap. They sent up a howl. Anyway, finally the numbers on the doors descended to 703. I slipped the key into the lock and went in. My roomie, Little All Bright Peterson, was on his bed with a lady who wasn't breaking with hotel policy. She was setting on top of him, and he was smoking a stogie and having a quaff. Little All Bright gave me a wave. "Five minutes, huh, pally?"

I shut the door and stood in the hallway for a very long time.

# THIRTY-ONE

BELIEVE IT OR NOT, the N.Y. Americans had a game that night. Most of them managed to grab an hour or two of shut-eye, and showed up no worse than half-cut. White Wings O'Brien was so advanced in his recuperation as to be hung over, and he didn't seem to recognize me from earlier that afternoon. Mind you, not all of the Amerks were come-to-naughts and ne'er-do-wells. A couple were well-behaved laddies who showed up on time, bright-eyed and ready to play. The other men treated them like lepers.

Muzzy Tobias came into the dressing room. Muzz was an obese man with a mole in the middle of his forehead, a big thing with hairs sprouting out of it. Every time I ever seen him, Muzzy was digging and rooting in his left ear. Usually he just used his pinky, but I saw him employ the odd tool, a pen or a pencil, a key or something. Muzz was a jolly sort of fellow, never took anything too seriously, so he was the right coach for the Amerks.

"Well," said Muzz philosophically, "it's Montreal tonight."

The men groaned. The Canadiens were the class of the NHL that year, what with both Morenz and Cleghorn.

"You all know Percy Leary," Muzz said. "He'll be put in with O'Brien and Clancy."

"Three Irishters," I pointed out.

"Yup," nodded Muzzy Tobias, "except for Clancy."

That's the kind of team we're dealing with.

After that rousing pep talk from old Muzzy, the New York Americans filed out onto the ice. We had all the pep and ginger of a funeral parade.

Sprague Cleghorn caught sight of me and grinned. I wished I still had that huge silver crucifix that Manny had given me.

"Lookee," said Cleghorn. "Little Leary is an *American*."

"I'm as Irish as ever I was, Spray-goo."

"If you're Irish," asked Cleghorn, "how's come it's everyone else on your team that's green?"

Some of the boys did cast a sheen, but you can't let anybody bad-mouth your side, even if your side are drunken yobs. So I dropped my mitts and went into a bit of the bob-and-weave. "Come on, Cleghorn," I snarled. "Let's see the kind of stuff you're made of." I tucked my shoulder and shuffled on my blades. I threw rabbit punches and roundhouses. Cleghorn stood there and watched. After a while he picked up his stick and brought it down across my head. That's all she wrote.

I came to early in the third period. My head hurt, or so I imagine, about the same as one of Blue Hermann's worst hangovers, where pain compels him to actually drive his gnarly fingers deep into his eye sockets. My head was bandaged pretty good, but I still worried about blood and bits of brain leaking through the gauze.

The club doctor was sitting on a nearby bench, smoking a cigarette.

"How many?" I asked him.

"Forty-odd," he responded. "You got some on the inside, some on the out. In a few days I'll have to open you up again."

"Much obliged." They'd taken off my sweater and skates, so I set about putting them back on. "What's the score?"

"Four-nothing," the doc answered. "Cleghorn's got a pair."

"Cleghorn? You mean to tell me he's still playing?"

The doctor shrugged. "He got a five-minute penalty."

"Five minutes for an attempted murder?"

The doc just shrugged again.

I put on my sweater—it was styled after the Yankee flag, bars and stars, all red, white, and blue—and laced up my skates.

I was some steamed. Five minutes for a split melon, that's what passes for justice in this sorry world. I stormed out and took a seat at the end of the players' bench. The other fellows were watching the game and exchanging pleasantries. It made me ill. I called over to Tobias, "You gonna put me out there, Muzz?"

"How do you feel?"

"I feel like someone's cracked my head open. But I also feel like I don't want to watch these pitiful Amerks pleasure-skate with hockey players from Montreal."

"Well, if you want." He whistled someone off. I hopped over the boards.

"All right, all right," I sang out, "make way for the Dublin hurricane!"

Some photographer made my picture right then, and it's in a number of books. There's me with my head all bandaged, the wrappings stained black with life stuff. My eyes have, I'll admit, a certain lunacy to them. The next few minutes are somewhat hazy in my memory. I certainly don't remember any noise from the stands, any cheering or suchlike, although Blue Hermann reported in the *Star* the next day that the fanatics had gone berserk. When it was all over, I'd scored three goals and assisted on two more, both of those tallied by groggy White Wings O'Brien. Bollicky Billy added a lone score, and the Canadiens were stifled.

Blue Hermann was waiting for me in the dressing room. He had his pencil out, his little notebook at the ready. "Comments?"

"I was just playing hockey. The good old shinny, as when I was a lad."

"Comment on what Cleghorn did to you?"

"Sprague was just playing hockey. Mind you, he and I got different concepts of what that entails."

"He hit you pretty hard."

"Not hard enough, sir," I told him. (That was the headline in Blue's column the next day—"Leary says Cleghorn didn't hit hard enough.")

Blue Hermann stared at me for a long moment. I didn't know that he was seeing me all blue. The booze had already ruint his eyes, you see. "Well," he said with a nod, "it was a good game, Little Leary. You are a tenacious bastard."

Outside the dressing room some urchins were waiting, wanting my John Henry. I obliged, telling them, "Eat yer veggies and don't never smoke a cigarette."

Then I noticed that there was a woman standing there in the hallway, one of the smallest women I've ever seen. I mean, she wasn't a midget or anything, but she was small. She wore her golden hair short on the back and sides, long in the front. On one side a hank covered most of her face. The other side glowed with a huge blue peeper, but it was an odd blue, the color of the sea. The girl was dressed in silver satin, and from underneath came the impression of nakedness. She came closer and spoke to me. She wondered, in a high-pitched voice that I'll confess approached silliness, "Does your head hurt very much?"

"It don't tickle."

The girl reached up and touched my bandages. It happened so quickly that afterward I wasn't sure it had taken place.

"Do you like music?" she demanded suddenly, and I do mean suddenly, the question just sort of fell out of the branches and landed in front of me.

"I suppose so."

"I *adore* it." The word "adore" took several seconds to speak. "Especially the new French romantics. Debussy!" Whoever this fellow was, the girl was mad keen on him. When she said his name she swooned backwards.

"Plays music, does he?"

"Well, you know, he's *dead*. But he wrote such *exquisite* music. My favorite is called 'Afternoon at the Farm.' "

"Uh-yeah."

The golden-haired woman said, "Let's go get your hat."

"My hat?"

"You had a hat trick, Jubal told me, so you get a hat."

"Where?"

"Back at the hotel, silly billy." The woman gave me a whack, I mean a Jesus-hard whack, balling her tiny hand into a fist and lacing into my shoulder.

"Well, okay."

"I'm Hallie," she said.

"Percival."

"Percival. A very romantic name. Will you be my knight errant?" Hallie whipped on a fur coat she'd been holding. "Will you slay me a dragon, Sir Percival?" This weird blithering set her to giggling. She grabbed my hand and led me away. We walked quickly and we walked mostly in silence. I tried to make conversation—where are you from, how long have you been here?—but all I got was one- and two-word answers— Kansas, three years. Hallie pulled me through the lobby of the Forrest Hotel and into the elevator. She pressed the big 8 button and up we flew. When the doors slid open on the eighth floor, I followed Hallie into the hallway. Her room was directly across.

"I'll just wait here for the hat, ma'am," I said, but before I knew what was happening I was pulled through the door.

There were two things in Hallie's apartment. One was a piano, a scratched and chipped monster that likely was a runaway from some honky-tonk in New Orleans. The other was a bed, a much classier affair. It was one of them four-posters with a canopy. It was covered with red satin sheets. This was the biggest bed I'd ever seen, especially given Hallie's stature. If she was having trouble sleeping at night, she could simply try another portion of the mattress to see if it had a soothing effect.

Hallie threw her fur coat onto the bed and then rammed her fists on her hips. "Do you want to hear me play the piano?" she demanded. The light cut through her dress and silhouetted her body. It was all I could do to come up with a nod. The foot pedals had special blocks attached so that her toes could reach them. She rested her fingers on the ivories for a long moment, her eyes closed, her breathing rapid and shallow, then she started to play. It was a slow piece of music, full of notes that twisted my insides. Hallie played well, and the melody was sweet and strange. I sat down on the corner of the four-poster, affecting to be a man at his leisure, but really I didn't know how long my legs would have held out. Hallie twisted her head

upwards as she played. The moon came through the window
and washed the color out of her face.

When she was done playing, Hallie jumped down from her
stool, went into a small cupboard, emerged with a top hat covering most of her face. Then the satin dress tumbled to the floor.
She was naked underneath. I understood that this was the
reward from Jubal St. Amour for my hat trick—this naked
woman. I was a married man. Hallie's nipples were small and
hard. I was the father of a gormless baby. Hallie moved across
the room, folded my head within her arms and drew it to her
breast. It had been a long, hard day. I pushed her away and
left the room.

# THIRTY-TWO

LONNY CHANDRIAN EXCUSES HIMSELF (executing a sort of half bow, a servile habit left over from his head usher days) and rushes off, telling us he'll be right back.

Iain comes down to my end of the table. If I touched that nappy head of his, I'm sure a spark about a foot long would leap up my arm.

By the by, about five or ten minutes back, a fellow Iain knew came into the Potbelly Lounge. This mook may as well have had Fugitive from the Law tattooed across his forehead, that's how furtive he was. This desperado sidewinded into the establishment, and he and Iain effected some business dealings. From where I sat, it looked mighty one-sided. Iain gave the mook most of his money and received a handful of white beans. I heard that story before. It's up the beanstalk with the lad.

"King, King, O mighty King," Iain says—his blue eyes have a glaze like metal—"we're going across the street to the Oxford. Yes, we're embarking on a crawl. My God, I love a good crawl. Up and down the boulevards, searching in all the nooks and crannies. Boldly going where no man has gone before. Remember, we mustn't interfere with any of the life-forms. No, no. Keep your golf shoes on, ladies and gentlemen, they are feeding the lizards alcohol!" Iain giggles and takes a pull at his bottle of beer. He shoves it rudely toward my wrinkled puss. "Care for a tug at the witch's tit, my liege?"

"A fine thing," I tell him. "You're supposed to be looking after me."

"I am, I am," Iain says, "I'm looking after your spiritual self."

"I'm game," croaks old Blue. "I'll go on a pub crawl."

"Hey," says Duane Killebrew, "tomorrow's my day off. I got all night."

"Weary as I am," says Claire, "I must look after my charges."

"This is excellent!" Iain screams. "Mobilization!"

"I am agèd and infirm!" says I. "I shouldn't be kept out past eight-thirty or nine. Here it is almost eleven."

"Oh, King mine," says Iain, "what good is your health if you don't live?" Iain presses his lips to my wrinkled brow.

"You are drunk."

Iain slams his fist down on the tabletop, hard and quick. Then he quiets as quick as he maddened. "Ladies and gentlemen," he calls out, "Mr. Ray Charles!" Iain closes his eyes and starts throwing his body sideways, back and forth. " 'It's crying time again,' " he moans. "Everybody, sing along."

Lonny Chandrian reappears. "You know, Mr. Clinton . . ." Lonny always had a dopey way of saying that name, separating it in half and biting it off with his too-big front teeth, "Clinton." "Mr. Clinton had a secret place down in the west wing."

"How do you know that?" I ask him.

"Urp." Lonny looks guilty. Mind you, I did ask him that question pretty churlishly. "When we rewired for the new scoreboard they had to install some generators and electrical equipment and . . . " Lonny shrugs. "We had to put the stuff *somewhere*, so one of the contractors said, well, it's hollow back here, so we knocked down the wall, Mr. Leary."

Iain is still rocking sideways and singing. "You there! You in the three-piece with the woman who has enameled hair! Please, sing along!"

"No dead bodies back there, I hope?" I ask Lonny.

Lonny never does seem to realize that I'm making a joke. "No, sir. There wasn't very much of anything. Just some old underwear and newspapers. A couple of empty champagne bottles. And this." Chandrian reaches into his jacket pocket and extracts the big crucifix, the one Manfred handed to me so many years back. "I thought maybe you might want it, Mr. Leary."

Iain catches sight of the cross, covers his eyes, and screams at the top of his voice.

Lonny hands the thing to me. It feels so heavy that for a second I'm certain it must be a different crucifix, but as I lay my fingertips to it, I'm filled with a familiar sensation. How in the world did Clay Bors Clinton get ahold of this thing? The only answer being, somewhere along the line he stole it from me. That wouldn't be overly difficult, being as I never could recall what exactly I did with the thing. But why would Clay want it? That question hits me so hard that I have to say it aloud, like it's been smacked out of my gut. "Why?"

"What's the matter, Leary?" asks Blue Hermann. "You got that old-time religion?"

It's all of a sudden suffocating in the Potbelly Lounge. This was the favorite of Clay Clinton's haunts. Many was the time I sat in here and waited for the man, often for hours on end. I fear he may walk in suddenly, just like he used to, wink at me with those steely gray eyes of his. "Percival, Percival, I've just porked the prettiest poppet!"

"Let's get out of here," I tell the table. "Let's go to the Oxford. Anywhere." I'm putting on my overcoat. Iain doesn't even realize that he is supposed to be helping me, on account of I am agèd and infirm.

"All right, kiddies," says the Claire thing, "I want everyone to join hands and follow me."

We hit the street. The Claire thing moves to the middle of Charlton and stops traffic like a cop. Our ragged parade slowly moves across. In the basement of the Oxford Hotel is a tavern for the riffraff. I been there before with Clay Bors Clinton. It's called the Boiler Room, for two reasons: one, it actually is a boiler room, at any rate the ceiling runs thick with pipes and such, and two, the house speciality is boilermakers, whereby the bartender takes a shot glass full of whiskey and sinks it to the bottom of a big draft beer mug. It's the kind of confection that appeals to those particularly bent on intoxication, and the Boiler Room has long had a reputation for being a rough-and-tumble kind of place.

We walk down six steps, through the double doors, and the first thing I see, sitting in a corner with his mouth wrapped around a boilermaker, is the gormless boy Clifford.

He's all alone at a big table—a sight that weakens my knees for a moment—and I cross over to him. Clifford looks up and sets his mug on the table.

"Poppa," he says.

"What are you doing here?"

"What am I doing here?" Clifford's hair is sprouting every which way, and he hasn't shaved for a couple of days. The tiny whiskers are pushing through his chubby face all gray and white. "It's King Leary Night at the Gardens! What was I supposed to do, stay away?" Clifford sees the people behind me and attempts a smile. It spreads out long and clumsy across his face. "Hey, hey, hey!" he says. "The King and his court. Mr. Hermann. Iain. Lonny Chandrian. Um, some tall guy. And, what the hell do you know, Duane fucking Killebrew! Hey, Duane-o!" shouts my son. "Sit down here and kill a brew!"

"You been drinking, boy?"

"Jesus Christ, Poppa," sighs Clifford, "do you think I'm this big an arsehole all the time?"

"This is my son Cliff," I tell those who don't know.

"Have a seat," instructs Clifford. "They make this drink here—it's called a boilbreaker. It gets you gunned."

We sit down with Clifford. (All except for Iain, who races off to play pinball. He rams a waiter and sends boilermakers every which way.) The whole crowded bar is interested in our arrival, because of Killebrew, of course.

Clifford orders a lot of those boilermakers, one for everybody at the table. I don't drink mine, but the others down their drinks and the drunkenness level is upped by about twenty-five percent.

"King Leary Night at the Gardens," marvels my son Clifford.

"They've had them before," I remark. "It's not like this is the first time I've been so honored."

"You know what else today is?" asks Clifford. "Rance's birthday."

"Uh-yeah." The big teevee screen over in the corner is showing highlights from the hockey game. I watch Killebrew execute the St. Louis Whirlygig. I get a feeling like someone is playing cat's cradle with my innards. There's me on the screen. Dropping the ceremonial puck. The camera zooms in for a close-up. I am a most unsightly man. The King waves to the multitudes. Now, they must be hard up for news, they're going all historical. They show old footage of the Gardens being erected. There's me and Clay in a news clip. Clay is laughing. What in the world did that man find so damned amusing?

"Want to know something funny?" asks Cliffy. He's talking to the whole table, his voice as loud as a tomcat in a trashcan. "You know what they used to call me at work? For a nickname, like? Except I didn't like it, and I asked them not to call me that, but they did anyway? They used to call me Prince. See, it's funny. My dad is the King, so I must be the Prince." Clifford shrugs and sips on his boilermaker. "I'm pretty fucking old and fat for a prince. Rance, now, Rance was a prince."

"Why the hell do you keep going on about Clarence? These nice people don't want to hear about Clarence. Talk about hockey or shut up."

Iain returns, raises his boilermaker, and drains off about half of it. "Ladies and gentlemen," he announces, "Mr. Lou Rawls!"

"Talk hockey," mutters Cliff. He nods at Killebrew. "Good game, Duane-o."

"Thanks."

"I never could play hockey. Too fat."

"You could have shed some poundage," says I. "It's no big deal, Clifford. Just don't eat so much."

"I tried to, Poppa. Once I drank nothing except fruit juice for a whole frigging week! I gained a fucking pound!" Clifford laughs with little joy. "Rance could play hockey."

"He couldn't skate right! I tried to show him, and he couldn't do it. He pushed off with his hind leg, he didn't move side to side. He skated like a girl, goddamn it."

Duane Killebrew says, "One time, my old man . . ." Duane-o shakes his head, a strange half smile on his face. "I'm playing peewee, right, and ever since I was like eight or nine I've been big news, and there's newspapermen at all my games and shit, but my old man, he was never impressed. Like to him, I was nothing special."

"Please, everyone," says Iain, "sing along."

"And this one game—I'm maybe eleven, playing two tiers above me, so all the other guys are fourteen—I scored fifteen goals. Fifteen fucking goals. That's one every four minutes. The final score is fifteen-one. Right? And the old man gets all over my case, because he says I was dragging my ass when they scored their one lousy point. Jesus." Killebrew hits his boilermaker.

"*Yeah!*" explodes Clifford.

"*I said, fucking sing!*"

"I never did anything like that," I mutter.

"Maybe not," Clifford admits, but then he sticks one of his short, fat fingers at me. "But you were never impressed, Pops. Like to you, we were nothing special."

Iain stands and waves a boilermaker in the air. "Leary, as your doctor, I suggest a drinky-poo. Tenderbar, bring the King, his majestic Leary-ness, a boilermaker!"

"I don't need a drink." My skin has turned clammy. I think I might faint. "I need for everyone to stop talking damn foolishness!"

"Ladies and gentlemen . . ."

"Uh-oh," says I.

Clay Bors Clinton appears in the barroom. I can feel my heart rattling in my chest. Clay is grinning like he's been exchanging jokes with the Almighty Creator. Clinton waves, calls out, "*Hello, Percy, my precious! Long time no see!*"

I can only summon the smallest of smiles.

# THIRTY-THREE

I REMEMBER THAT AFTERNOON AT THE FORREST, me and Little All Bright Peterson were playing gin. I was demolishing Little All Bright (Alvin, his right name was), because I was by way of being a gin-playing genius. He was no kind of a genius at all, Little All Bright, except for he was pretty good at luring women up to our hotel room and making me stand outside in the hallway for hours on end. Be that as it might be, on this particular day, early in the hockey-playing year, my second season with the loathsome Amerks—I'd been home for the summer, and impregnated Chloe with Rance—me and Little All Bright were simply playing cards.

Speaking of Chloe, she was sorely afflicted with lumbago. Much of her time she spent in bed—her tiny fluttering heart usually keeping her there, anyway—gingerly propped up on pillows and sofa cushions. Impregnating her with Clarence was no easy matter, my friend. It was done amidst caterwauling and confusion. Sometimes I wonder if that had anything to do with the way Clarence turned out, a scuzzy pornographic type who seldom bathed.

So Dummy Bakker came running into the room, intent on telling us something. Now, the funny thing here is that Dummy Bakker was a deaf-mute, and aside from waving his hands in the air to let us know something was up, he did little more than perplex us for the better part of five minutes. Dummy kept grabbing at his own throat as if to strangulate himself. Whatever he was trying to communicate had more to do with me than with Little All Bright, that's as much as I could gather. Then White Wings O'Brien came into the room. He was ashen and shaking and crossing himself and looked like he needed extreme unction. "Sweet Mary, Mother of God," he whimpered, cracked as per usual, "they've come to get me."

"What goes on around here?" I demanded.

Then I heard a *thud*, the unmistakable sound of someone walking full tilt and oblivious into a wall.

"Hold on here." I turned to Dummy Bakker (I'd sooner talk to a deaf-mute than to the besotted White Wings). "Is there a bunch of monks out there?"

Dummy was watching my mouth work, and when I said that word "monks" he clapped his hands together.

I jumped up from the card table and flew to the hallway. I ran into Simon the Ugly and it was somewhat akin to hitting a brick wall. Except a brick wall didn't catch you on the rebound and commence to squeeze the air out of you under the pretense of administering a joyful hug. "Percival!" said Simon the Ugly.

"Look, Isaiah," said Brother Andrew, who had become an even squatter fireplug since I'd last seen him, "it's Percival."

"I can see that it's Percival!" shouted Brother Isaiah. This was a keen stunt as his milky blue bossed eyes weren't even pointed in my direction. "He looks just jim dandy."

Theodore the Slender was apparently on a diet, and it was a few moments before I noticed he was there at all. Theodore was holding a hotel key, and he waved it in the air. "Let's find our room," he said. "We have plenty of time to talk to young Leary the arsonist." (Brother Theodore never was one to let you forget your misdeeds.)

"What's your room number?" I asked.

The thin man examined the key and read off, "Seven eighteen."

"Seven eighteen? They put you on this floor?"

"Surely," nodded Isaiah the Blind. "We asked for the floor with all the hockey players. We are, after all, hockey players." Brother Isaiah grinned in a manner that, if it weren't for his being a man of the cloth, I would be forced to describe as shit kicking.

"Yeah, but . . ." I stammered.

At this moment a door flew open and Voiceless Richie Reagan came out in pursuit of the big blonde bimbo who was in accordance with hotel policy. She barreled down the hallway in our direction. Most of us were able to scatter, but Brother Isaiah stood his ground in the middle of the corridor. The bimbo smacked into him and spun him like a top. Then Voiceless Richie hit from the other side and reversed him. Brother Isaiah the Blind was still grinning when he finally came to a stop.

"Seems like a nice place," he told us.


Now, I don't think it was any mere coincidence that those Brothers happened to be there that night, the night when Manny and I finally squared off against each other, jousting as it were, head-to-head. Mind you, I had played against Manny before, but only when he'd been on the bottle, and those nights Manny couldn't usually muster much energy or ginger. We tended to avoid each other during those games, and if the script should call for us to bump into each other, we would do so with no particular enthusiasm. Manfred was appointed captain of the Paddies after Clay traded me, but Clinton was forced to relieve him of the big *C* after some drunken shenanigans. Manfred wasn't even the Paddies' best goal scorer at that time. Some young mick named Bobiash was. That's how sadly things had deteriorated, the Paddies were without a heart and their main man had the name of Bobiash. I don't know what kind of name that is, but I know it ain't Irish.

One time we played up in Ottawa, and as I skated out onto the ice I heard a voice calling, "Go you Lucky Number Nine!" Janey was sitting front row, her feet up on the railing. She'd been drinking. Her skirt had ridden back and I could have seen her frillies except that my stomach buckled at the thought of looking. I toyed with the blade of my stick, scraping up bits of snow and ice. Janey had a purplish blue eye and she spun me some yarn about how she'd walked into a door. Manny whirled out of the dressing room like an autumn leaf. "Hey, Percy!" he called, a crippled smile on his face. Veins were bursting in his eyes.

I sidled over to Kip Meaghen, one of our biggest defense-men. "If he comes down the boards," I whispered, "take him out hard."

When Manny did come down he rode Meaghen into the boards so heavily that Kip concussed and didn't wake up for three days.

But Manfred's game was gone. He couldn't fancy-skate, he couldn't pass, and every shot he took at the net just bounced pitifully off the goaler.

I had no reason to believe that things would be different that night. I was surprised to see Patty Boyle put Manfred out for the opening face-off (the usual strategy was to hold the hung over Ozikean in reserve, awaiting moments of despera-tion), and there was something odd, boyish and teasing, in the smile that Manny gave me as I skated towards him.

"Ho," he said lowly.

"Hey, Manny." I hunkered myself down in the circle. I always had a unique style when taking face-offs, getting lower than most players. "How's things?"

"Good, Percy." Manfred squared up, and the referee came to drop the puck.

Well, I won the face-off, for all the good it did me. For some portion of a second I was in possession of the puck, then Manny applied the full force of his weight and almost sent me into the crowd. Ozikean started up the ice. That first rush, it was like everyone was too stunned to move. Manny fired on Shrimp Worthers, and the Shrimp just ducked. Ottawa had a one-naught lead, and Manny had an NHL record for the fastest goal, something like four and a half seconds. (Duane-o got that one last year, scoring in two-point-whatever seconds on an overly zealous French Canadian Catholic who was giving himself a few extra passes with the Holy Cross. Manfred him-self used to do that, but he abandoned the procedure some-where along the line.)

The only applause came from the four black-robed monks who sat in the third row back, center-ice, and generally car-ried on like rubes on bad gin.

I skated back to the face-off circle. Manfred was grinning at me. "What's news, Manny?" I asked him.

"Oh, not too much. I gave up drinking."

"Did you now?"

"I had to, Percival. I was dying."

The ref dropped the puck, and I did the Silver Platter. This was meant to humiliate Manny, giving him the rubber and then taking it away. Mind you, the plan came a cropper. I let Manfred have the puck, and he damn well vanished with it! That did it. I charged up behind him and worked my stick in between his legs. Manny tumbled to the ice like a felled tree. I claimed the puck and turned toward enemy territory. This piece of rubber was worth a tally for damn sure, except for the fact that the referee had whistled the play dead and tagged me with a tripping penalty. I argued that as well as I could, but I didn't have much of a case. The Patriots scored twice during that short-handed spell—Ozikean himself got one—so by the time five minutes had been played, us Americans were on the short end by a score of three to naught. The Brothers of St. Alban the Martyr were pleased with this. The rest of the Madison Square Garden was upset, chiefly with Little Leary. I determined to make it up to them.

There was a whistle at some point, an offside, and as we reformed I noticed Manny skate out of his way to get close to the boards where the monks were sitting. Brother Isaiah talked to him, pointing out various positions on the ice. Isaiah's pointing finger and bossed eyes were at odds, but Manfred nodded studiously as if the world were suddenly making arithmetical sense. The Patriots scored on the next play, and they scored by virtue of Manfred either being at or passing to these locations indicated by Brother Isaiah the Blind.

At the end of the first twenty, the score was five-naught for the Paddies.

Blue Hermann was waiting for me outside the dressing room. His head was covered by gray clouds from his cigarette. "What gives, Leary?"

"Manny's playing good." Newshounds have no sense of when a fellow wants to be left alone.

"*Good?*"

"Every now and again, everything rolls right for you. Tonight is Ozikean's night."

"It certainly isn't yours."

"Thank you kindly, Mr. Hermann."

I was determined to do better the second frame, so I dogged Manny's every step. I threw so many checks at him that my body turned purple, and the most effect I could muster was to wobble him a little, destroy his picture-perfect form. I could stop Manny, but every time I did the referee would assess my conduct as illegal. I'd want to argue. "Why sure, I know that it's normally against the rules to give a mook the double-hander across the back of the shins, but that's *Manfred* out there, and the boy is making me look like a greenhorn!"

And between whistles, Manfred would hustle over so that he could chat with the monks. The brothers were doing all the coaching, seemed like, but Patty Boyle didn't mind as long as the score was seven-one, which it was after two periods. And as if all that wasn't bad enough, the lone Amerk tally was perpetrated by White Wings O'Brien. He was playing better than yours truly, and the little git was three-sheeted.

It was a sorry atmosphere in that N.Y. Americans dressing room. Muzz Tobias just kept shaking his head. Whatever was in his ear was currently burrowing into his brain. Muzzy had practically his whole hand up his ear. "Can't figure it," he said, ace coach that he was.

"It's those priests!" Little All Bright piped up. "Those priests are helping Oz."

"They ain't *priests*," I told Peterson. "They're monks."

Bollicky Bill Stubbs asked, "How's come you know so much about it?"

"Those are the fellows from the Bowmanville reformatory, and me and Manny was both there, so that's how come I know so much, Mr. Stubbs, and by the way you are looking even more ugly today than usual."

"So why," demanded White Wings, "aren't they telling you stuff?"

"Why?" I jumped off the bench and glared at my teammates. "Why? I'll tell you why. Because I haven't asked them."

"Well, for shit's sake," screamed Coach Tobias, "go ask them!"

So I hit the ice early, and I skated over to where the brothers were sitting. They seemed to be expecting me; they all started to grin as I drew near. Isaiah the Blind beamed bright as the sun. "Hello, Percival," he said quietly, nodding in my general direction, then somehow nailing me square with his bluey walleyes.

"Hi."

"You can't fight Manfred," said Isaiah, just like that. "He's too strong for that now. Be as the grass in the wind, Percival."

"Uh-yeah."

"And," Brother Isaiah went on, "you worry too much about putting the puck in the net. *The vision is yet for an appointed time, at the end it shall speak and not lie: though it tarry, wait for it: because it will surely come, it will not tarry.* In other words, Percival, concentrate on the game along the boards. Play hard in the center. Be as a piece of music, young Percival. There is more to a song than the last note."

I muttered, "He's making me look like a goat."

"You're making yourself look like a goat," said Brother Isaiah. The other monks nodded.

"How come he's all of a sudden so much better than me?"

Isaiah the Blind shook his head gently. "He's better than you at his game, Percival. But remember: *'Go to battle in thine own person.'* You are a breeze through the Irish hills. A little lick of dragon flame. If Manfred catches you, you're sausage meat, but who can catch the wind?"

I nodded. "Down by six, twenty minutes to play. Grim."

"Numbers are for shit," announced Brother Isaiah with finality.

"Why did you come tonight? Why this game?"

The monks laughed as if I'd said something funny, or as if I myself was crack-minded and mouthing morsels of weirdness. Brother Isaiah waved at the ice, and came damn close to missing. "Play hockey, Percival. We like hockey."

About a minute into the final frame, I found myself with the rubber over in the corner, Amerk end of the rink. My first thought was: *How in hell am I going to tally this one*, and then I told myself not to worry about that. Play the game in the corners, in the shadowed caves. I cleared my mind and worked at the rubber with my blade. I noticed that Manfred was coming at me, so I braced and solidified myself, and then I realized that Manfred was simply too big and strong, that I was going to get crushed and mashed and flattened like a flapjack. So what I did was, I blew like the wind. Manny hit me and I let him. Manfred went into the boards like a freight train. I rolled off to the side, taking the puck with me. Patriots kept coming at me, so I just slipped this way and that, a shadow, a zephyr through the lowlands. Before long I was in the clear, standing before the Ottawa net. Scoring the goal was as easy as spitting.

I looked into the stands. Brother Isaiah was nodding. I wouldn't lay money that he was nodding at me, but he was nodding and that made me feel a lot better.

Well sir, I scored four times in that final twenty minutes. A hat trick with a feather in it, that's what I like to say. Some people said it was the finest display of shinny playing that they ever witnessed. Other people—all they talked about was the game played by Manny Oz. He was impressive, that's for damn sure. All of New York City argued it the next day, which one of us had played better. As Blue Hermann put it in the headline for his column: "Who is King of the Ice?"

# THIRTY-FOUR

IAIN IS TUGGING AT MY SHIRTSLEEVE and telling me to wake up. I wasn't asleep. I was merely cradling my head in the crook of my arm, shielding my weary eyes from the thestral Clay Bors Clinton. Even though he hasn't seen me since he died in 'sixty-seven, Clay is in no hurry. He is currently taking advantage of his status as ghost. He stands on top of a chair and stares into the abyss of a fat lady's cleavage. Then Clay's eyes spark, and he fulfills a lifelong ambition, strolling nonchalant and invisible into the women's john.

"Wake up," says Iain. "I have decided to toss away my hook, King. I've decided to transmogrify radically. It'll be disgusting to watch. I'm gonna become amorphous, undifferentiated tissue. Gruesome." Iain takes a sip of his boilermaker and starts to cry.

Clay follows a woman out of the head. He is rubbing his hands with glee, and as the lady turns to sit down, Clay Clinton holds out his hands like eagle talons and takes a rush at her bubbies. Clay passes right through her and vanishes again.

"Ladies and gentlemen," says Iain, kicking back his chair and standing up, "Mr. James Brown!" Iain begins to dance, his eyes closed, his neck craned back, his face set in a kind of painful ecstasy.

I lay down my head.

Clay Clinton has his young man's face and his old man's potbelly. He is wearing a three-piece. Then again, Clay would dress up fancy to do his gardening. Not that he ever did any—I suspect it would come as something of a surprise to Clinton that seeds could be planted and flowers result. All in all, Clay B. Clinton looks damn good. Death has been kind to him.

"Wake up, my liege," says Iain. "I've brought you a boiler-maker."

"Take it away."

"*Go on,*" urges Clay. "*It beats the pants off ginger ale, Percy, my punk.*"

"I have had alcohol before. Do not forget I drank a glass of champagne in one-nine one-nine."

"*Champagne is alcoholic?*"

"Not good enough for you, eh?" Iain has been fed through the Wringer of Life seven or eight times but is still unctuous with festive befuddlement. "I know! The King needs to have this potion tested for him. Who better than I? I'm almost completely transmogrified now, I'm not afraid of anything." Iain drains my boilermaker. "It's fine. Tenderbar!" shouts Iain. "Another butt of malmsey!"

"Why did you take the crucifix, Clay?"

"*You weren't using it. I needed it.*"

"What did you need it for?"

"*Drink your drinky-poo. Don't you want to know what it's like to be tipsy?*"

"Why don't you tell me? You been tipsy enough times."

"*For me, tipsiness was characterized by falling in love with the most proximate object. Sometimes, fortunately, it was a young lady. Occasionally it was a rather attractive young lady. But often, you know, there was no lady within miles, and then I'd fall in love with all manner of strange things.*"

"I admit it," says Iain, "I'm tipsy. Know how I know? Know how I know that I'm tipsy? Because I feel this oneness with the cosmos. Like the universe is a big toilet bowl and God has just flushed."

"Wake up, daddy."

"I am awake." I rear my head off the table, rub my eyes. Clay Clinton has vanished. "I think I should go to bed now."

Blue Hermann is struggling upwards with his thick oaken canes a-wobbling. "I think I should go to the head now." His voice alarms the patronage, and after he's spoken all you can hear is the *beep-beep* of the pinball games.

"I'll come with you. I'm your fucking nurse! Waiter, we are shipping out, me and the noble Blue! Upon our return I want to find that table loaded with mealie beer!"

Those two move towards the Men's sign.

"I was on my way to the bathroom, you know, when I slipped on that toy fire truck of Clarence's."

"Yeah, but, Poppa!" That's my gormless boy, Clifford. When Clifford gets drunk he gets confused. Right now such things as breathing and sitting are baffling the hell out of him. I brook no interruptions.

"Duane!" I call out. Duane-o is talking to Lonny Chandrian, nice boy that he is. "Come here, Duane, and I'll tell the tale of how my hockey-playing career was ended."

Cliffy says, "That's not a good story, Poppa."

"I'm talking hockey player to hockey player."

Killebrew slides his chair down. "Tell away, Mr. King."

"What happened was, we had three or four days off around Christmas. So I went back to Ottawa. Christmas Day was nice, I recall. Jane and Manny came over. Clay and some redhead. Manfred made a big turkey. Hugest thing you ever saw. He made a stuffing and all sorts of veggies. Eat yer veggies, Duane, please don't forget."

"*Perhaps I should have married that redhead, Percy, my pet. She was very acrobatic in matters sexual, none too squeamish.*"

"Never mind about that now. After dinner, we all sat around and exchanged gifts. Manny had knit me a scarf."

"*Do you remember what I gave you?*"

"You gave me *underwear!*"

"Underwear?" asks Duane-o.

My boy Clifford looks so confused it breaks my heart.

"Hey!" Iain sticks his head out the bathroom door. "Call Ross McWhirter at the *Guinness Book of Records!* The Blue man has unleashed a mighty torrent, and there's no end in sight!"

Here's that strange Claire thing smiling at me. The diamond in his tooth is almost blinding. "It's getting late, my dearies. Claire needs sleep. And I'm not just playing trombone in the Phantom Zone, I am tired."

"*Do you remember what I gave the boys for presents?*"

"I damn well do. Fire trucks!"

"Poppa . . . "

"*Am I to take it from your tone that fire trucks are somehow inappropriate gifts for young boys?*"

"Four minutes and seventeen seconds!" Iain and Blue Hermann are back. Iain grabs the waiter by the shoulder. "Fetch me a flagon of gruit."

"Gruit?"

"A mixture of ale and bog myrtle."

"I am telling the story of how my hockey-playing days were ended."

Blue Hermann is grunting, seating himself. "It happened in Ottawa, at your home."

"Well, I'm off home to the little lady." Lonny Chandrian stands up. He's got no "little lady" at home, he's got a tractor trailer that wears a girdle. I met her at one of those Maple Leave do's. Mrs. Chandrian is a terrifying creature.

"Goodbye, Lonny."

"Good night, King."

"The King of All the Hockey Players!"

"Yes, sir!"

"*Loof-weeda!*"

There's an old Indian at the table next to us, sleeping with his chin sunk onto his chest. When I say my nickname, he wakes up and grins sheepishly. "Sorry about that," he mutters, and then he falls back to slumber.

"Miss Claire is like *cataleptic*. I'm talking major motor malfunctions. I must go journey to the Land of Nod." The Claire thing stands up, the hank of hair flip-flops across his face. "King, see you on the morrow. I'll pick you up at the hotel. Duane—"

"I'll just go to the studio. I can get a lift."

"Right. Ta-tas and bye-byes!"

"Poppa, let's go now."

"What happened was, we had three or four days off around Christmas—"

"*I remember! I gave your wife a nightgown!*"

"That's right, a nightgown you could see right through. She might as well have been naked as in that nightgown."

"I beg your pardon," says Duane Killebrew, "I don't really understand how a nightgown figures into all this."

"Maybe I'll just have a wee keltie!"

"Never mind about the nightgown. I suppose she looked nice enough in it. She was a very pretty girl. Ill health beat the tar out of her, mind you. Towards the end she looked like the Frankenstein monster, scarred up by all the operations. But I was talking about the fire trucks."

"You're still mad about that, aren't you, Poppa?"

"Clifford, be quiet. So Christmas Day, Chloe took the lads out for a toboggan ride, because their Uncle Manny had given them new toboggans. I was all alone in the house. I was walking to the bathroom and all of a sudden, *bang*, I fell on my knee and mashed it up, and my hockey-playing days was over. Mind you, I don't blame Clarence—"

"It was me."

Duane stands up. "I better go. I'm meeting this girl."

"Well, Duane-o, it's been a real pleasure."

"*Let's go with him, Percival. Let's go meet the girl.*"

"Simmer down, dead man."

"Did you hear me, Poppa?"

"Cliffy, I'm saying good-bye to Mr. Killebrew."

"It was *me* that left out the fire truck. I was playing with it. Rance wouldn't leave his toys lying around. He was too neat. I left it out."

"You're saying it was you who left the truck on the floor?"

"Yes."

"Why didn't you tell me this before, Cliffy?"

"I didn't want you to be mad at me."

I am bone weary. I look at the gormless Clifford. He is big and fat. Life has slapped his mush and dealt him a few stern ones to the gobbles. His wife ran off with the equipment manager from the South Grouse Louses, they haven't won a game in years. I heave a sigh. "From now on make sure your toys are put away."

# THIRTY-FIVE

I'VE FINALLY GOT AHOLD of this dream I've been having. It is a weird one, my friends. My wife, Chloe, set great store in dreams, you know. She had a book, *The Dictionary of Dreams*, and every morning she would look up her sleeping fancies. They always meant the same thing, *death*, which I could have told her.

So the dream, this extravaganza, takes place at Manfred's funeral. Historically, it was a dull affair, not that I demand great excitement at funerals. But in my vision hellzapoppin'. The Amerks are all there, pissed as newts. There are also some actual newts. In my dream, the joint (a church that has had no upkeep or maintenance) is rampant with lizards, snakes, and blindworms. Hallie is there in a state of undress. Her body is unnaturally white, as though there never had been contact with sunlight or the outside world. Hallie is playing music for the funereal proceedings, leaping upon the keyboard of an old pipe organ. My wife, Chloe, likewise naked, is pumping the bellows. The music sounds of thunderstorms, men lost at sea. Hallie accompanies it with a loud moaning. In this she is joined by Poppa Rivers.

With the appearance of Poppa Rivers, we are entering nightmare territory. Gruesome, the man is. Naked to boot. Hey, am I the only one here with any clothes on? (I take that back. I seem to have abandoned my customary modesty. The bony little Leary rump is there for all the world to see.) Poppa Rivers's manhood is enormous. It's not like I go around looking at such things, but this particular waterspout is hard to overlook. Poppa

Rivers is covered with dried mud, the dirt sunk dark and deep into his many wrinkles. He has a drum fashioned from a cow's skull, rattles from a snake. Poppa Rivers plays along with Hallie's music. The unruly New York Americans dance, White Wings and Dummy Bakker, all of them, and all of them have brought naked bimbos along from the Forrest Hotel. Blue Hermann stands off to one side, taking notes.

Poppa Rivers spies me, and his arseholes-for-eyes pop open, and he comes dancing over. He appears to be doing the ha-cha-cha, a sashay from the Boom Boom Room. "*Loof-weeda!*" he screams. "You dumb fuck!" Then Poppa Rivers spins around and brandishes his wrinkled, mottled buttocks in my face. His fingers spread his cheeks and *Mayday! Mayday!* Little Leary's entire body horripilates. It gets you-know-who to laughing. Yes, sir, Clay starts laughing, that laugh he had, like life was a circus and he had a free ticket.

Clay has appeared with Janey Millson on his arm. They both are naked. Janey's body has a nice softness to it, although her breasts are a tad duggy, dragged down by gravity, worried by Life. Those two show up and I realize that this isn't Manfred's funeral (despite the enormous oaken casket over in the corner) this is the nuptials of Clay and Janey. Hallie changes the organ music appropriately, drawing out a *Twilight Zone* version of "Here Comes the Bride." Chloe pumps the bellows so hard that she has an asthma attack. Clay and Janey walk down the aisle. There is drunkenness and fornication going on all about them. Poppa Rivers scurries up to the pulpit; apparently he is going to do the service. "Dearly beloved," he begins— the man can barely suppress his giggling—"we are gathered here in the presence of God and this dumb shit over here—" Poppa Rivers wags his crooked finger at me "—to join this man together in you get the general idea. You may fuck the bride."

Clinton begins to do so. Their coupling strikes me as particularly wanton.

Then there is a bellow, and the top of the casket lifts off. Manny "The Wizard" Oz, royally rummed, scronched, and whiskey-whipped, bolts upright and surveys the situation.

Manfred takes to the hills like a wild creature.

# THIRTY-SIX

"YOU'RE CUT OFF."

I wake up and suss out the situation. We are being tossed, specifically Iain. That's going some, you get tossed out of the Boiler Room. In the fifties there was a knife murder here, and I believe they let the perpetrator finish his drink. But this stocky bartender is gathering up glasses and wiping the tabletop, affecting an air of nonchalance, and saying as how we can't have any more.

"Why not?" screams Iain.

"You've had enough." The bartender has the tone of voice of a lad answering history questions in grade school.

"Yeah, well, listen up, buddy-boy," says Iain. "I am a paramedic. I know when I've had enough. I've had enough when a Sherman tank can roll over my tootsies and I don't even notice. Now, bring us more boilermakers before I rearrange your gnarly puss."

"Just leave, pally."

"Fuck you!" Iain reaches up and grabs the fellow's collar. The fight is over before I'm done putting on my overcoat. Blue Hermann finishes up all the drinks before the waiters can fetch them away. Then the two of us slowly make our way across the room and out the door.

Iain is all bruised up and purple. He fair glows in the dark. He has a cut on his forehead and is spitting blood. "I lost a frigging tooth!" he cries. Iain is on his hands and knees hunting for the thing. What he's going to do with it when he finds it is beyond me. His glasses have vanished as well. Blue strolls around, using one of his canes like a blind man's stick, and he finds them.

Iain saddles the glasses across the bridge of his nose and labors upwards. "Well, at least I got in a few good licks." With the back of his hand, Iain drags a loopy thread of blood across his face. "Didn't I?"

Blue Hermann, Ace Reporter, shakes his head sadly. "Not even close, son."

"Yeah, but I sure gave those guys a tongue lashing. You should have heard it. Your ears would be burning." Iain sighs heavily, wobbles in the moonlight. "Where now?"

"Bed," the Blue man and I say as one.

"Me, I'm ready for love." Iain giggles, stumbles over to the other side of the walkway. "Just joking. Not ready for love. Totally unsuitable, in fact. Not built for it. Oh, well. How's about a little drinky-poo?"

There is further commotion in the tavern doorway. My son Clifford is battling all three of the bouncers and two of the heftiest waiters. Cliffy is handling himself well, wielding his magnificent belly like a battering ball, unleashing smooth, straight punches with his beefy hams. The gormless boy is biting his tongue with concentration, and his eyes are reddened by rage. His opponents give him the sort of respect they'd give to a rabid dog. For the most part they stay their distance, only venturing in when there's a chance to do true and permanent damage. Clifford smacks one on top of the head and drops him. Then another (who has been standing away from the fray, surveying the action) spies Cliffy's Achille's heel. The lout rushes in and elbows my son soundly in the gut. The air rushes out of his body and with a cry of "Poppa!" Clifford timbers. The bouncers and waiters clear out of the way. They wipe their hands. One of them even affects a disdainful spit, but it's obvious to us and to them that they were lucky. They hurry inside before the gormless boy can lumber to his feet.

"Fuck a duck," says Cliff.

"What were you doing, boy?" My throat is almost too tight for speech.

"I thought Iain was in a fight!" he moans.

"Well, *technically*," says Iain.

"We showed them," says Clifford. He's made it as far as his knees. I don't like to see him on his knees like that. "We didn't pay for that last round."

I attempt to haul him up. He won't budge. Iain and Hermann come to assist, and with some effort we've got the lad on his huge, fat feet.

Iain is urinating against the side of a building. Actually he's just spraying the edifice owing to gravity and such similar natural forces; he's aiming for the Dogstar Sirius.

My gormless boy decides to join Iain. He reaches around his belly and with some toil draws out his short, squat tool. His beer-fueled stream lands only inches away from the high toes of his shoes.

I tell him, "You can't drive, boy, you're too drunk."

"No probs, Poppa. I can drive."

"Remember what happened," I tell him.

"What happened, Poppa?"

"To your brother."

Clifford replaces himself. He needs to hop up and down in order to do his zip. "Lemme see. My brother drove into a telephone pole. I don't think I want to do that."

"Drunk, he was. Drunk as anything."

"Poppa, you don't think it was an *accident?*"

"All right. Enough." Blue Hermann speaks quietly, but his voice registers. "Let's go to our room. Clifford can take a room at the hotel."

"It's kind of pricey," says Cliffy.

"*I'll* pay," says I.

"Well, then, fuck a duck."

As quick as that, it starts to snow. The flakes tumble downwards, big and wet. You can feel them as they settle onto you. Iain darts around, plucking snowflakes out of the air. "I just know," he tells us, "that two of these boogers are the same!"

"They all look the same to me," grumbles Blue Hermann.

Clifford splays out his palm and waits for things to land in it.

*"Oh, well, 'it's lovely weather for a sleigh ride together with you . . .'"*

The man can't carry a tune in a suitcase.

*"Percival, my precious,"* he hails me. *"Let's you and I have some sort of a contest. A race, perhaps. Or a fight!"*

"No fair, Clay. After all, I am old. Agèd and infirm."

*"Don't complain too much, little one. I'm dead."*

"Clay?" asks Blue Hermann.

"Can you see him, Blue?"

"Did you say *Clay*, Leary?"

"Aha!" Iain has both hands held out, his thumbs and pointers pressed tightly together. "These two!" he shouts. "Identical!"

Clifford is giggling.

Blue Hermann looks like he's got hair again, the snow piling up on top of his gleaming bald pate. "My sister said, come live with me in Florida. But me, I decide to stay in Canada. Brilliant."

I says, "You may have made something of a gaffe there, Blue-boy."

"Well," the scribe says vaguely, "I had promises to keep."

Then all of a sudden I get beaned by a snowball! It's a soft, mushy one, packed only hard enough to sail it through the sky, and it explodes across my forehead. "What bastard done that?" I scream. Meantime, Iain is giggling like a circus seal. "Two can play at that game!" I shout. What, does he think I've forgotten how to fashion a snowball? I even got my own method, quick and efficient. First I take a handful of snow and squeeze it hard, squeeze it down to about the size of a walnut. I set that down and roll it back and forth, side to side, and it quick picks up a couple layers, each about an inch thick. Then I compact that, apply a rub for luster and glaze, and I am armed. The problem with snowball fights (actually, what gets your heart beating like a marching band) is that while you're making your snowball, someone else is making theirs. You're crouched and semiprotected during the construction, but once you stand up to fire, you're a dead duck. This is where the Inner Eye becomes very important. You have to aim *before you stand up*, visualize it in your mind. I stay hunkered and imagine where Iain is. I can hear his wheezly giggling (another reason never to smoke cigarettes, they give away your location during snowball fights), and I picture him there. He is standing up, something tells me, which means that he has a snowball on the ready. I got maybe half a second, tops. I clear my mind. No sense waiting. I pop up and unleash. There's a *whoosh* and a gagging sound and the boy is choking on snow! "Ha-ha!" Now I bolt for cover. I've maddened Iain; he uncorks even though I've gone weavy. The snowball whistles past my ear.

Then I get beaned in the back of the head. This one stings! This one had a quarter inch of ice around it. If I didn't know any better, I'd swear that it was a prefashioned snowball, made the night before and stored in an icebox. They ought to make those things illegal. Someone is assisting Iain. There's no way he could have made two snowballs to my one. "No fair!" I shout. "No fair, you bastards!"

I go down.

I didn't see the slick of ice, buried as it was underneath the soft, new snow. But my fancy dress shoe doesn't stand a chance.

The pain in my left leg is enormous. I decide against moving for a while.

A little red toy fire truck rolls in front of my eyes. It says CLARENCE ARMSTRONG LEARY in big bold capital letters. Son of a gun. I didn't even know the lad could print.

I will not be King of the Ice now. Not with Manfred out there. He's as big as a mountain, but he moves like the wind.


"Percival, my prince! Are you all right?"

"My leg, Clay. Can't move my leg."

"No, no, of course not. Cartilage damage, Little Leary. Your hockey-playing days are done."

"But—"

"But the good news is that Pat Boyle, the slimy pederast, is no longer coach of the Patriots. I want you!"

"Sure! I can coach the lads, Clay-boy. I'll fill the bucks full of vim and vigor."

"Fine. Now, Percival, we have a problem. I have been offered no less than four players and quite a chunk of cash for one of our players."

"Do it! We need men out there! Manfred can't do it all alone!"

"The problem being, Percival, my pet, it's the big Man-Freddy they want."

"Manny? You want to trade Manny?"

"Of course I don't want to, Leary-deary."

"Who's the other team, Clay?"

"The offer was tendered by a very good friend of yours. One Jubal St. Amour."

"The Amerks?"

"The New York Americans."

"You can't trade Manfred to the Amerks."

"And why not?"

"Because . . . they're a wild crew. I don't think he could—"

"He hasn't had a drink in years."

"Yeah, but you don't know what it's like down there."

"He's a professional hockey player."

"This is so you can get Janey, isn't it, Clinton?"

"That thought was the farthest thing from my mind. In fact, let's just leave me out of this. It's up to you, Percy, my pretty. Do we trade Manny or don't we?"

"Let me think about it."

"You don't need to think about it. Your mind is made up."

"Well . . ."

"Yes or no, Little Leary?"

"Trade him. Trade him to the Amerks."

"God have mercy, Percy. At least I was in love."

"And I," says I, "am King of the Ice."

# THIRTY-SEVEN

THE SUNLIGHT IS LEAKING THROUGH THE WINDOW, but it is weak and cautious, far more trepidatious than, say, the maid, who stormed in here twenty minutes ago with her vacuum aimed like a bazooka. She took a look at the three of us and fled in terror.

I can't blame her. Over there is Blue Hermann. He lies on top of his bed sheets (but somehow knotted in them), naked to the world. As he snores, his mouth falls open, his maw both darkly gray and red as blood.

On the chair over there, folded up like yesterday's paper, is Iain. That boy was bad pissed last night. He kept me and Blue awake for almost an hour with whiskey-inspired lunacies. As he talked, Iain kept throwing little white pills into his mouth. He dug out Hermann's secret stash of hooch and made short work of it. Sometimes he'd be laughing, and the next breath would find him close to tears. About every four minutes, Iain would introduce Ray Charles. "Ladies and gentlemen, Mr. *Ray Charles!*" After one such intro, Iain tumbled asleep. That's what he is now, asleep, snoring fitfully, his long legs twitching like a mechanical dog's. Iain has accumulated a total racktime of about fourteen minutes, and that was spent crumpled in the chair.

He wakes now, still tight as a tick. "The King is dead," he mutters. "Long live the King."

Iain's eyes are red, and by far the brightest thing in our gloomy hotel room. "Ladies and gentlemen," Iain announces, "it is showtime." He springs, staggerish, to his feet. "Ladies and gentlemen," Iain calls out in the morning stillness, "Mr. *Ray Charles!*" Iain begins to stamp his feet awkwardly, closing his eyes and twisting his face side to side, his features clenched in demonic abandonment. " '*It's crying time again . . .*' " He leaves off abruptly. "Kinger, Kinger, make my day."

"How could I do that, son?"

"Why, tell me what day it is!"

"Sunday."

"I hate Sundays," Iain broods. "The righteous hit the streets."

"Do me a favor, lad."

"Sire, for you I would do most anything."

"See if you can hail Cliffy on the blower for me, will you?"

"Why, sure!"

I practice for the advert a bit while the besotted Iain talks to the desk clerk. Here's what I say: "Hello to all my friends across Canada and Newfoundland! This is King Leary, here with his good buddy Duane-o Killebrew to talk about the good old stuff, Canada Dry ginger ale. I been drinking it all my life. People ask me why."

"Why?" croaks Blue Hermann, who is struggling to extricate himself from his bedclothes.

"Why the hell not?" I jump into my trousers. "It's as good as anything else, I'll allow. But, you know, I maybe should have tried some other stuff. Coconut milk, maybe. I never in my life tasted coconut milk, and might be it's the puppy's butt."

Iain blows trumpety noises through his crooked, swollen lips. "Ladies and gentlemen," says Iain, "Clifford Leary and his fabulous tummy-tum-tum! How's it hanging, Big Cliffy?" Iain listens for a bit and then chuckles. "We won't tell you-know-who."

"Won't tell me what?" I grab the phone out of Iain's hand. "Tell me whatever it is, Clifford. I'm your father."

Iain locates an empty whiskey bottle and with some vigorous shaking manages to coax out a few meager drops.

"It's nothing, Poppa."

"I know what it is. You got a woman in your room with you."

"No I don't."

"Why not?"

"Beg your pardon, Poppa?"

"Never mind, Clifford. I'm just phoning to say good-bye."

Cliffy yawns and I'm reminded of the gormless baby sucking on his mother's tit. Cliffy never cried as an infant, but he yawned a great deal. "Hey, Poppa, I'll see you a week Sunday. The Louses are going to play the team from Hope."

"I wish them luck, boy. You stick with those Louses, Clifford. I know they'll win soon."

"Oh, yeah. I'm gonna stick with the Louses all the way."

"Now, Clifford . . ."

"Poppa?"

"Cliff, I want you to listen very carefully to what I'm going to tell you. It's about the accident, when I hurt my knee."

"I'm sorry, Poppa."

"Cliff, I was reading the newspaper. I want you to know that. I was reading the newspaper, the sports pages, and I had to go to the john, and I kept reading it as I walked down the hallway. I was reading the newspaper and not watching where I was stepping, and that's why I stepped on the toy fire truck. So just don't worry about that anymore."

"But—geez. I wish Rance had of known."

"Let's not worry about Clarence. There's nothing either one of us can do about poor Clarence. Let's just make this thing right between me and you."

"Well . . . sure."

"All right, son. I have to say good-bye."

"Bye-bye, Poppa."

"Stick with the Louses, son."

"Okay. Bye-bye."

Naked Blue Hermann is staring at me. "King," says the ancient scribe, "they wouldn't have published a paper on Christmas Day."

The Claire thing wafts into the room. He's dressed oddly, a pinkish sweater that descends all the way to his knees, and great big furry boots. He also has a Slavic fuzzy of the sort that the Rooskies like to wear. "Wakey, wakey!" the Claire thing shouts. Then Claire catches sight of the denuded Blue Hermann, who has managed to sit upright on the side of his bed. The Claire thing stops dead in his tracks. "Medics!" he shouts. "Medics!"

"Claire-baby!" says Iain. "You look in fair fith and kittle!"

"The wonders of slumber."

"I wouldn't know about it," Iain mumbles. "Luckily for me, there's always Better Living Through Pharmaceuticals." The lad tosses some pills into his mouth.

"King," says the Claire thing, "you are looking magnificent."

"Listen up. Friends, drink the good old Canada Dry. It is sweet and bubbly and can make you burp."

"Oh, for gawd's sake, don't say *Canada Dry!*"

"Why not?"

"They're the big competition. I mean, we hate them with a passion that verges on monomania."

"You ain't Canada Dry?"

"No, no. My client is *Acadia Dry*, Canada's best-selling ginger ale–type beverage."

"*Acadia Dry?* That's the swill that damn near poisoned me on the train!"

"Ah, you've had some."

"How can that fart water be Canada's best-selling beverage?"

"King, I'll level with you. It's cheap. Real cheap. Like a can costs all of a quarter."

"You charge people a quarter for the privilege of poisoning themselves?"

"King, I'm an advertising whore, right? What did you expect the old pro Redford to say? I'm sorry, I can't take the did-I-mention *multimillion*-dollar account because people who really know their ginger ale say the stuff stinks? Which I didn't even realize until just now. King, Mr. Leary . . . are you crying?"

"It's all so damn *complicated!*"

"Hmmm?"

"When did all this happen? Did that Serling fellow make a general announcement that we were living in the Twilight Zone?

Did those Dogstar People get into our beverages?" I'm leaking from my nose, from my eyes, my mouth is filled with catarrh.

"Kinger," implores the Claire thing, "don't leave me in the lurch. Don't say you won't do it!"

"I never said I wouldn't do it."

"I mean, my Lord, the stuff can't be *that* bad."

"It's plenty bad, Claire. But I'll do the advert."

"Thank you!" The Claire thing simmers down. "Now let us leave, the limo awaits."

Iain stumbles over to help Blue Hermann get dressed, although Iain is more of a hindrance to the procedure. Blue has to wear this underwear gear that resembles diapers, due to his problem with incontinence. But unless you know exactly what God's got in store for you, don't laugh.

Blue struggles to his feet, supporting himself with the oaken canes. Exertion beads his upper lip with sweat.

"Attago, Blue-boy," I tell him. "You're doing just fine."

Blue slaps that grin on me, the one he used when he was a young man. For a second, in my mind's eye, it's like he *is* young again, even to the extent of having a bubbly-bosomed girl dangling on his arm. This sort of thing has been going on quite a bit, this confusion. It has ceased to startle or worry me.

We go downstairs in the elevator. Music leaks out of a hole in the ceiling. We walk through the lobby of the hotel, into the day.

It looks like the welkin dumped about a foot of snow on the earth last night as I slumbered. Everything about the world is white and quiet. But the air is warm, and already the gutters are furious with melted snow. Maybe the snowfall was winter's last huzza.

Guess who's sitting in this sleek black limousine? Clay Bors Clinton, of course, hung over as can be. Oh, I know that, seeing as how Clay is a specter, he didn't have anything to drink last night, but being hung over in the morning is force of habit to him. He rubs his eyes and focuses on me. "*Morning, squire,*" he moans, "*Christ, I feel awful. Awfully awful.*"

"Guess what? It wasn't Rance left out the fire truck. It was Clifford."

"*Hmmm.*" Clinton doesn't seem interested. The Claire thing has opened up a newspaper, and Clay is reading over his shoulder, even though things don't apply to him anymore.

"You don't seem too surprised."

"*I'm not.*" Clay reaches out a ghostly hand and prevents the Claire thing from flipping over the page. Claire assumes that he must have been interested in some article and his eyes peruse the print looking for it. "*It doesn't make much difference which of the tykes left it out, Percy my precious. You tripped over it.*"

"It ruint my hockey-playing career, you know. And Chloe, remember, Chloe used to say that I never could forgive Rance for leaving out the truck. But if it wasn't even him—"

Claire has opened to the stock market pages. Clinton's eyes light up with fire. "*Jiminy!*" he cries. "*Look at the money to be made!*"

"If it wasn't even *him*—" I persist.

"*Yes, Percival?*"

"Well, that's . . ." I gaze at the city streets through the darkened limo window. I have come a long way since nineteen double naught. So has the world out there. "That's monstrous."

"*Aha!*" exclaims Clay. "*Now we're getting somewhere. Little P. Leary, something of a natural.*"

"Monstrous? What's monstrous?" Iain has tumbled into a Blue Hermann fitful doze, and my words startle him back into waking.

A little red sports coupe overtakes us, overly close, prompting our chauffeur to blast the horn. The driver of the red sports coupe pushes the gas pedal down, changing gears with arrogant noise. He burns away, hurling slush. "I didn't know," I whisper. "Worse, I never even thought."

We pull onto a street that's in the bad section of town, a lot of tenements, sorry little brownstones. Brave and valiant in the midst of all this is an old church. The stained-glass windows are riddled with marble holes. The huge oaken doors haven't seen fresh paint in years. Without thinking, I raise a hand to cross myself. I'm startled to see my liver-spotted claw tremble. I don't know if that's from palsy, fear, or exhilaration.

At any rate, I decline to make the cross with it. To hell with that noise.

Almost next door to the church is something called Solstice Video Studios. As we pull into the parking lot, bells start ringing. The church doors open and people spill out into the warmish winter air. They are poor people, largely black. Most of them are smiling, one or two are even laughing out loud.

Iain watches them and starts to cry. I pretend not to notice.

Meantime, the queer birdy Claire is flitting around trying to get things organized. He's alarmed because Duane Killebrew hasn't arrived yet. There's fourteen cars packed into the studio's tiny parking lot, and how Claire knows that one of them isn't Duane-o's is a mystery.

"Like," Claire bellows, puffs of steam firing from his nostrils, "we have technicians here getting maybe triple, quadruple scale and a half for working on a Sunday. Get the idea? And, I should mention, we have Gordon Pennylegion waiting inside. Is this man cheap, my children? No. Mr. Pennylegion is not cheap. We're talking heavy-duty exorbitance. So all right, let's start without Killebrew. Iain, do you think you could manage to get the King inside? I'll sweeten the pot for you, baby. Do you know what's inside that building? Booze. All sorts of it. And you! You, fat stuff in the putrid off-white! Take Mr. Hermann into the Green Room. Follow that dipsomaniacal male-nurse person."

A silver car with flames painted along the sides pulls into the parking lot.

"Well, well, well," says the Claire thing, buckling his fists onto his hips, "look who's decided to arrive. Mr. Hockey himself, the fab Duane!"

Iain is steering me toward the studio doors. He's more wobbly than I.

Duane gets out of the passenger's side, a girl from the driver's. She appears to be seven foot tall, big busted as a dance hall queen. Killebrew spots me and waves. "Hey, King!"

"Morning, puppy!" I return.

We push through the door, my scrawny shoulder left to do most of the work. The walls inside are covered with photographs. I'm reminded of the old shanty groghouses that Manfred Ozikean loved so dearly. The people in these pictures are famous Canadian television personalities. I don't know them from various Adams and holes-in-the-ground. Iain steers me down a hallway.

The Green Room is green. It's got sofas and a little bar set up in the corner. Iain sets me down and goes behind to where the booze bottles are. He looks at labels and selects something crystal clear. Iain drains about half a glassful before asking me what I want. "Kinger-Binger? A spot of the good old stuff?"

"Beer."

"Come again?"

"I want a beer."

"Beer?"

Fat stuff in the putrid off-white steers Blue Hermann into the Green Room. Blue spots the wet bar and starts grinning his grin, a cat with a gobful of mouse. "Alphabetical order, thank you, Iain," he says.

"The King is having a beer," says Iain.

"The King is dead," croaks the hoary scribe. "Long live the King."

Clay Clinton spins around the corner into the room. "*My, my!*" He is appraising the bar. "*What wouldn't I give for a little taste.*"

Iain hands me a tall pilsener glass. His hands are shaking pretty badly. The brew slops over the side. I salute them all and drain off a little bit of the beer. The foam tickles my lips, and my first draft is thick and bitter. It's a distinctive taste, this beer. I give it another try.

"Well?" they ask me.

"That's what all the fuss is about, is it?"

They nod.

I pull down another gulp.

"Well," I proclaim, "I don't see that—"

The burp starts somewhere in my great toe. It jumps electrical up my legs and tingles my groin. It heaves around my guts for a split second, spinning my innards like a wash cycle. Then the burp leaps upwards, almost squeezing my nipples, and it has me by the throat. My head spins back and forth—maybe it even does a complete three-sixty. The belch is magnificent and holds in the air like a cloud. The reverberations are slow to die. It is certainly the best burp of my entire lifetime. It has drained me, left me exhausted.

I manage to smile at my companions.

# THIRTY-EIGHT

I AM IN THE GREEN ROOM, WAITING. They are setting up lights and cameras in the studio. The director has been taking Hitler lessons. He is screaming at everybody and has created an atmosphere of intense hatred and mistrust. Apparently this is crucial to the making of fine television adverts. It doesn't bother me, though. I sit on the sofa and wait. Pennylegion's assistant, Kim, is wearing a blouse that you can see through. She has small Japanese breasts that bounce a lot as she races around instilling in people the fear of Pennylegion. This girl is having quite the effect on Blue Hermann. He is so excited that I suspect blood is actually coursing through his veins. And Clay, well, Clay's phantasmic eyes are bugging out of his head, as if he's never seen a bubby before in all his days.

Kim screams at me about something, but I watch the heave of her breasts and grin. She leaves disgusted, reducing me, Blue, and Clay to wheezy old-fart laughter. Kim is slim hipped as a boy and from the rear (as she storms away) she looks to be no more than twelve years old. And we are still giggling when a voice says, *"Here you guys are!"* My blood chills. Manfred Armstrong Ozikean comes into the Green Room.

I think I mentioned before that Clay's spirit has his young man's face and his older man's stout belly. When first laid eyes upon, that's how Clinton appeared, but things are always changing. Sometimes the ghost is sixty-seven years old, preyed on by disease and bullied by the pugnacious heart, and sometimes Clay is eighteen and still a mite pimple faced. It is this

Clay, a young brash one, that is currently engaged in pursuing Kim around the Green Room. Myself, I'm used to these Sirius transmogrifications, and even if it is a bit frightening, it's the least I deserve. But I'm unprepared for Manny. Manny is melting, Manny is unglued. It's as though he fled the grave without any practice at managing his wraith. Manfred grins toothlessly, his mouth gray, his empty eye sockets a deep black. "*Percival!*" he says, and then, catching sight of Clinton, Manny grins even wider. "*Clay!*" he booms.

Clay won't be distracted from the Kim girl. He's bouncing along backwards in front of her, his hopping timed to the fury of her breasts. "*Freddy! Pull yourself together!*"

Manny sheepishly tries to keep body and soul intact, but various limbs and accoutrements continue to drop off.

Blue Hermann begins to shiver, and for a second I think that he must see Manfred, then I realize he's shivering because he's taken poorly. Sweat has beaded on his face. Manny drags himself across the room and stares at Hermann for a long moment, if a fellow who has neglected to equip himself with eyes can be said to do that. Manny reaches out a spectral hand and touches Blue's wrinkled brow. Hermann instantly tumbles into a sweet slumber, even commences a loud and gnarly snoring. The snoring amuses Manny, who steps back, chuckling. "*What a racket!*" he announces.

Here comes the Pennylegion creature himself. He stands five foot nil, wears a baseball cap, and carries a clipboard. The purpose of the clipboard is to beat against his thigh. Pennylegion looks in most regards to be somewhere in his early thirties, but his hair and beard are peppered with gray. "People, people, people!" he bellows. "Can we keep the fucking *noise down!!??*" He stops in front of Duane Killebrew, who is sitting on a couch with the long-limbed girl. Pennylegion snaps his fingers a few times. "What, what, what is it, *Killebrew?*"

Duane-o nods.

"Killebrew, here's what the hair says. The hair says, *remember the seventies?* Killebrew, we lose the fucking hair."

"I like his hair," protests the show-biz type girly.

"I'm sure you do, honey. That's why you're, what, what is it, you're a *receptionist* or a *facialist* or something, correct-a-mundo?" Pennylegion snaps the fingers on one hand and uses the other to beat the clipboard against his thigh. He must have one hell of a bruise there. "Hair people! Where are the fucking hair people?" Some hair people, two young women, charge in and set upon Duane with hedge clippers. "Now," says Pennylegion, "where is this hockey legend?"

"*Who's that, you?*" whispers Manfred. Typical of Manny to whisper even though he's a vision that appears only to me.

Kim drags Pennylegion my way. She makes terse introductions, annoyed at me for being unable to take my eyes off her bubbies. "The point is, we are making a commercial for ginger ale," Pennylegion grumbles. "We are not making fucking *Night of the Living Dead.* This creature should have been in makeup hours ago. I don't see how we can have him resembling a humanoid before next fucking Thursday. Makeup people! Where are the fucking makeup people?" A girl bolts forward. Pennylegion grabs her elbow and waves at me. "You pull this off, I guarantee the fucking Pfeiffer Award." Pennylegion turns to go away, but I halt him.

"Hey, you! Pup!"

"*Pup?*"

"Listen, pup. This is the thing. Any time now I expect to have my arse hauled out onto the carpet in a major way. I would appreciate it if you'd just calm down."

"You tell him, King!" says Killebrew, whose golden locks are being shorn.

"Fucking hockey players," Pennylegion mutters. He and Kim wander away. The makeup person attacks my puss with a powder puff. The girl is maybe seventeen years of age and very smiley. All the time as she does my makeup she talks, but I don't pay much attention. She calls me "dahlink." "Look up, dahlink. Look over there, dahlink." Over there is Manny Oz. He is sitting down, his huge hands resting on his knees, and he looks as delighted as a child at the circus. "*My goodness gracious me,*" he sighs. "*What a world.*"

"Worst part of it is," I tell him, "this is typical."

Iain comes over with a couple of sheets of paper in his hand. "All right, Kinger," he says, "I'm your script coach." He tosses one of the pages at me. His drink has an olive in it. Ever notice how serious booze hounds like to put olives in their drinks? Without the olive it would be too much like they were pouring liquid solvent down their gullets. "Your part is underlined in red, sire," Iain says sloppily. "I shall read the part of Duane Killebrew, finest hockey player on the planet, which is what . . . ?" Iain ticks off with his fingers. "One, two, *three* stones from the sun. Okay? Here we go. Ahem. First, a small sip of the pulque. Ahh. Now. '*Winning the Stanley Cup was a lot of fun, but it was a lot of hard work, too.*' "

I have to hold my sheet at arm's length to pull it into focus.

IT WAS THE SAME FOR ME BACK IN 1919.

"It was the . . . same for me . . . back in one-nine one-nine."

"King, I don't think they want you to say '*one-nine one-nine.*' "

"That's when we claimed the goblet—one-nine one-nine!"

"Yeah, but people don't say that, '*one-nine one-nine.*' Only you say that."

"It was the same for me back in nineteen nineteen."

"Aren't you hockey legend Percy 'King' Leary?"

AND AREN'T YOU FUTURE HALL-OF-FAMER DUANE KILLEBREW?

"And aren't you . . . future hall-of-famer . . . Duane Killebrew?"

Manny gets up, at least most of him does. He roams around the room, investigating its corners and contents. His passage across to the other side was a rough one, from what I understand. It was undignified.

"That's what's so bad about it, boy. It can steal your dignity."

"What's that, Kinger-Binger, an ad lib?"

"The booze, I mean."

" I'm just having a wee nog and pomperkin. What the fuck could be more civilized?"

"He was all alone in a hotel room."

"It's not my fault all's they have is shandygaff and rumbullion, so of course I get drunk. What did everyone expect?"

"All alone in a hotel room."

"*For the early part of the evening,*" Manny Oz says, "*Hallie was with me. We had some wine and some cocaine. We talked for a while, and then we loved each other. Hallie had to go somewhere. She gave me a bottle of whiskey for a present. I wondered why she'd given me a present. Well, it was New Year's Eve. Then I felt very far away from home. Very far away. So I took the whiskey and I drank it all, very fast. And while my brain was still buzzing from that, I broke the bottle across the windowsill and cut myself. Here and here. Then I went to the bed and lay down. It was not a bad feeling, Percival. I felt happy just before the end.*"

"You didn't cut yourself, Manfred. You died of something called 'alcoholic insult to the brain.' "

Manny shrugs. "*I remember what I remember.*"

Clay floats toward me. "*Do you think Jubal and I would have let it be known that Manfred was a suicide?*"

"You knew this?"

"*Well, St. Amour implied as much to me, yes.*"

"Why didn't you tell me?"

"*You can see why I need that crucifix! You never even noticed it was gone.*"

"I thought it was with my hats."

"*Hats? What hats?*"

"The hats I got for scoring real, true hat tricks, which is three goals in a row in the same period."

The Claire thing and Pennylegion are standing in front of me. The director's thigh is taking a furious beating from the clipboard. "Fine, fine," he says, "the old fart is visiting relatives in Flip City."

I have to be sneaky here. "I bet you didn't know that, did you, Mr. Pennylegion?"

"Know what, what?"

"That a true hat trick is three goals all in a row, all in the same period."

"A piece of information that has inexplicably eluded my grasp all these years."

"I thought maybe you could use that fact in your advert. Like this here. Friends, a true hat trick is all three goals all in a row in the same frame. And a true ginger ale is this crap here."

Pennylegion and the Claire thing exchange trepidatious glances. Then they get excited, they start to nod rapidly and energetically. They make for the doorway. I study the dragon's head on top of my walking stick. It bears a distinct resemblance to that loutish growtnoll Pennylegion.

Blue Hermann is awake. "You ought to get paid extra for that, Leary."

"Blue, how did Manny Oz die?"

"You know."

"Tell me the truth. Did Manfred break a whiskey bottle over the windowsill and cut himself on the wrists?"

Blue's eyebrows—each comprising one or two snowy white tendrils—begin a slow climb up his forehead. "If something like that happened," he says finally, his voice quiet and inhuman, "Jubal St. Amour would have paid a lot of money to the coroner of New York City to alter the death certificate. And if there was a newshound who knew the scoop—because, for instance, he went to the Forrest Hotel to wish Manfred a Happy New Year—then Jubal would have given him a lot of money to never say what he saw. And that newsman likely would have taken the money—because he needed it for booze, mostly—and then he might have moved away from New York. Maybe to Toronto. So he would not be at liberty to discuss what happened to Manfred Ozikean."

"But he couldn't have done it. Manfred was a Catholic."

"Manny died without a God."

"I'm glad Hallie was with him, at least for a while. She was a hell of a girl."

Blue Hermann tilts his head, bewildered. "How do you know all this?"

Iain goes down spectacularly, almost as if he was hip-checked by the ghost of the son of a bitch Sprague Cleghorn. "Whoopsy daisy!" Iain lies there motionless for a while. "All right, all right," he says. "I admit it. I am a drunker and a lowly, lorn shebeener." He crawls back to his feet. "But what the hey. A little drop of usquebaugh never did no one no harm!"

Iain searches the floor for something to blame for his tumble. Then his brain skips off in another direction. For some reason Iain starts to pretend that he's playing the saxophone, and he blows a lot of razzes and spit through his lips.

"Calm down, boy."

"*Loof-weeda!*" calls Iain. "Care for a drinky-poo?"

"I want a drinky-poo," snarls Blue Hermann, the ancient scribe.

"What's your pleasure? A little dram of Nelly's Death?"

Blue lifts his palsied claw and waves it in the air. "Gimme the top shelf in a pail."

Manny and Clay are talking over in a corner. They are sharing laughter, which surprises me. I assumed they'd not have much to say to each other. I am sitting alone, wondering what is so damn funny.

# THIRTY-NINE

"NICE HAT TRICK you got last night, Duane."

The lights are bright, blinding bright. I can't see nothing except whiteness. It makes me very nervous. There are strange dark forms out there—Pennylegion and the Claire thing. They seem less real than even Manfred and Clay, who elected to stay in the Green Room, unimpressed by the fact that I am making a television advert.

"Thank you, King," says Killebrew.

*King* is right. Lookee here. I got the old Ottawa Paddies jersey on, and it's got the good old number seven stitched on the back. It ain't the genuine article, though, because my jersey was cotton, and this is made out of some Space Age material. I'm baking inside of it, and my undershirt is soaked through.

"But a true hat trick is three goals in a row in the same period." And when you get that, if you happen to be employed by the notorious gangster Jubal St. Amour, Hallie plays the piano and then strips off. She stands naked in the moonlight. "And when you get that," I go on, "you get yourself a real top hat." I got one behind my back, the idea being that at the end of the commercial, I'm going to place it on Duane-o's head. They pay big bucks for this caca.

It's Duane's turn to do the talking, a true ginger ale is Acadia dregs. I'm glad I don't have to say that. I still have some pride. Uh-oh, my turn. "I been drinking it all my life." Or at least, since a party in the parish hall when I was fifteen. That was when Manny first tasted liquor, and don't tell me that Clay Bors Clinton didn't give it to him. I went back and got the flask so's Clay wouldn't be found out. Always covering up for the lad.

"*King!*" screams Pennylegion.

"Yo?"

"You always get stuck on this line!"

"What is it again?"

"Duane says, 'Why do you like Acadia Dry ginger ale?' and you say, 'Because it's bubbly and delicious; it feels like leprechauns are dancing in my throat.' "

I am pursued by ghosts and goblins. How am I supposed to remember so foolish a speech as that? I heave a sigh and tell them that I'll try once more. When the line comes, it eludes me. I am thinking about Hallie, something that happens whenever I hear those words "hat trick."

"Because—" I start.

"*King!*" screams Pennylegion.

"Because it makes me *pissed!*" Manny and Clay come bursting out of the Green Room, their arms thrown around each other's shoulders. "It makes me feel more alive! It tingles my innards and causes burps of glory!"

"King!"

"It is bubbly and delicious. It tastes like leprechauns are dancing in my throat."

"King, you talk like Muggs fucking Mahoney! Don't say 'troat.' "

"It's the same way I been talking all my life."

"Take it from Duane's line: 'Why do you like Acadia Dry ginger ale?' "

Duane says his line. He's very good at this—doesn't even sweat. I'm more than pleased. Between you and me, he is the new King. I'm going to tell him later on. Uh-oh. I have just failed to put the hat on Duane's head. This is, to judge from Pennylegion's reaction, a crime ranked just below treason. The cameras roll again. I reach up and place the top hat on Killebrew's curly head. Then we both grin at the camera. I have been told by Kim (who finally donned a sweater, put off by my leering, my best achievement today) to keep my mouth closed when I smile. Most television viewers expect more than the one tooth. It is very hot under the lights and wearing the plastic Ottawa Paddies sweater.

Down I go, felled as by a Cleghorn two-hander.

Now this is interesting. This is, I suspect, the Twilight Zone. It isn't death, I know that much, because you don't die from making television adverts. I just overheated and fainted, so now I'm in this Twilight Zone affair. It's like my boy Clarence's show on the television. My son Rance was a writer and a poet.

There he is there. He is just a little git, can't weigh much more than one thirty-five, maybe five foot six. He's got a face that looks like it enjoys getting punched up. Rance's nose is so small and squashed that it's easy to overlook. He's got dark little eyes and he squints, suspicious about everything. But, I have to admit, Rance has a nice smile. He keeps it slid up sideways on his right cheek, and he puts a dead-end cigarette butt in it and puffs away happily.

"Clarence!" I rush toward him, stop myself short.

"Pops," he nods. Rance reaches up and tilts the coal miner's cap he wears, making a kind of formal salute.

"It was the gormless Cliffy left out the fire truck, Clarence."

"Which fire truck is this, Pops?"

"The one I tripped over, thereby busting my knee. And if I hadn't busted my knee, I probably would never have done what I done to Manny, because I would have fought him for it fair and square."

"Fought him for what?"

"For being the King."

Rance makes a farting sound, flips away his spent butt. "There ain't no King, man."

"The hell you say. Newsy Lalonde was the King, but I fought him for it and I won. And Sprague came at me, but I held him off. Eddie Shore come at me, and we battled long and hard, but I held him off. And Manny, Manny . . ." I stop to breathe. There is little fresh air in the Twilight Zone. "I knew Manfred wouldn't make it, Rance. I knew what would happen."

Clarence lights up another smoke, plays with it between his yellowed fingers. "You shouldn't have oughta gone and done it, Daddy-o."

"No," I agree. "They don't even have Manny in the new Canadian Sports Hall of Fame."

"I dedicated 'The Stink of Grace' to him, you know."

"This is how you honor your Uncle Manfred? By dedicating pornography to him?"

"Give it a rest, baby."

"Your mother almost died of embarrassment."

"No, she didn't."

"Well, *I* did! Every morning it would be in the papers, how this poem was obscene. And it wasn't even good old-fashioned obscene, it was—" I can feel my face redden.

"It was which?" Rance flips his eyebrows up a bit.

"It was *queer* stuff."

"Oh, is that what the problem is?"

"You're a fairy!" It is hard to breathe in the Twilight Zone. "How could you do that to me?"

"Old fart."

"It makes me ill, my own flesh and blood."

"Wrinkled codger."

"Fruit."

"Wizened molelike yob."

"Flaming pansy-poof!"

"Gnarly maggoty man, curled up under a rock!"

"Little girly bum-boy!"

"Crinkled grub! Revolting roundworm!"

In 1954, we had a party at the Toronto Gardens for Christmas. All of the Leaves came, bringing with them their tykes and wives. It was for a pleasure skate, everyone floating across the ice, looking so much like Sunday afternoon on the Rideau. I came with my wife, Chloe, who was by this time confined to a wheelchair. God had done a number on her legs. Chloe was the provincial champion for the Girls' Under-Eighteen Hundred-Yard Dash in 1916, but apparently such feats don't impress the Almighty. So I wheeled Chloe about on the ice. She whistled along with the recording of organ music. My son Clifford was also there, thirty-three years old, already the owner of a big belly. He brought his wife, Janine (who spent the entire time flirting with Eddie Pierce, the equipment manager), and he brought the infant Thom, who is my grandson. Thom stayed mostly perched up on Cliffy's shoulders. Clifford laughed a lot that day, and he had fun being with all the hockey players.

Clinton played Santa Claus. He gave all his players tickets to resorts and leisure spas for them to use over the summer. He gave me underwear, it seems like he was always giving me underwear. I don't know why; I had enough. Clay now, Clay would lose underwear like nobody's business. He could lose two or three pair a day, and I'm sure the globe is still littered with Clinton's gotchies.

Janey was there. I'm sure Clay hadn't spoken to her for months. But Jane came. Her legs were as thick as Chloe's were thin, inordinately stout for some reason. Jane still kept herself fine, her hair was nice and all, but she really didn't look too well. Mostly it was her eyes. They had turned a somber shade, there was no sparkle to them. They were dead eyes. Janey talked to the hockey players, laughing and such, but I knew that it was studied and practiced.

And Janey said to me, "Hello, Little Brother."

"Sister."

"Merry frigging Christmas." And then she started to cry, but it was quick and hard, and she snuffled and wiped it all away with the back of her hand. "Lucky Number Seven," she said, "let's see that move."

I didn't know what she was talking about.

"Let's be young once more. Up ahead there's Bertie Corbeau."

"The Little Napoleon standing behind him, guarding the net."

"First things first, Little Brother. How do you get around Corbeau?"

"I execute the St. Louis Whirlygig, Sister, a feat of majestic grace!"

"Do it."

"The Whirlygig?"

"Do it, Little Leary."

"Janey, I'm fifty-four years old."

"Little Brother, it would make me happy."

"Well, for you."

I gave over the handles of Chloe's contraption to her sister. Then I did a couple of squats, trying to limber up the pins. The Maple Leaves stopped to stare, digging each other in the ribs and whispering. "I'm about to give you boys a wee lesson," I told them. "When you got a defender up ahead—not no whussy like you fellows play, I'm talking about someone mean and nasty like Joe Hall or Billy Boy Henderson—then here's how you get around him." I launched myself down the ice. Santa Claus gave me a big thumbs-up as I passed. Once I crossed the blue line, I leapt skyward. The Whirlygig itself was a beauty, and I loved the feel of the cold wind as it wrapped me in its arms, but my ankle buckled on the landing. One little ankle wobble and say good night, sister. So my ankle gave, just a little bit, but by the time that worked itself up to my hip I was careening. I hit the ice—taking most of the fall with my right elbow, which caused no end of pain—and slid into the endboards. My head met the wood with quite a thud, but I got a nice hard head.

*"Eeyuh!"*

It sounded like there was a drunken vulture up in the light stanchions.

"Eeyuh, eeyuh, *hooo!*"

I could hear the spray of mucus, the popping of corset buttons.

"Hee, hee, hee, *haaaaa!*"

I lay on the ground and grinned, listening to the sweet sound of Janey's laughter.

A pair of skates approached me. They were white skates, with pics on the end. What was surprising to me was that they were attached to a man's legs. I heard a voice ask, "You all right, Pops?"

I felt giddy, maybe breathless from exertion, for sure cheered by Jane's guffaws. (I could hear her still at it; by this time she'd be buckled over and dropping to her knees.) "What the hell you got sunglasses on for, lad? The glare off the ice hurt your eyes?"

Clarence helped me on to my feet, not that I needed much assistance. I pulled the butt out of his crooked grin. "Don't never smoke a cigarette," I snarled.

Rance looked foolish, that's my estimation. He was wearing sunglasses and sporting one of those pointed beards that just cover the chin. He was wearing clothes that were too tight, all of them black as midnight.

"What were you doing, Poppa-reno?"

"Well," I said, wiping the bits of ice from my body, "Mrs. Clinton wanted to see me do the famous St. Louis Whirlygig."

Janey was trying to stifle her laughter in Chloe's bony shoulder.

Clarence cupped his hands around his mouth and hollered down the ice. "Aunt Janey!"

Janey looked up, tears and God knows what running all over her face. She waved, blew my son a kiss.

"Here you go, ma'am."

Clarence dug in his toes and started off. It didn't take him long to get his speed up, but dammit, he was skating like a *girl*, pushing off the front of his foot, his hands held aloft for balance. But I'll give the boy this much, he executed the stunt. It damn near took my breath away, that's how surprised I was. He went up into the air, turned a neat three-sixty, landed on a pin. Even the hockey players were impressed. Some of them applauded. And Rance wasn't through. He turned around, sailed backwards, and then he leant forward and brought one leg off the ice. Backwards on one foot! I'll tell you a secret, I can't do that, never could. Mind you, I can't imagine why I'd want to. You can't elude Sprague Cleghorn with one leg in the air and headed arseways. Still, I did try it one day when I was all alone on the ice, and I was unable to pull it off.

I watched as the Maple Leaves exchanged glances. Some of them shrugged, others merely pursed their lips and thought about it. Finally one of them—I believe it was Ed Nielson—got up his nerve and tried it. He ended up flat on his face, and there was a good deal of laughter. (Hearty laughter, too. What with Janey's sea-cow braying, no one felt bashful about letting loose.) Someone else tried it, with no better a result. It wasn't long before everyone was attempting this little stunt of Clarence's, and there was much gaiety and falling down. Even Clay Bors Clinton gave it a whirl, still wearing his Santa Claus garb, and he did pretty good for a middle-aged fat man. I stood in the middle and watched.

"Well, that's my boy," I said aloud. "He can do the St. Louis Whirlygig to boot!"

And amidst all the chuckling and cackle, I heard one of the players say, "Not bad for a *queer*."

# FORTY

THEY HAVE HAULED ME INTO THE GREEN ROOM, laid me out on the couch, put a cold compress across my wrinkled brow. Pennylegion is currently out in the corridor shouting, "Lunch!" but he shouts it so loud and mean, the sound tearing the flesh along his throat, that no one will have any appetite left. But they clear out of the little studio. Pennylegion, the Claire thing, and Kim go off to discuss strategy. Iain is likely off in search of more booze. There's a room full of hooch here, but you know what alkie sopheads are like, they are always wandering off to find another soggy heaven. So Iain is not around, even though I could well have been undergoing some life-threatening episode, a heart attack or brain explosion.

So I am all alone in the Green Room. Even the spirits of Manny and Clay are taking a lunch break. Except I hear a scraping out in the hallway, the sound of slow and painful movement. There is a labored breathing, heavy as fog, and mixed into the croaking suck of the intake is a scream of air. If it is another ghostly specter, it's the worst yet, and Manfred was gruesome beyond belief.

It's Blue Hermann, pulling himself into the room on his thick oaken canes. He glares at me on the couch. "Whew," Blue sighs, fresh from Life's Weary Wringer.

"Hermann." I nod. My voice is feeble, likely more so than it need be.

Blue lurches for the bar. It takes him a few long moments to get there, and when he does Hermann goes into a bit of a feeding frenzy, sucking on a multitude of jugs, his toothless maw pumping like a pup's on a nipple. When he is recovered sufficient he turns to me and says, "I was so scared you'd died."

"Yeah?" Blue Hermann ain't such a bad sort, you know. He was a *newspaperman*, after all, so he can be forgiven much of his sharky rancidness.

The Blue man pulls on his drink. "Yeah," he nods, the melting flesh blurring on his face, "I was afraid you'd gone and died before I had a chance to beat the piss out of you."

"Say what?"

"Clay made me promise I'd do it, but I have to admit, I really want to."

"I'd say your medication's misfired, Hermann. Clay was my best friend."

"Clay was your *only* friend, you bastard."

"What about . . .?" I keep my counsel. "So why would Clay make you promise such a thing?"

"That's what he said. '*Make him hurt.*' " Blue shrugs. "So I'm gonna lay a beating on you."

"That's very humorous, buck. In case you ain't noticed, you are invalided and *I* executed a St. Louis Whirlygig yesterday."

"In case you ain't noticed, Leary, I am *armed.*" Blue hefts up one of the walking sticks and waves it in the air. There is a *whooosh*. Point well taken. My own staff, the one with the dragon's head, is resting over in the far corner. I start to get a bit nervous, especially since I am prone on the couch, and Hermann could make it over here with two or three well-executed lurches.

"Hermann! Your brain is on the sizzle. Clay was my bosom companion. We were like brothers. They wrote books about us. Why would Clay make you promise to beat me up?"

"He said,'*Make him hurt.*' "

Blue lurches, and I pop off the couch. "Hold on there, Blue-boy."

" '*Make him hurt.*' " Hermann takes another lurch, and this one has a bit of a side step to it, which blocks the avenue of escape I was about to pursue. He takes his third lurch and is within striking distance.

" 'Make him hurt, Blue.' That's what Clay said. *'Promise me. Make him hurt.'* " Hermann raises his right-hand cane and takes a bead on my bald crown. " *'It's the only way to save him.'* "

Well, folks, I still have some of the old Irishter quickness, because his eyes pop as I hit him in the stomach. He didn't even see me move. I don't hit him hard, mind you, I just apply the fist to his lower belly, where he stores the little oxygen he uses. Then I step around him neatly. "Just calm down, Hermann!" I realize he's about to go over. I make a move toward him, even get my hand around his brittle rib cage, but he buckles and crumples and slips through my fingers. There is a sharp *crack* as his head meets the arm of the couch. Blue Hermann gives up his remaining air and his last two drinks. The carpet in the Green Room, formerly green, begins to turn purple in a halo around Blue's head. I see blood trickle from his hairy ear. No scream will come. Blue Hermann is motionless. Can you imagine leaving two old farts like us on our own? Inexcusable. I stand over Blue's body, hoping to hear a groan or a rusty wheeze. I hear nothing. It seems strange that Hermann could come so far and then give up the ghost so easy. It's like Blue's body eagerly tossed the old ghost heavenwards. His features are calmed by the fingers of Death. He hasn't looked this good in years. Blue is almost handsome again. He is smiling and contented.

I grab my dragon-head swagger stick. I flee.

# FORTY-ONE

ALL THE CARS HAVE VANISHED except for the silver one, the car that has red-and-yellow flame licking down the length of it. The windows are tinted dark, so I can't see inside, but I can see enough to know that it is occupied. It is a treacherous undertaking, the crossing of the parking lot. The sun and wind are staging a major coup, trying to replace the stubborn winter with fragile spring, and the ground is now half-water, half-ice, slick as bacon fat.

I manage to achieve my destination, and I apply my whorly knuckles to the window on the passenger's side. The blackened window rolls down, and Duane-o is grinning at me. He wears a cowboy hat and silver sunglasses that hide his eyes. "Feeling better, sir?"

"Duane, I need your help. I got to get to this new Sports Hall of Fame."

"What about the commercial?"

"We're on the lunch break, ain't we?"

"Yeah, but—"

"It's important, Duane. It's most damn important."

Duane turns his head and says, "Hallie?"

"What did you say that for, Duane-o?"

"I was just asking Hallie if she'd mind driving us over to the Sports Hall of Fame," Killebrew explains.

I duck my head to look past him. It is some tall woman with more teeth than regular people. "Your name's Hallie?" I ask her. "I knew a Hallie. Not very well, but I knew her." I try to smile at her. I'm afraid she might be alarmed by my tooth-less gums (I actually have one tooth, as you know, but it is near the back), so I let the smile slip away from my crinkled puss. "What do you say, Miss Hallie? Will you drive the old King over to this Sports Hall of Fame? There's something I got to do."

This girl Hallie nods. "Hop in."

Duane opens the door, steps out, leans his seat forward. I scuttle through to the back seat.

I watch the melted snow move along the gutters.

"What do you tell the tykes, Duane?"

"Come again, King?"

"*Percy*. Call me Percy. I ask, what do you tell the tykes when they come up for the old John Henry?"

"Oh." Duane shrugs. He's got one arm around Hallie's shoulders. "I tell them, you know, pay attention to their folks."

"Good."

"Get an education."

"That's important."

"I tell them, stay away from dope."

"Dope? The tykes is on dope?"

"Hey, they're starting pretty young."

Hallie nods. "I did grass when I was eleven."

"Dope, you say? Mother of Jesus." The sun is bullying the snow away. Over there a big shelf of the white stuff dislodges from a roof and slides earthward. It lands with a muffled sound, but I am reminded of fireworks. "Duane-o, I guess you know what it is I got to tell you," says I.

"What's that, Percy?"

"Well, son, you are the King now."

Duane almost giggles. "Perce, things have changed in the National Hockey League. We don't really have a—"

"There has always been a King. It was Newsy Lalonde before me. I had to fight like hell to get it away from him. Manfred helped, for all the good it did him. And I was the King for many years. But now I am an old, old man, and unde-serving, what's more. You are maybe the best there ever was—although I would have loved to have gone toe-to-toe with you in my prime—and you are the King. That's all there is to it."

Hallie says, "King Killebrew."

"What do I do?" asks Duane. "Just start telling people I'm the new King?"

"You'll be surprised. It will just happen. You'll be walking along the street and an old fat man with a little dog will walk by, and he'll look up and smile and say 'Good afternoon, King.'"

Duane says, "That kid down in Pittsburgh isn't going to think much of me being King."

"Oh, yes indeed. That's one of the best things about being King, they'll come at you, come at you hard, and you'll get pumped up and your spirit will feel like it might break your bones, it's so big, and you'll play with your whole heart."

Duane nods slowly, turns around and grins at me. "Sounds good."

"But now, hey, you're still a pup. Keep eating yer veggies, and try to have a good time now and again."

"King—Percy—there's something I have to tell you."

"What's that, son?"

"I hate fucking *veggies!*"

The sunlight is playing on the road, dancing in the melted snow. "So do I, Duane. So do I."

And when Clay Bors Clinton died, four thousand people came by the Toronto Gardens to look at his bloated body lying in state. I wanted to go in by myself, and the coppers held back the multitudes as I did that. His face was still rum ruddy, despite an inch of powder and cream, and Clay wore a smile like he'd pulled something over on us all. Maybe he had. And I looked down upon him and I spoke. "You bastard." Then the tears came. They burned my eyeballs, and my efforts to contain them produced the oddest sputtering noises since Mr. Ford first made automobiles. "You bastard," I said, "you left me all alone." I leant forward and pressed my thin lips to his forehead.

I heard a strange shuffling sound, and I reared up, alarmed, spun around with meanness in my heart. It was Janey Millson Clinton, all clad in black. "Hello, Little Brother," said she. Her voice had acquired a huskiness. "Lucky Number Seven."

I was a mess, tears and snot and such slick on my face. I nodded and wiped at it with the back of my hand.

Janey's left leg was harnessed in some sort of metal brace. Jane took a step closer to the coffin, and I saw that this left foot got dragged behind. The right leg was round and thick, no difference 'twixt calf and ankle. Janey walked with the use of a cane, and her gait caused her to buckle in the middle and hump her back. She drew nearer the coffin, her gray eyes calm on Clay's powdered face. Janey smiled up at me. "Looks good in makeup, doesn't he?"

I'd managed to clean myself up, mostly. I held out a hand and Janey accepted it without thinking. When she came within a foot of Clay she let go and rested her hand on the bier. She let out a small stream of air with relief and blew a lock of gray hair from her forehead.

"Well," I said, twisting my little miner's cap between my hands, "I just—"

"I know." Janey nodded. "Me too."

It looked like no blood was getting to Jane's face, that's how pale it was. Her lips were colored a bright red, and I was reminded of the coloring books my sons used when they were small, because in neither case was an effort made to stay between the lines. Clarence would color outside on account of his general perversity, Clifford due to his gormlessness, and I wondered about Jane Clinton until I got a whiff of her breath and realized that she was tanked. She nodded as if I'd said something. "Pissed," Janey acknowledged. "What can I say?"

I muttered, "It's a hard time."

Jane looked back at Clay. "Bastard," she whispered.

"Mustn't speak ill of the departed," I told her.

"It's a compliment," she said. "He worked damn hard at being a bastard."

"Sister, I must be off."

"*Where?*"

"Beg your pardon?"

"Where must you be off to, Little Brother? Your whole world is gone."

"I got some work to do in my office. I'm working on a block-buster trade." I allowed as only a matter of some gravity would let me escape the enclosure. Janey saw through my little lie, was kind enough to ignore it. Her knuckles had blanched under the strain of supporting herself upright.

"I want to explain to you," Jane said, covering a burp, "why I never chose between them."

I quickly turned to Clay, almost hoping that he might say something. He just grinned, enjoying my discomfort.

"Well," said I, licking my lips, "you did choose, didn't you? You chose Clay."

"You three chose for me. You and this one sent Manny to New York. It was an evil thing to do, and there was a time when I wished you in hell, Little Brother. But really, you know, Manfred himself started back on the drink. Nobody poured the stuff down his throat. And I realized some time back that he did it for me. To choose for me. He chose aloneness, though he knew it would kill him. And left me with Clay." Janey reached down and brushed a little forelock of snow white hair from Clay's brow. It popped back mischievously. They say that your hair keeps growing after you're dead. Clay's hair behaved badly.

"And I'm bloody pissed off that you three had the gall to choose for me," declared Jane. "Because why couldn't I have two loves?"

"I'm sorry?"

"You think you're all such princely wonders, don't you, you men? Each of you is all a woman could want. Far from it. I think that you men might be better off forming little committees, three or four of you at a time, and approaching women on that basis. Pardon me, will you take me and my mates to be your lawfully wedded husband? Then we might stand a chance at this game."

"Let's go now, Janey."

"Between them," Janey told me, "I was properly loved. Manfred was all fire and passion, Percy, and made me feel alive. He also got drunk and beat me. And when he wasn't drinking there was a sadness in him that I couldn't touch. This one here was all refined and gentlemanly and made me feel royal. But he could be cold as a dead fish, Little Brother, and you know it every bit as well as I do, and at the bottom of it he just didn't care for other people. Except maybe for you, Little Brother. I believe Clay did care for you.

"So between the pair of them, don't you see, I had a fine lover. And you three had the damned nerve to choose for me."

"It's the way the world rolls, Janey."

"Do you remember, Little Brother, once I asked you why you never fell in love with me? I know the answer to that now. It's because you did."

I nodded slowly. "Come away, Little Sister. There's people waiting to get in."

"Professional mourners, I hope. I don't seem to have a tear to spend on him."

She took my arm and we left that place.

# FORTY-TWO

THE LAKE IS WILD TODAY. Whitecaps rumble everywhere, kissed by light. The clouds move like bumper cars at a fairground. The Sports Hall of Fame looks a little silly next to all that. It was designed by an architect who liked glass and sharp angles, and the edifice itself resembles a broken ginger ale bottle. The building is squat and ugly, the most ambitious thing about it being the parking lot, acres and acres of black tarmac. There's maybe ten cars, all parked in a clump near the front entrance. Hallie drives at these cars, her foot heavy on the pedal, steering with one long elegant finger. She slams on the brakes, whips the wheel, and we scream into the parking lot. "New Canadian Sports Hall of Fame," she announces.

Duane says, "Let us see what we shall see."

I put my gnarled hand in my pocket and feel the cool metal of the crucifix. I am a bit short of breath, because I know the place is full of hobgoblins, gremlins, and the like.

"Man," says Duane-o, savoring the air, "it is *balmy* out here."

Hallie even takes off her buckskin jacket, slings it over her shoulder. This lady's got bubs, brother, but I don't have the time to tell you about it.

Just outside the main door is a little box, like an ice-fishing hut, wherein sits a little old witchy woman selling tickets. They cost a fin apiece, if you can believe that. Duane has to pay. I don't got no jack.

As we approach the front portals a Godlike voice rings out, "Welcome to the new Canadian Sports Hall of Fame!"

"This place is wild," chuckles Killebrew. "They got it all wired for sound."

The prime minister's voice sounds, telling me what a glorious sports history Canada has. Yeah, yeah, yeah. The prime minister is an Irishter, you know. The president of the U.S. of A. is an Irishter, too. And although this might be a bit unpatriotic of me, it seems odd that this is so, because for centuries we been watching how well us Irishters govern our own country (piss poorly, anyone would admit), so it strikes me as foolhardy to give these mooks free rein over other nations. If the Mexicans ever elect an Irish president we're in heaps of trouble.

"Where's the Hockey Section?" I demand.

"The other end." Duane-o points down a long hall filled with booths, exhibits, and incessant chattering, even though the place is largely empty. Whose bright idea was all this recording of voices? We start off down the hall, but Duane is like a little kid. "Check this out!" he cries, and then he hauls Hallie over to a booth. I hobble up behind them and listen to the voice. It tells me that Babe Ruth once played baseball in Toronto.

"I knew the Bambino!" says I. "He was great buddies with Blue—" I hush up about Blue Hermann. It was all his own fault, attacking me with his oaken walking sticks, mouthing gibberish all the while. I launch off again toward the hockey exhibit.

"Hey!" Now Hallie wants to go look at a skiing exhibit. Skiing is foolish, if you want my pronouncement. If you want to go down a mountain fast, hurl yourself over the side.

You couldn't get a mountain steep enough for Clay B. Clinton. He'd don sunglasses and a long scarf and launch himself with abandon. I'd wait for him at the bottom of the mountain, usually shivering.

*"Now that, you see, is the difference between thee and me."*

For a second I think this is one of the recorded voices, so I pay it no mind.

*"You see my point, Percival?"*

Clinton has apparently found some beyond-the-vale hooch, because his face is ruddy and he is weaving slightly. *"That is to say, you like to go fast under your own steam. I, on the other hand, am willing to give myself over to gravity."*

"There's a great many differences between me and you, Clayton. That strikes me as one of the less consequential."

*"I see. Quite the blow you dealt the Blue man, Percival, my porcupine."*

"It was his own damn fault. And what's this about you making him promise to beat me up?"

*"Did he tell you about that? What a naughty liar-liar-pants-on-fire."*

Up ahead stands Manfred A. Ozikean, transfixed by a video pertaining to golf. Manny never played golf, but it doesn't take much to transfix him. *"Hey!"* he says as we draw near. *"This guy shot two holes in one on the same day. Sumpin', eh?"*

"I shot a hole in one," remembers Clay.

*"You never. The ball nestled about three inches away from the cup. You got there before anybody else and toed it in. I seen you do it, Clay."*

*"What's three inches in the grand scheme of things?"*

"Football!" hollers Duane-o, and he and Hallie are off again. The football exhibit is huge, Canadians being very fond of the sport, willing to play it in all sorts of ghastly weather. I've watched games where you couldn't see nothing but formless masses slurping around in mud and drizzle.

I say, "We ain't got no time for football!"

Killebrew is shouting along with various voices. "And Faloney goes back, back, and then he *throws* the ball!" Hallie pretends to be the receiver and she highsteps away, reaching heavenward with a long arm. Her sweater hikes up and you should see what I just saw.

"Touchdown!" Duane and Hallie shout together.

*"Hey!"* Manfred has become transfixed by something else, in this case, curling. Listen, people, curling is *not* a sport. There might be winners and losers, but anything that travels that slowly don't qualify as a sport.

Duane and Hallie come up behind me and both throw an arm around my scrawny little shoulders. "Almost there," says King Killebrew.

"I built the Gardens in nineteen forty-seven," says Clay.

"Yeah, yeah, we know all about it."

"I started assembling the Glory Teams of the fifties."

"Shovel it harder, Clinton! It was *me* done that, director of hockey operations!"

Clay doesn't stop for my interruptions. "We won nine Stanley Cups," he says, and I detect a metallic edge to his voice. I realize that I have been listening to a recording. It has an airy echo to it. Clay is already at the exhibit, melting with emotion. His recorded voice trails off, the music swells, an announcer says, "Yes, Clay Clinton was certainly one of the prime architects of Canadian sport!"

I go over and look at the setup. They got two pictures of the Toronto Gardens, one when she was first built, one as she looks today. They got some photos of the various Maple Leaves teams. They got a big rendition of the picture you've all seen, the one where Clay is pouring champagne over my head. This was one-nine four-nine, and we'd just won our first Stanley Cup with the Leaves. We were two happy geezers in that photo. For historical purposes they got a picture of Clay as a boy, the little lad staring at the camera insolently; they got him as a young man in his officer's uniform, his Cracker Jack decorations covering his breasts; and they got a wedding photo, him and Janey.

Manfred takes a look at the exhibit and smiles oddly. He is not transfixed. "*Hey!*" He is entering the Hockey Section proper. "*There's Howie!*" Manfred walks over to view a photograph of Howie Morenz. Clay stays to hear his own life story one more time.

The Hockey Section is where most of the people are. There's as many as twelve or thirteen milling about, not counting tykes, which is far too many for my purposes. There's even a security guard, which could be real trouble, except he looks to be seventeen years of age and stupid to boot. "Duane," says I, "I need your help."

"You got it, Perce."

"You got to distract these people away from here, down to the other end. I need to be alone for a few minutes."

"What are you going to do?"

"I just need to be alone."

"I suppose." Duane doffs his cowboy hat and removes his mirrored sunglasses. He takes a few steps into the Hockey Section and all hell breaks loose. It's the tykes that notice him first, and they attack his kneecaps like a swarm of bees. The grown-ups are a touch more shy, and they wander over, affecting only the slightest curiosity. There's one mook who's downright disdainful. He casts a haughty look at Killebrew and shrugs his shoulder, *no big deal*. Then he remembers something, namely, that he forgot to pay more attention to whatever exhibit is right by Killebrew, so he snaps his fingers, gives his forehead a tap, and heads off.

The tykes are pressing Duane-o for autographs. "I'll sign," he tells them, "but it'll have to be away down there." And Killebrew leads them, security guard included, back down to Baseball.

And left alone, I prowl through the Hockey Section of the new Canadian Sports Hall of Fame.

I give a nod to Howie Morenz, who I once pretzeled in a play-off game. He could have been the King, maybe, except for his heart wasn't strong enough. By that I don't mean that his left ventricle blew, I mean that when he found himself out of the game at the age of thirty-five (busted leg) he just died. Some people say he died of a broken heart. I know I've said that people can't die of a broken heart, but I'm changing my opinion some. Maybe Howie did. Maybe Manfred did too, except for there was so much blood and booze around no one could tell.

Lookee there. Sprague Cleghorn made the Hall of Fame. I thumb my nose at his photograph. Way to be, Spray-goo. You son of a bitch.

Newsy Lalonde. Cyclone Taylor, my hero when I was a lad of seven. (Oh, Mr. Taylor, why did you forsake us for the Renfrew Millionaires?) The Conacher Boys. Aurèle Joliat. Francis Clancy. All in the Hall of Fame. All dead as well. Except for me, and I'm feeling poorly. Hey there, the Chicoutimi Cucumber, good old Georges Vézina. Goalers, you know, are crazy men. Why would you stand there and let people pelt you with rock-hard rubber? I dig my hand into my pocket and wrap it around the crucifix. Lookee. Eddie Shore. He took a run at me, came at me bullish, but I held him off. Tough man, Eddie was. Another son of a bitch. I take a quick tally. Fully three-quarters of the men in this Hall of Fame are sons of bitches! That's a mind-boggling statistic.

You take this fellow right here. A boy of twenty-one or -two, staring at the camera, a brash young cocker. Couldn't weigh more than one-forty, but he thinks he's got a firm grip on the world's gobbles and he ain't about to let loose. He's a son of a bitch, don't you just know it. His jersey has a big O on it, standing for Ottawa, and in the middle of that O is a sham-rock. This is a joke, you see. His team is called the Patriots, but because most of the men are Black Irish like this pup, people call the team the Paddies, and the shamrock is their emblem. And, oh yes, the lad has a C stitched over his puny heart. And that means a lot to this fellow. I wouldn't smile so much if I were him; which, of course, I am.

What else we got in this display case? An action photo of me in my New York Americans garb, scoring a goal on—let me have a closer look—scoring a goal on Tip Flescher. In this photograph I am airborne. I loved being airborne. You look at fifty action photos of the old King, I bet I'm off the ground in thirty-five of them.

That there is a photograph made in 1915 of the All-Ontario Boys' Hockey Champions, from the Bowmanville Reformatory. That's Brother Isaiah the Blind. There's Theodore, Andrew, and the huge unsightly creature is Brother Simon. I am circled, sitting in the front row because I'm a touch on the short side. Towering above me, grinning into the camera, with no circle made around him, is Manfred Armstrong Ozikean.

A picture of the Maple Leaves throwing me a birthday party. It was only my sixty-fifth, but the boys didn't figure I had many left, ha, ha! In this other photograph, Clay and I are standing in the doorway of an airplane and waving either good-bye or hello. I don't remember any such occurrence.

Now this is an interesting article. It is a New York Amerks jersey, as you can see. The design of the sweater was based on

the Yankee flag, which is why it's covered with bars and stars
and is red, white, and blue. *But,* you see them little rust brown
spots that cover the shoulders? You know what that is? That,
my friends, is dried blood, and it came from my crown, and it
leaked in the year one-nine two-six, which is when that bastard Sprague two-handed me. As I told Blue Hermann so many
years ago, he didn't hit me hard enough.

My spine tingles like it's made out of fur. There is the one-
nine one-nine lumber, that is to say, there is the very selfsame
stick with which I scored the Stanley Cup–winning goal. Cy
Denneny took Odie Cleghorn out along the boards. *Kaboom!*
The boards sounded like thunder in the mountains! The puck
comes out to me, Little Leary.

"*And Percival, my own, perseveres up the ice!*"

"*Yeah! And then I saw Lalonde coming at Percy!*"

He came at me like he wanted to put me in an envelope
and mail me to his great-aunt in Cleveland. And then I heard,
*pssst!*

"*Pssst, Percy!*"

I drop the rubber between my pins. I'm escaped. I hear a
sound like the world is blowing apart. That's Manfred and
Newsy colliding.

"*And a more gruesome, barbaric exhibition I have never
seen.*"

"*Lalonde had his elbows up high,*" remembers Ozikean.

"*Well,*" remarks Clay, "*it marked the end of your face as
we knew it.*"

"I circle like a hawk, distant, above the world. The puck
pops onto my blade. Up ahead is Bertie Corbeau. I execute the
old Nureyev, he ends up with his jersey on inside out. There
isn't a sound in the stands. In the world. Nappy Minton moves
out of his goal crease. Remember him, boys, the Little Napoleon? His eyes were different colors. Little Nap moves out,
and he leaves a piece of light no bigger than a silver dollar sitting over his right shoulder. And I shoot that goddamn puck!"

"*Hey!*" shouts Manfred.

"*Yes!*" shouts Clay.

"Quiet down!" I take a long peek down the hallway. The
people are still clustered around King Killebrew. He is laugh-

ing and signing autographs. I see someone moving through the front door. Oh, no. I got to hurry now.

I take Manfred's crucifix from my pocket. "It's all I've got," I explain.

"*Never mind, Percy,*" says Manfred. "*It doesn't matter. I don't deserve to be here. I was just a drunk.*"

"Don't never say that. Look at all these sons of bitches. You were a good man, Manny. You weren't just a drunk. You were the mountain, and the wind."

"*I think it's a very touching gesture,*" says C. B. Clinton. "*A trifle maudlin and mawkish, but basically touching.*"

I shrug. "It's the least I can do." The crucifix feels cold and heavy in my hand.

He is getting closer.

I raise up my dragon-head walking stick. I take a deep breath and summon whatever strength is lying around in this wrinkled carcass.

"*King!*"

His shout mixes with the tinkling of broken glass. I didn't think I'd do it first shot out of the box. My walking stick is pulled out of my hand, tugged away. Shards tumble around my arm, bouncing off my sleeve mostly, but one or two carve across my wrist. I'm startled to see blood spit out, covering the crucifix. Some of the blood spurts onto the Amerks jersey. The blood is red and gleaming. I am not alarmed by this blood, although I'm a little surprised that my puny little being holds so much. And there seems to be no end in sight, but I got no time to watch. I lay the crucifix down on top of the Amerks jersey. *He is getting closer all the time, and his shouts have alarmed everyone. Now Duane-o is coming back towards me, too, him and his girlie.* My finger is slick with red stuff—my whole hand is—and I reach out and draw a lopsided circle around Manfred's face in the 1915 photograph. My walking stick is buried beneath sheets of broken glass. I grab the one-nine one-nine lumber and light out. There is a Fire Exit not ten feet away and I allow as I can make it before anybody catches me.

"King!" he shouts.

"Come on, boys!" We hustle for the big metal doors. I lay my shoulder against one, and I reckon that if I didn't have Manny and Clay there with me I couldn't even budge the thing. But I get through, find myself in a gray stairwell. There's stairs leading up and there's stairs leading down. I can't decide. I put the hockey stick between the handles of the double doors and fall back against them. Goddamn, there is a lot of blood.

I hear a weak thud from the other side, his drunkenness making him clumsy. I hike a thumb at my friends, tell them, "Lad drinks too much."

"King!" he shouts from the other side. "Let me through."

I giggle, which I admit is somewhat unseemly. We are like children playing at a game. Clay laughs, too—always willing to laugh, old Clinton—and Manfred grins and shrugs, tossing off the weight of the world. I catch sight of Manny's black eyes bearing on me. I nod, take a moment or two to catch my breath.

Iain presses the doors, but between the one-nine one-nine lumber and whatever substance remains in my blood-emptied carcass, the thing stays closed.

"Son!" I call out. This stills him. "Put your ear close to the door. I need to say something to you."

I hear a bustling, a hard knock as he lays his muzzy noggin against the cold steel that separates us. "What?"

My lips have dried like yesterday's worms. My tongue is little better than sandpaper, but I run it over my flappers a couple of times. It might be best to get this out as quickly as possible. "Son, because you love me, I'm asking you for this promise."

Manny is mouthing the words along with me.

"Stop drinking this—"

"What, King?"

I raise my voice. "Because you love me, I'm asking you for this promise, that you will stop drinking this liquor that hurts you so badly."

I struggle to my feet. Manny and Clay each have ahold of an elbow, and I couldn't do it without them. "Do you promise, boy?"

"I promise. Now let me through. You're bleeding."

But I got places to go.

I run down a little flight of six stairs and punch through a door marked Emergency Exit. This sets off a fire alarm, and the building starts making a noise like a slot machine paying off big. The sunlight blinds me. The earth is melting, the snow going so quickly that it almost leaves behind steam. Up ahead, their arms around each other, their feet fairly skipping, are Clay Bors Clinton and Manfred A. Ozikean. "Boys . . ." comes out of my throat, but it is a quiet sound and does not carry on the warm wind. Manny and Clay don't slow for me. I try to dig in, but that only makes the ancient pins buckle. The snow feels good on my face. I am very tired.

When I wake, night has fallen. The sky holds a moon, a big silver moon. Everything is washed in its light. I hear my name, and slowly I climb to my feet. Over there the monks are out on the ice. Brother Simon the Ugly flies through the air, Andrew the Fireplug steams around the boards. Brother Theodore stands in the center of the ice, his eyes closed, preparing to fire the puck. And Brother Isaiah the Blind is waving to me.

I join them in the circle.